D0839993

Marianne Brandis

The SIGN of the SCALES

The Porcupine's Quill

CANADIAN CATALOGUING IN PUBLICATION DATA

Brandis, Marianne, 1938-
The sign of the scales

ISBN 0-88984-164-0

I. Title.

PS8553.R29S53 1993 jC813'.54 C93-093487-3
PZ7.B73Si 1993

Published by The Porcupine's Quill, Inc., 68 Main Street, Erin, Ontario N0B 1T0 with financial assistance from The Canada Council and the Ontario Arts Council. The support of the Government of Ontario through the Ministry of Culture and Communications is also gratefully acknowledged.

Distributed by Scholastic Canada, 123 Newkirk Road, Richmond Hill Ontario L4C 3G5.

Copy-edited by Doris Cowan. The cover is after an original watercolour by Patty Gallinger.

The author gratefully acknowleges the help of Linda Davies at the Toronto Marine Museum; Michele Dale at the Marine Museum of the Great Lakes in Kingston, Ontario; the staff of the Todmorden Mills Museum in Toronto; and the staff of Black Creek Pioneer Village, especially those in the Lasky Emporium and Post Office.

I also wish to thank Dr. Margaret Angus, Richard Neilson, and Professor H.R.S. Ryan, all of Kingston; Professor Ryan was assisted by Dr. Shirley Spragge, Diocesan Archivist of the Anglican Diocese of Ontario in Kingston, and Mrs. Lillian Birks, of the staff of the Diocesan Centre in Kingston.

York

Upper Canada

1832

Chapter One

Whenever the front door of McPhail's Hotel opened, a discreet but authoritative little bell tinkled. Mrs. McPhail would go and see who had come in. If it was someone asking a question, she answered it. If it was people wanting rooms, she signed them in and, if necessary, summoned Joseph Tubb to help with the luggage.

On this windy afternoon in April, Mrs. McPhail was out and her niece Emma Anderson was signing in a new guest. He was a neat, slender, middle-aged man in beige pantaloons and a cutaway coat; he had taken off his overcoat and tall hat when he came in and laid them on the reception counter in the hotel lobby. He was a very gentlemanly-looking person, but his voice was gravelly, and Emma was having trouble with his name. She had already had to ask him once to repeat it and now, with the hotel register open in front of her and the pen poised, she asked again. Mrs. McPhail insisted on having the guests' names correct.

'Mr. Michael Harbottle?' Emma asked.

'Michaels-Harbottle,' he said patiently. 'With a hyphen. That's the full surname.'

He pulled a small leather case out of his waistcoat pocket and laid one of his cards on the counter in front of her. She copied the name carefully; halfway through she had to dip her pen in the ink again.

The card gave his address as Albany, New York; she wrote that down too.

'Thank you, sir,' she said, laying down the pen and corking the ink bottle. When she looked up she caught him watching her. He had shrewd brown eyes with a smile lurking in them.

'You're doing fine, young lady,' he said. 'Just fine.'

Emma flushed with irritation. The words sounded like a compliment, but the man's smile suggested that she was doing fine for a raw beginner – which was not a compliment at all. She had been signing in guests for nearly a year now, and it was only because of the man's complicated name and hoarse voice that she had seemed slow.

He must have interpreted the blush as a sign of uncertainty. He chuckled. 'No, no, don't worry, you didn't make any mistakes. But a girl as young as you can't have been doing this for very long.'

This was a further annoyance to Emma, who was used to being taken for older than her actual age of fifteen, rather than younger. But it was impossible to say anything. Mr. Michaels-Harbottle was a hotel guest and must not be contradicted.

Instead she gave him a tight-lipped smile. 'Let me show you to your room, Mr. Michaels-Harbottle.'

She came around the end of the counter and picked up the valise standing near his feet. It was heavy, but pride forced her to carry it as though it were light. He took his coat and hat from the counter.

Before going upstairs, she opened the door on the other side of the lobby. 'This is the dining-parlour,' she explained. 'We serve breakfast and dinner. You may arrange for midday luncheon as well, but you have to request it specially. There is no bar, but we always have alcoholic beverages on hand, particularly whiskey and a variety of wines, and you have only to ask Mrs. McPhail or me if you wish for anything.'

Again there was a gleam of amusement in the new

guest's eyes. Now Emma was sure that she must be doing something wrong. Or maybe he was a very important man, whose name she should have recognized at once. But then he wouldn't arrive with only one valise, nor walk up from the wharf where, he said, he had just arrived on the Niagara boat.

She led the way up the stairs to Room Three. Inside the door, she set his valise down.

'Do you wish to have your hot water now, sir, or later?' The guests were always brought hot water before dinner so that they could wash, but they could also have some when they arrived at the hotel.

'Later. I have business which will occupy me all afternoon. I may be dining here. My plans are not very definite. Do I need to notify you whether I will be here for dinner?'

'Since you are alone, sir, no. We appreciate notice for larger parties.' She made a small curtsey. 'I hope you enjoy your stay with us, Mr. Michaels-Harbottle. Please let us know if there is anything you require.'

'Thank you, I will.'

She looked for signs of the slightly mocking smile, but he had stopped paying attention to her.

As she went downstairs, Emma suddenly realized that he might have been amused by something wrong in her appearance. She froze for one alarmed second, then ran down the remaining steps and went to the mirror in the lobby.

But no, she looked just as usual. Her acorn-brown hair was, except for the frizzy short bits around her face, still gathered into the single thick braid down her back. There were no smudges on her face; there was no dirt on the white kerchief spread over her shoulders and tucked into the V-shaped neckline of her black dress.

She heard the door of Room Three open and close. Mr. Michaels-Harbottle would be coming downstairs and setting off to do the business he had mentioned. She darted behind the counter and, when he appeared, glanced up from the register in which she was pretending to search for something.

'Good day, lass.' He nodded, opened the door, and, once out on the veranda, put on his tall hat and walked away towards the centre of town.

Emma stared after him for a moment or two. She had just shaken herself and picked up the sewing which she had been doing earlier, before the new guest's arrival, when the door at the back of the lobby opened.

It was Mrs. McPhail, the owner of the hotel, back from her afternoon's errands. As always, Emma cast a quick, assessing glance at her face and hands. Mrs. McPhail's firm, rather attractive face seldom showed much emotion, but when she was angry her hands clenched and loosened spasmodically.

This time, however, perhaps because her hands were busy untying the strings of her bonnet, it was her face which gave Emma an inkling that there might be something wrong. Between Mrs. McPhail's eyebrows was a small vertical furrow.

'Well, Emma,' she said.

Normally Emma would at once have reported the arrival of a new guest. But that little line between Mrs. McPhail's eyebrows kept her silent. Something was wrong. Perhaps Mrs. McPhail had heard bad news, or perhaps she had discovered something objectionable that Emma had done – or some misdeed committed by John, Emma's younger brother, who lived at the hotel but worked at Blackwood's livery stable just down the street. Both of them sometimes did or said things which earned them a scolding from Mrs. McPhail.

So Emma said, 'Good afternoon, Mrs. McPhail,' and waited for further signs.

Mrs. McPhail came behind the counter and went into her private room. Emma could see her laying her cloak and bonnet neatly on a chest.

'Come in here, Emma, please.'

Emma knew that tone of voice and felt herself going cold. What had she or John done this time?

'Leave the door open,' Mrs. McPhail added, 'so that we can keep an eye on the lobby.'

Emma, settling herself into the chair beside Mrs. McPhail's desk, met her aunt's cool grey eyes. Mrs. McPhail was a widow in her thirties, a businesswoman and a highly efficient hotel-keeper. She was the half-sister of Emma's and John's father, now dead, and the children's legal guardian. But they never called her 'aunt'; the blood relationship counted for much less than the fact that she was their guardian and Emma's employer.

'Well, now,' said Mrs. McPhail. 'I've just been to Freeman's.'

Emma nodded. Freeman's was a shop at the east end of town; Mrs. Freeman, who was ill, was an old friend of Mrs. McPhail's, and Mrs. McPhail visited her from time to time.

Emma had never met either Mr. or Mrs. Freeman or their teen-aged son, whose name she had forgotten, nor had she ever been to their shop. Still, she asked politely after Mrs. Freeman's health.

Mrs. McPhail shook her head dismissively. 'Oh, there's no change. That's not important now. What is important is the shop. Some years ago I invested money in it. Abner Freeman needed funds for new stock and some renovations. It seemed a good investment, and it was. He repaid me gradually. Last autumn I made him another loan. And then three months ago his wife had to take to her bed because of rheumatism. Before that she helped in the shop, and she was good at guessing what the customers wanted. She would help her husband decide what to buy from the suppliers.'

The line between Mrs. McPhail's eyebrows deepened slightly.

'Is Mrs. Freeman too sick to help make those decisions still?' Emma asked at last.

'I don't know. She's completely bed-ridden, I believe. Of course Abner Freeman could perfectly well do it himself, watch what people buy, make a note of what they ask for. No, it's more his state of mind. The ... the determination has gone out of him. If something isn't done he'll go under, go bankrupt, and he and his wife will be paupers. I suppose he could get some other kind of work, but if his job took him away from the house he'd have to pay someone to stay with his wife ... or the son would have to support them....'

'Does the son help in the shop?'

'He's not clever enough, apparently, and he doesn't want to. He drives a brewer's dray part-time.'

'So he could help support them in other ways.'

'Probably. Though I gather that he is unlikely to get work that pays well. And if the shop fails....'

If the shop failed, Mrs. McPhail might lose her investment. Emma had learned enough about business to understand that.

'If Mr. Freeman found other work, he could gradually repay you.'

'Not with a wife who is probably going to need more and more care. That would drain off a considerable portion of his earnings. She's a good woman; I wouldn't want her to....' Mrs. McPhail met Emma's eyes.

Emma understood this look. In dealing with the world, Mrs. McPhail usually seemed to consider business more important than people. At least once this had led her towards dishonesty. When Emma's parents had died two years ago in a fire, their farm had to be sold so that Emma and John and Mrs. McPhail could divide the inheritance. It had been sold to Mr. Blackwood, a friend of Mrs. McPhail's; he had tried to resell it to a Major and Mrs. Heatherington at a very large profit which he and Mrs. McPhail would divide between them. Emma had helped to prevent that swindle; the Heatheringtons had indeed bought the farm though at a much less inflated price.

But at other times Mrs. McPhail managed to combine good business with a concern for people. She employed the Tubbs – Joseph, his wife, and their son Joe – who were a bit simple. She paid them less than she would have paid more intelligent people, but she did give them wages, board, and lodging. In addition, she was on a committee which helped penniless immigrants find work so that they did not become beggars or criminals.

Clearly this was another of those cases; both humanity and good business made Mrs. McPhail worry about Abner Freeman's shop.

'What are you going to do?' Emma asked.

Mrs. McPhail was silent for a few moments, staring out of the window. When she turned to Emma, she spoke decisively.

'I want you to go over there.'

'Now?'

'I don't mean just for a visit. I want you to go every

day to work in the shop and help look after Rose Freeman. You're to be tactful, of course. You're just helping Abner Freeman out. But see what you can do to brighten the shop, attract customers, improve sales. See if you can put some heart into the place. And some heart into Rose, who needs company. Mrs. Molloy comes every morning to do the housework, and Charlie Freeman, the son, looks after the hens and the pig, but.... Maybe it just needs organizing.'

Emma, watching her aunt's face carefully, saw the decisiveness fade once again into uneasiness or puzzlement. There seemed to be something that Mrs. McPhail was leaving unsaid, and this time Emma could not guess what it might be.

After a moment's wondering, she returned to what her aunt had actually said. 'So I'm to work *there* all day, rather than here?'

Mrs. McPhail nodded. 'For a few weeks, perhaps. I want that shop to keep going and even improve. Keep an eye on things and see what you can do.'

'What about my work here?' Emma had a full schedule, as chambermaid and waitress, in the hotel. She rose at five o'clock and was busy until bed-time, with about two hours off in the afternoon if nothing was pressing. Only in the last two weeks had she had some help from Ruth, an immigrant girl whom Mrs. McPhail had hired to assist with the spring cleaning; no one knew how long she would stay.

'Ruth can do most of it,' Mrs. McPhail said. 'You can do some work before you go to the shop – clean these downstairs rooms first thing in the morning, as usual, and have your breakfast. And you ought to be back in time to wait on table during dinner. But I'd like you to begin training Ruth to do that, so that she can take over if ever you're not back in time.'

Emma nodded, though she was silently calculating that this new schedule would make her days even busier than they were now.

'When do I start?'

'Tomorrow morning.'

'Do the Freemans know that I'm coming?'

'No. The idea only came to me just now. But I'll send Joe Tubb with a note.' Mrs. McPhail paused for emphasis and focussed all her attention on Emma. 'Now I want you to realize that this is important. You have to be tactful, and cheerful, and do what the Freemans tell you. Is that clear?'

Before Emma could answer, she received a nod of dismissal. But when she had got to her feet, Mrs. McPhail added, 'And keep your eyes and ears open. Use your wits. If you run into problems, come and talk to me.'

'Yes, Mrs. McPhail.'

Only when she was out in the lobby did Emma realize that after all she had not been scolded for some mistake or misdeed. But the realization did not cheer her up. This new assignment made her uneasy. She was on the point of turning back to have another word with her aunt – but she didn't know what she wanted to ask, couldn't pin down what it was that worried her.

***

For the rest of that afternoon and evening, Emma was so busy that she had no time to worry. She had to set the table for the guests' dinner, explaining the procedure to Ruth as she went and showing her where everything was kept in the big dresser near the dining table.

She waited on table during dinner and cleared up afterwards. In the intervals she attended on Mrs. Reynolds, one of the guests, whose baby was sick; it was Emma who ran up and down stairs to help with the bedpan, a vomiting bowl, a clean towel, a tray of dinner for Mrs. Reynolds.

The servants always had their dinner after the guests, but Emma's was a scrappy affair tonight, interrupted by waiting on Mrs. Reynolds. Then, while Ruth helped Mrs. Tubb with the dish-washing, Emma tended the parlour fire and supplied the guests with the whiskey, tea, and candles that they ordered during the evening.

At ten o'clock she was finally free to go to bed. She went to the outhouse in the yard and, back in the kitchen, filled her bedroom jug with hot water.

'Has John gone upstairs?' she asked Mrs. Jones. Mrs. Jones was the cook; she spent almost all her waking hours in the kitchen and kept track of the other servants' comings and goings.

'Yes, everyone's in. Even that Joe Tubb. Mrs. McPhail was looking for him earlier.'

Mrs. McPhail had wanted Joe to take a note to Abner Freeman announcing Emma's arrival tomorrow morning. But he had been out, probably rambling around town in his aimless and half-witted way. Now it was too late to deliver messages; tomorrow morning Emma would have to carry her own introduction to the Freemans.

Mrs. Jones locked the back door and made sure that the windows in the kitchen, scullery, and larder were closed. Then she and Emma trudged upstairs, carrying their candles and jugs of hot water, up one flight to the floor where the guests' bedrooms were and then a further flight to the attic where they themselves had a tiny bedroom each and John slept on a pallet in the open space among the odds and ends of furniture and other stored objects. The Tubb family slept over the wash-house behind the kitchen, and Ruth at home with her parents.

Emma had expected to see John already asleep on his pallet but instead she found him in her own small room. He was sitting on her bed, trying to thread a needle. His breeches were lying on the bed beside him; he had a blanket wrapped around his legs. Beyond him, the window, shaped like a quarter of a pie, reflected parts of the room.

'Oh, there you are,' Emma said, setting her candle on one of the shelves and her jug of water on the floor near the washstand.

'One of the suspender buttons came off my breeches,' he said, looking up with a grin. 'I thought I'd try to sew it on myself, seeing as you were so busy, but I can't even get the needle threaded.'

'You have to let girls be best at *something*. Here, I'll do it.'

He handed over the needle and thread, the breeches, and the button. He watched carefully as she threaded the needle and tied a knot in the end of the thread.

'What were you so busy with?' he asked.

She didn't answer immediately. Her tired mind churned with the day's images: Mr. Michaels-Harbottle and his sardonic amusement, Mrs. Reynolds fretting over her sick child, Mrs. McPhail's worries about the Freemans and their shop.

'Do you know anything about the Freemans?' she asked. 'You know, the people who have the store in the east end of town?'

John was a good person to ask. One of his chores at Blackwood's livery stable was to run errands. He knew almost everyone in York. He was observant, and he had a good memory and a knack for picking up information. After their arrival in York a year and a half ago, he had found his way around town much faster than Emma had done. Even though he was only thirteen, she trusted both his knowledge of facts and his assessment of people.

Now he shrugged. 'Not much. The shop's a bit too far away from the centre of town to be a real success, though it's used by the people who live near there and beyond the Don River. Trouble is, the people living in those squatters' shacks in the marshes along the river don't bring in a fat profit. I bet they don't pay their bills half the time. But Freeman keeps going somehow. His prices are supposed to be a little lower than those in other stores. His wife used to help, but now that she's sick....'

'They have a son, don't they?'

'Charlie doesn't get along with his dad, so he doesn't help in the store. He drives a dray for Doel's brewery.'

'He isn't very bright, I gather.'

'So they say, but I can't see anything wrong with him. Why d'you want to know all this?'

'Mrs. McPhail is sending me to work there – help out with Mrs. Freeman and in the shop.'

She spoke casually to hide her uneasiness about the new assignment. But John was not deceived. He gave her a long, speculative look.

'Is that so? Are you pleased?'

'I'm not sure. I can't quite see.... I wonder if Mrs. McPhail is up to something. That's why I asked you. Do you know anything more, anything that...?' She looked at him, not minding now if he realized how she felt.

He frowned in thought, his fingers picking absent-mindedly at the edge of the blanket wrapped around him. 'One thing – watch out for Abner Freeman. He's got a temper, and they say he's a bit of a bully.' Abruptly he looked up and met Emma's questioning gaze. 'He may not be too happy about your being there.'

'Why not? I'm going to help.' But even while she was speaking, she realized that John was right. A man such as he had described might resent an outsider, might suspect interference. That would make her assignment still more difficult.

She pondered for a moment, then finished sewing on the button and bit off the thread with her teeth. She reached over to put the needle into the pincushion on the shelf over her bed, and lifted the breeches, shaking them out to check if they needed any more repairs. As she did so, she heard a slight clink, as of coins in the pockets. This was not unusual; John often received small tips for the errands he ran. But the sound of the clink, and the weight of the breeches, suggested more than the two or three coins which he might earn in tips in a single day.

She nearly asked him jokingly whether he had robbed someone, but that would seem like fishing for information, and she and John had been taught by their parents to respect other people's privacy. So she said nothing, and apparently John did not realize that she had noticed anything. He was on his feet gathering the blanket around him. He took the breeches, thanked her, picked up his candle, and left the tiny room.

Emma undressed, washed, and got into bed. But she had too much on her mind to sleep at once. John's breeches pocket, holding perhaps eight or ten coins, so far as she could judge – how had he come by so much? She knew that he had a hiding place in the attic where he kept his money. He would have emptied his pockets last night, so the clinking she had heard was made by what he had earned today. But could he really earn so much in tips in one day? And it couldn't be wages because he had mentioned getting paid last week and would have hidden the money then.

Should she have asked him after all? If it was money honestly earned, might he not have told her?

Not necessarily. He was a reserved person, hiding his private life and going his own way.

And then there was the arrangement about her going to work for Abner Freeman. She was not eager to go. The hotel was a familiar place now; she knew the work, knew her fellow servants, felt at home. John's description of Mr. Freeman worried her. So did Mrs. McPhail's instructions to 'keep an eye on things'. There was something behind this plan, something that Mrs. McPhail had not put into words. Emma felt as though she were being sent into a pitch-dark room, told to keep her eyes open, but not given a candle to see by.

But of course she was not literally going into the dark. She *would* be able to keep her eyes open and see whatever there was to be seen.

Certainly, though, she would have to be patient and careful as well as watchful.

Chapter Two

The main shopping district of York was along King Street, eastwards from Yonge, parallel to the shore of Lake Ontario and about a block north of it. On King and its side streets, along with the stores, were many of the public buildings: the court house, jail, and market; the District Grammar School and the Masonic Hall; St. James' Anglican Church, the Scots Church, and the Methodist chapel. East of this area, near the marshes at the mouth of the Don River, were the burned ruins of the original Parliament Buildings, a blockhouse, and a windmill still under construction. By then King Street had curved north-east and changed its name to the Kingston Road before crossing the Don River by means of a covered bridge.

Mrs. McPhail had told Emma that the Freemans' store was close to the road that turned off to the windmill. Emma did not know the area well; she had been here only once, when she and John, on a fine Sunday afternoon in the previous autumn, had gone after church to see the enormous flocks of migrating birds that always stopped over at the Don marshes. Lured by the weather and the Sunday-afternoon sense of freedom, they had crossed the two mouths of the Don and walked some distance along the peninsula, which at this point was a narrow bar of land with the bay on their right and the lake stretching out like an ocean on their left. A group of horsemen had passed them, probably heading for the track on the peninsula where horse-races were held. But Emma ignored them; she had stood with the wind buffeting her face, the huge lake reaching from her feet to the United States, and had felt tiny and chained down but full of unimaginable potential.

That glorious feeling had vanished very quickly, and she barely remembered it now as she walked towards Freeman's store. The tininess and the chains were, in any case, more real than the potential. She *was* only a tiny speck in a vast world, and she *was* apparently locked into a job and a routine which, though not unbearable, gave her little chance for developing. Already this morning she had done more than two hours of work in the hotel, sweeping and dusting the stairs, lobby, and dining parlour, lighting the fire, setting the table for the guests' breakfast. She had bolted some breakfast herself and now, at about eight o'clock on this chilly morning in April, was on the way to her new assignment. She had her cloak wrapped closely around her. In her pocket was a note from Mrs. McPhail explaining her arrival to Mr. Freeman.

She was feeling no happier about the work facing her. But as she walked along the fairly solid edge of the muddy street, she remembered other times in her life when she had faced something unknown and frightening. She recalled walking from the Wilburs' house to Dundas to consult her late father's lawyer about Mrs. McPhail, and later making the decision to go with Mrs. McPhail to a new life in York, two occasions when she had gone blindfold into a strange world. She had survived, and she had even learned and achieved something. You had to push on, take all the strangeness as it came, hope that your wits would save you if you got into difficulties. It was a bit frightening, but somehow she would get through it.

These thoughts took her along King Street, past the

shopkeepers opening their stores for the day, through the Saturday bustle that was all the busier because Saturday was market day. Being preoccupied, she did not give much heed to it all.

Before long she was again among houses with gardens. Here she had to begin paying attention so that she could find her way to the Freemans'. Besides, in spite of all the unfamiliar things facing her, she enjoyed being out at this time of day and looked around her with pleasure. A rooster crowed, and a girl of perhaps eight crossed a yard leaning against the weight of a milk pail. Alongside the road was a ditch filled with scruffy brush and weeds and, here and there, a pool of water. Near one of these puddles a red-winged blackbird clung sideways to a bare stem, giving his sweet whistle. Invisible frogs sang.

A little further on, a block away to her right, were the burned-down Parliament Buildings – the new ones replacing them were farther west, in the newer part of York. Here, at this eastern end of town, there had actually been two sets of Parliament Buildings, the earlier ones built in the first years of the town's existence and burned down by the American soldiers in 1813, the second ones built on the same location and burned accidentally in 1824. Now the people of York dumped garbage in the ruins; it was the gulls screaming and wheeling over the site that attracted Emma's attention.

A cart loaded with lumber creaked up behind her, going only a little faster than she was walking. To make herself heard, she shouted, 'Where is Freeman's store? Do you know?'

The driver pointed to the right and a short distance ahead, at a log house with a small barn behind it and a few fruit trees in its back yard.

'Thank you!'

She slowed her pace, yielding for a moment to anxiety, inspecting the place to learn what she could before going in.

Abner Freeman's house was not actually on the Kingston Road but just off it, facing onto a lane. Presumably the shop occupied one of the downstairs rooms, but there was no shop window to mark it. There was an upper floor, probably a room or two under the slope of the roof. The building behind it was not actually a barn but a straggle of sheds; hens scratched along the edge of the road, among the flattened, bleached grass left over from last year, and a pig could be heard grunting. The place looked rather neglected; there was a broken pane in one of the downstairs windows, a muddy track leading up to the front door, the beginnings of a rail fence which had never been completed. Emma, coming from the trim and neat respectability of her aunt's hotel, felt her courage sink. Mrs. McPhail's talk yesterday had suggested that the store was a prosperous business suffering a temporary set-back, but it actually looked as though it had never been a success.

As she turned into the lane, the front door of the house opened with a tinkling of an unseen bell and a woman came out to stand on the door sill and shake a dust-cloth. This couldn't be Mrs. Freeman, who was bed-ridden, so it must be the charwoman, Mrs. Molloy.

The woman saw Emma and nodded, probably taking her for a customer.

'Good morning,' Emma said, picking her way along the least muddy edge of the path. 'Is Mr. Freeman in? I have a message for him.'

She need hardly have asked. Through the open door

came a bass-voiced bellow of rage and then a softer male voice protesting inaudibly. Probably Abner and his son, Emma thought. She looked up to meet Mrs. Molloy's eyes.

'Aye. He is.'

At first Emma had thought her a sour old thing, but now she caught a glint of grim amusement in the eyes and at the corners of her mouth. That cheered her more than anything else so far had done.

The bellow was not repeated, but the deep voice made some snarling comment and a door slammed.

'Ya wanna see him?' the woman demanded of Emma, jerking her head towards the house behind her. 'Are y'a customer? Store don't usually open till nine, but I guess....'

'No, I've come to give him a note.' She drew it out of her pocket. As Mrs. Molloy reached for it, Emma hastily added, 'No, no, I have to give it to him in person.'

Mrs. Molloy shrugged and turned without a word. Emma followed and found herself in a narrow passage. Two doors on her right were closed; another, on the left, stood open and revealed the room which served as a shop, with a counter behind which rose shelves of merchandise. The only things not typical of any small shop were two comfortable chairs, one in front of the cold fireplace and the other near one of the two windows. The latter was occupied by a sleeping cat.

At the end of the passage, in the doorway to the kitchen, stood a big, burly man in shabby clothes.

'Well?' he growled. Then, evidently realizing that she might be a customer, he said, 'Yes'm?'

Emma would very much have liked to run away. Already she was afraid of this man with his rough voice, red face, and unattractive manner. But there was no going back. She drew herself up, gathered all her resolve, and held out the letter.

'My name is Emma Anderson, sir. This is a letter from Mrs. Harriet McPhail.... That is, if you are Mr. Abner Freeman.'

He took the letter and pushed past her into the shop. Though not invited, Emma followed and stood in the doorway, watching him break the seal and unfold the letter. He looked up to scowl at her, then walked closer to one of the two windows and, by its light, read the note.

From where she stood, Emma could see the side of his face, the slightly bent back, the hand that trembled as it held the paper. Now that he was not glowering at her, she could see him more objectively. He was an unappealing figure, but Emma remembered that he had a sick wife. He did not look like a man who would have much patience with sick people – nor, for that matter, someone who would feel comfortable in a shop. He looked much more like an ordinary labourer. The oddity puzzled her, and something about the way he was poring over Mrs. McPhail's letter made her feel almost sorry for him.

Before she had time to wonder at this unexpected twinge of sympathy, he turned on her, head still lowered. He stared at her from under his eyebrows with a sharp and suspicious question in his eyes. He even opened his mouth as though to put the question into words. But he changed his mind and, shrugging, pushed the letter into his pocket.

'Sure. I guess you kin stay. Your aunt....'

She waited, but he only shrugged again and turned away.

After a moment of staring at his back, she said,

'What would you like me to do first, Mr. Freeman? My aunt said that I was to help you by working in the shop and caring for Mrs. Freeman. But I don't know anything about shopkeeping, so you'll have to explain it to me.' She tried to speak politely, though his behaviour offended and worried her. What had Mrs. McPhail let her in for?

He did not reply immediately; he was standing with his hands in his pockets, staring out of the window. For a little longer he stood like that, and Emma wondered what to do. Then he turned towards her. His face had settled into heavy, unattractive lines, but he looked as though he had made up his mind about something.

'All right, then. This here's the shop, as you kin see. It'll take a while till you find your way around. There ain't no prices on the stuff – they're all in my head. This here's where we keep the cash.' He went behind the counter and pulled out a drawer under it in which lay some coins, whole ones and the halves and quarters into which they were sometimes cut to make change. 'But there ain't much cash, ever. Most of 'em bring in stuff to barter, or buys on credit – I keep track of it here.' He laid his finger on a ledger with a marbled paper cover, very shabby and battered. 'If people come in when I'm not here, you kin write down what they buy and get 'em to sign, and then I'll figure out the cost. If people want to know the price before they buy, ask Rose – that's my wife. Sometimes, o'course, we haggle a bit, and sometimes they bring in a dead chicken or a bunch o' carrots and ask how much sugar that'll buy. I'll tell you some more later.'

Emma nodded; much of this was familiar to her. Because of the shortage of coins in circulation, a great deal of business was done by barter or, as Mr. Freeman had explained, by letting the customer run up an account until harvest-time or some other opportunity for paying. She wondered if she herself would have to decide the value of a dead chicken, but that was something she could ask later.

Although this was familiar, there was, however, a great deal she'd have to learn. She hoped that Abner Freeman was the sort of person who could explain things clearly and who wouldn't mind her asking questions, but she wasn't too sure. At this moment he was standing with his hands in his pockets staring unseeingly ahead of him.

She had kept her cloak on until she was certain that she would be staying. Now she lifted it off her shoulders. That attracted his attention. When he looked at her, his face was perhaps a little less unfriendly than it had been.

'I'll have to show you all about the scales 'n' things,' he said. 'But I guess you ain't met my wife. Come along. You kin hang your things out here.' As he led the way into the passage, he pointed to some pegs against the wall and continued walking towards the back of the house.

The kitchen was warm but untidy. Like most kitchens, it was the main room of the house, with a long table, benches, a chair, a few papers lying on a shelf, the usual kitchen equipment. Mrs. Molloy was bending over the fire stirring something that was cooking in the big kettle hanging over the flames. On the table behind her were potatoes in a basket, a piece of knitting, a litter of unwashed dishes.

'Over here,' said Mr. Freeman, going towards an open door.

Beyond the open door was a very small bedroom,

barely twice the width of the narrow bed it contained and obviously carved out of the kitchen so that the sick woman could be close to the centre of the family's activities. In the bed, propped against several pillows, lay Rose Freeman, a bony woman with wispy hair and a heavily lined face.

'This here's Emma Anderson, Rose,' Abner Freeman said.

The woman in the bed had been staring sightlessly ahead of her. Now she drew her mind from wherever it had been.

'Emma Anderson?' She smiled. 'Oh, you must be Harriet McPhail's niece. She's talked about you.'

'That's right,' Emma said. 'Mrs. McPhail sent me to help Mr. Freeman in the shop and to look after you a bit.'

'Ain't that nice of her?' Abner Freeman said in a big, hearty voice. It was the tone that people use to speak to invalids and the aged – or to disguise their own feelings. Emma was not sure which it might be, but she noted it. Mrs. Freeman gave her husband a glance as though she also observed the false heartiness. The glance could mean something different, though – or nothing at all. Emma did not know these people yet and could not guess at the unspoken matters lying between them; for the time being, she told herself, she had better not puzzle over them.

'How are you feeling?' she asked Mrs. Freeman.

Before the sick woman could answer, there came the tinkle of the bell on the front door and a man's voice shouting, 'Abner?'

'Customer,' Abner Freeman said.

His departure was a relief to Emma. Rose smiled again. 'Sit down, Emma.' She gestured towards a stool beside the bed, and Emma saw that her hands were knotted with rheumatism, the skin stretched shiny over the knuckles.

She sat down on the stool. 'You must tell me what I can do for you, Mrs. Freeman. I helped look after a sick lady once before.' This was Granny Wilbur, a member of the family which had taken Emma and John in after the death of their parents. Emma always remembered her with love and respect.

'It's very kind of you, my dear. I'll need you mainly when Mrs. Molloy isn't here. She only comes in the mornings. Sometimes,' Mrs. Freeman added in a whisper, 'she misses a morning on account of the pains in her legs.' She made a small grimace that suggested doubts about whether the pains were real or just an excuse. Emma smiled politely; this was no time to start taking sides on the question of Mrs. Molloy's legs. Instead she looked for a neutral subject to talk about.

'I haven't met your son Charlie yet,' she said, 'but I've heard about him.'

'He's a good boy, is Charlie. But he and his dad don't get along very well. That causes a lot of....' She lifted her hands in a small gesture of helplessness.

'Yes, I can imagine.'

Emma, observing the signs of rheumatism in Mrs. Freeman, wondered why the family continued to live in this part of town, which was close to the marshes and notoriously unhealthy. True enough, the small window in Mrs. Freeman's room was shut tight – the air was heavy with the sweetish odour of sickness, the rancid smell of bed-linen and clothing not washed often enough, and the fumes of cooking from the kitchen – but still the bad air of the marshes would surely find its way in.

Of course she could not ask Mrs. Freeman this, but maybe sometime she would inquire of Mrs. McPhail.

That thought suggested a question which she could ask. 'You and Mrs. McPhail are very old friends, aren't you?'

'Oh, yes, I was a servant in Mrs. McPhail's family when she was just Miss Harriet Anderson.'

'You *were?*' Emma uttered the words in a gasp of breathless surprise. 'Then you must have known my father!'

'Oh, yes. Not well, of course, because I was just a servant.'

'Then you can tell me....' Emma paused; her mind was suddenly so full of questions that she didn't know what to ask first. Since coming to York she had tried to find out something about the early lives of her parents, who had lived in York before getting married and moving out to the edge of the settlement to clear a farm for themselves.

Before she could form a question, she saw Mrs. Freeman's eyes shift. 'Here's my husband. I guess he's looking for you.'

Very reluctantly, Emma got to her feet and followed him. She would dearly have loved to stay with Mrs. Freeman and ask about her father, who had died before she was old enough to see him as a person. Emma had once asked Mrs. McPhail if there was anyone in York who had known him but had been told that there wasn't. Had Mrs. McPhail deliberately overlooked Rose Freeman? Or perhaps she considered it morbid of Emma to want to know – morbid, or silly, or needlessly distracting. Maybe she had just forgotten that Rose had known him, or thought that Rose would have nothing to tell. Maybe in fact she *had* nothing to tell, but still

Emma would ask when she had another opportunity.

For the moment, however, there was nothing she could do except follow Abner Freeman to the front of the house for her first lesson in shopkeeping.

They had barely entered the shop when the bell on the front door tinkled again. Emma turned to see who it was.

A little boy appeared shyly in the shop doorway. He was barefoot and dressed in a ragged shirt and breeches. By its legs he carried a dead duck, its colourful feathers rumpled and muddy. A drop or two of blood fell from its bill, landing on the floor and making Emma want to dart forward to wipe it. The duck, held up by the child's thin arm, was nearly as long as the child himself was tall.

'Yes, Willie?' Freeman asked. 'What d'ya want now?'

'Ma says ... flour,' the child whispered.

'Okay. You take the duck to Mrs. Molloy in the kitchen and come back here for the flour.' He turned to Emma. 'One of the kids from the shanties in the marshes.'

He got an old newspaper from a pile and spread it on the counter.

'At least it's flour she wants,' Emma commented.

'You thought they'd ask for whiskey? Well, they do sometimes, though they also got stills to make their own.'

He opened one of the barrels standing along the side walls of the room and filled a scoop with flour, carrying it back to the counter and emptying it onto the newspaper. 'The better sort o' customers brings their own containers but them shanty folk got no containers to speak of. Just what they pick up at the dump. So I use this paper for them. If you see old papers lying around anywheres, like at the hotel, you could bring 'em along.' He added another scoop of flour to the pile. Then he bundled the newspaper around the flour and reached under the counter for what at first looked like string but turned out to be a length of woollen yarn.

'How do you decide how much flour to give them in exchange for a duck?'

'I just guess, each time, but I weigh it and write it down. I kin figure it out later.' As he spoke, he laid the package of flour on the scales and weighed it. Then he opened the ledger-like book and wrote in it.

'How will I know?'

He brooded for a moment. 'Do just like what you've seen me doing now. If you write down what they bring and what you gave 'em, I kin decide whether they owe me something or I owe them.'

'Can they have whatever they like, when they come in bartering or asking for credit? I mean, suppose someone comes in and asks for ... let's say brandy, or whiskey, spices, tobacco ... expensive things, not something like flour that's basic food. How do I know that the customer can be trusted to pay you in the end? He might be a very poor man, or he might be a complete stranger who'll never show his face here again. Then you'd never get your money.'

As she was speaking, the little boy came back. Abner pushed the parcel of flour to his side of the counter. 'Here, Willie, but first make your mark in the book like I showed you last time.' He turned the ledger around, then dipped the quill in the ink bottle and handed it to Willie.

The child looked in awe at him and then at the pen. He took the quill slowly and clumsily. Mr. Freeman put a blunt finger down at the place where he wanted Willie to inscribe his mark.

'Make a nice neat cross now, Willie.'

The child's head came only just above the counter, and when he leaned closer his nose was barely an inch from the paper. Pressing so hard that the quill squeaked, he drew a shaky X.

'That's fine,' Mr. Freeman said, turning the book around again. 'See, I'll just write in, "Willie Jackson, his mark". Your name *is* Jackson, ain't it?'

Willie nodded, though Emma suspected that he was doing so to be cooperative rather than because he knew what his surname was.

'Okay, that's all,' Mr. Freeman said. 'You kin go now. Carry the parcel carefully.'

When the bell had tinkled again to signal the child's departure, Mr. Freeman said, 'You was asking something. I forget what it was.'

Emma had to think for a moment; she had been completely absorbed in the little drama and had been surprised and moved to see the big, rather unattractive man dealing so gently with the child.

'Oh, yes, I asked whether you give credit for everything, and to everyone.'

Abner gave it some thought. 'O'course *I* know my regular customers,' he said at last. 'But you kin check through the book and see if they got credit before and paid their account, or if they're still in debt, or whatever. I'll show you the book in a minute. If you're not sure, give credit only on basic food and medicine, not on brandy and stuff like that, what I call luxury goods.' He gave an odd, twisted grin. 'Funny ... I never had to explain it to anyone before. Rose and I sort of worked it out together when we started up. But I guess that's what I do. You kin always ask Rose. She knows who the regular customers are. Here, I'll show you the book.'

He again opened the big volume in which Willie had made his mark. It was indeed a sort of ledger, recording the dealings between Abner Freeman and his customers. In return for goods and provisions from the store, Abner received not only ducks but also wood ashes (which no doubt he sold to the soap factory), firewood, a whole range of farm produce, and services such as the shoeing of his horse or the loan of a cart. Sometimes he didn't even specify; the customer paid him in what was recorded as 'merchandise'. When he considered that an account was cleared, he drew diagonal lines through the various transactions which comprised it. The entries were not very neat and sometimes barely legible, but they had a sort of order.

Then he showed her how to use the scales, with the weights to be put in one pan and the merchandise in the other. 'This scales here is for little things. I got a big scales out back for things like sacks o' flour or wood ashes. Show you later.'

Finally he took her around the shop, lifting the lids of tubs of molasses and flour and raisins. He pointed to the kegs of brandy and whiskey lying on their sides on a home-made rack. He led her past the shelves behind the counter – a whole wall of them except for the space taken by one of the room's two windows – and pointed to the medicines and spices in their labelled containers. He pulled out drawers to reveal candles, soap, quill pens, sewing supplies, writing paper, fish hooks, nails and screws. Under the counter were crocks and jugs and a litter of cups and saucers, glass dishes, shoe laces, empty ink bottles, mouse traps, and many other things. From the rafters hung fire tongs and pokers, coils of rope, crow-bars, hammers, lanterns, and a bird cage. As he went, he mentioned some prices which Emma tried hard to remember.

'We ain't got everything that people might want to buy. No boots or cloth or things like that. People go to the stores in town for them.' He gestured towards the centre of York. 'We got stuff that people might need urgent-like, or not want to go into town for. Like a man might need a couple o' nails for his shed door that he's fixing. This fellow that came in this morning is working at the windmill, one o' the carpenters, and needed some rope for something, so it's handier for him to come here.'

He was just opening the cash drawer, which Emma had already seen, when the doorbell rang again. A thin woman carrying a basket came in, followed by a small boy.

'Morning, Mrs. Thompson,' Abner said in a reasonably cheerful and friendly voice.

'Morning, Mr. Freeman. How's Mrs. Freeman today?'

'So-so, I guess you'd have to say.' He glanced at Emma, who had drawn back, and jerked his head to summon her forward. As she came towards him he said to the customer, 'This here's Emma Anderson. She's helping out. Just tell her what you want. I'll watch and see that she gets it right.' And he went to sit down in the chair by the fireplace.

Emma was startled and nervous at being so abruptly put to work. She had been the customer often enough, doing errands for her aunt or Mrs. Jones, but now in an instant she had to change roles and become the shop assistant.

'Yes, Mrs. ... Mrs. Thompson?' she said, hoping

that her voice sounded right. 'What can I do for you?'

Mrs. Thompson touched the hair at the side of her face in a preening gesture, as though she too felt exposed to an unusual amount of attention.

'Well, let me see now. I'd like some tea – not the dearest kind, because I can't afford it. The other.'

Emma pointed to the big tin canisters holding the two different kinds of tea, giving the prices that she had just learned from Abner Freeman. 'This tea is forty cents per quarter pound, and this is thirty-two cents.' When Mrs. Thompson made her choice – she made a show of being tempted by the more expensive sort but in the end decided on the cheaper – Emma picked up a scoop.

'How much would you like, Mrs. Thompson?'

'Two ounces, please, dear.'

Emma scooped up some tea, guessing at the amount by remembering her own shopping, emptied the scoop into one pan of the scales, and laid the two-ounce weight in the other pan. Her guess had been close but a bit too generous; she scooped a small portion of the tea out again.

'A little more,' said Mrs. Thompson.

'That will bring it over the two ounces,' Emma said, one eye on Abner Freeman for a signal. Some merchants gave skimpy measures, others were generous. She hadn't had a chance yet to find out which kind he was.

He gave no sign, but he was watching her carefully.

'No, it won't,' Mrs. Thompson protested. 'I always gets just that little bit more and it's still two ounces. Ain't that so, Mr. Freeman?'

Abner lumbered to his feet and came behind the counter. Without a word he took from Emma the scoop that contained the bit of tea. With his other hand he shook the pan of the scales as though to see how much was in it. He tipped the bit of tea in, used the scoop to stir all the tea around, took up a small amount with the scoop, moved the weight around in the other pan. When he had finished, the proportions in the pan and the scoop were exactly the same as Emma had measured. Nevertheless Mrs. Thompson gave a satisfied nod.

'There you are, Mrs. Thompson.' As he turned to empty the scoop into the tea canister, he caught Emma's eye and gave her a tiny wink. Emma, who was facing Mrs. Thompson, could not wink back but understood very well what he had just demonstrated. Mrs. Thompson liked to have a bit of fuss made; she wanted to be sure that her purchase was weighed very carefully and to see that her sixteen cents' worth of tea was treated with the greatest possible seriousness.

'Mrs. Thompson'll have something to put the tea in, I'm sure,' he said, returning to his chair.

From her basket, the woman produced a battered tin tea-caddy, into which Emma poured the weighed tea.

'Anything else, Mrs. Thompson?'

'Boot black, please, dear.'

This came in bottles, so there was no measuring involved. There were several different kinds; Mrs. Thompson discussed the quality of each. Emma patiently listened to what Mrs. Thompson thought about the different kinds, what her husband thought, what her friends and neighbours thought.

They would certainly have gone through the same procedure with a paper of pins and two cakes of soap, except that Abner stocked only one kind of each. When Mrs. Thompson had everything she wanted, Emma added up the cost. She didn't know whether Mrs. Thompson was one of the people who regularly received credit – when she had time she would look through the ledger and memorize some names and the details of the arrangements that Mr. Freeman made. Mrs. Thompson, as it turned out, paid cash; she counted out the coins and put the purchases in her basket. She again patted her hair and gave Emma a patronizing little nod.

'You did that very well, dear.'

Emma was amused. 'Thank you, Mrs. Thompson. It was a pleasure to serve you.'

Mrs. Thompson collected her little boy, who had been stroking the cat. She nodded again to Emma, gave Abner a kindly message for his wife, and left.

Emma took a deep breath. That hadn't been so bad. She realized that she could draw on much of what she had learned in the hotel about dealing with the public, and that only the actual handling of the merchandise and remembering of prices would be new to her.

Chapter Three

That morning, Emma served two more customers. One was a brisk woman who became feverishly impatient with Emma's careful weighing out of a pound of raisins; the other woman brought three small children, who ran shouting about the shop and had to be constantly watched lest they hurt themselves or damage something. By then Abner had stepped out to talk to a friend of his who was driving by; Emma could see them on the road, the friend sitting on the seat of his wagon and Abner standing beside. She could have called him in had she needed to, but clearly he was leaving her to manage as well as she could.

When the woman with the rackety children left, Emma perched on a stool used for reaching the top shelves and the merchandise hanging from the rafters. The shop was suddenly quiet, and Emma had leisure to look around. As she did so, she remembered Mrs. McPhail's comment about putting some heart into the place.

She wished that she could have seen what the shop was like when Rose Freeman had been well enough to work. Apparently she had given it a pleasant atmosphere, and clearly she had made a good impression on people because all the women customers had asked after her. No doubt she had been patient, friendly, and interested in them.

That, surely, was something that Emma could try to imitate. She was thinking that she would have to learn the customers' names as quickly as possible, and then wondering whether there was any point in doing so when she might be working here only for a few weeks, when Mrs. Molloy put her head around the door.

'Ready for dinner, dearie? Where's Mr. Freeman?'

'Out on the road talking to someone.'

Mrs. Molloy opened the tinkling door and screeched to Abner, who nodded and took leave of his friend. Emma followed him to the kitchen.

Already seated at the table was a young man whom Emma took to be Charlie; she had seen him about town driving a brewer's wagon but had never known his name.

Abner performed introductions. 'Charlie, this here's Emma Anderson, come to help out.'

The words were mumbled and awkward, and they reminded Emma that Abner did not get along well with his son. In addition to learning about shopkeeping, she had to become acquainted with the Freeman family. At the very least she had to learn enough to avoid being tactless or foolish. So far she had gained quite a few impressions about Abner Freeman – in fact, all morning she had been revising her first image of him – but she knew much less about his wife and son.

'Hello, Charlie,' she said.

Charlie half-rose from the bench and gave her a wide but somehow tentative grin. He was a tall, lanky young man with a mop of brown hair long enough in front to shadow his eyes. Hair also furred the backs of his hands and curled from the open neck of his shirt.

Emma remembered what Mrs. McPhail had said about Charlie not being very bright. She compared him to Joe Tubb in the hotel. Joe was clearly feeble-minded; he had a blank face, nearly round, with small eyes like currants. He sometimes laughed abruptly for no reason, and his vocabulary contained only a dozen or so words, though he seemed to understand more. Charlie looked normal. But if he were clever he'd surely be doing something more challenging and rewarding than driving a brewer's dray part-time, loading and unloading barrels of beer.

As he sat down he glanced at her again. This look had something more personal in it, not just the formal response to an introduction. The broad, vague grin came back for a brief moment, but the brown eyes under the thatch of hair regarded her with friendly warmth. There was something attractive about Charlie, something that shone unexpectedly from behind the rough exterior and caught Emma by surprise. As she sat down, she hoped that she wasn't blushing.

The meal consisted of stew and bread. Mr. Freeman drank whiskey – rather a lot – while Charlie and Mrs. Molloy drank beer. Emma was offered both but declined; she saw that tea had been made, presumably for Mrs. Freeman, and asked whether she might have a cup.

'Charlie has to hurry,' Mrs. Molloy said. 'He's got to work this afternoon.'

'Delivering beer?' Emma asked. It was a silly question but she wanted to be friendly.

He nodded. 'Out to the fort.'

'You must know York very well.'

He shrugged and gave his wide grin. 'Mebbe.' Then he bent over his plate and resumed spooning stew into his mouth.

There was no further conversation. Five minutes later Charlie drained his beer and left. A minute or two after that, Abner also got to his feet.

'I'll be in the shop for the next half hour,' he said to Emma. 'You do what you like. After that, you're in charge for a while.'

When he had disappeared along the passage, Mrs. Molloy said, 'Better stay here, dearie. He usually has a sleep after dinner, sitting in one o' them chairs in the shop.'

'Maybe I could have a little chat with Mrs. Freeman,' Emma said, remembering that she wanted to ask about her father's youth.

'She sleeps too.'

Mrs. Molloy put away the left-over food in a cupboard, stacked the dirty plates, and brought out a basin for washing dishes. Emma took a dish-towel from a peg and prepared to help.

As she lifted down the towel, she noticed an oval-shaped board standing against the wall in the corner. She might not have noticed it specially except that it had a picture painted on it – a picture of a weigh-scales, painted in a yellowy-gold colour on a dark background. It was the gold that caught the light. The board looked like the sort of sign that might hang out in front of a shop or a pub, depicting the kind of business it was and usually giving its name in the form of a picture.

There was no sign-board out on the road to identify the Freeman shop; if there had been, Emma wouldn't have had to ask directions of the carter this morning.

'The Sign o' the Scales,' Mrs. Molloy said.

Emma looked up. 'The Sign of the Scales? Is that what this shop is called?'

'That was the idea. Scales, see, for weighing stuff.' Mrs. Molloy used her two hands to show imaginary merchandise being weighed. 'That board there used to hang from a post out beside the road until it was knocked down by a wagon. They ain't got round to putting it up again.'

'It's a nice sign,' Emma commented, taking up the

dish-towel. 'If it were out there where passers-by could see it, it might bring in more customers. It would swing in the wind, and the gold would catch the light....'

It was the Freemans' affair, of course. But the fact that Abner had not erected the sign again after it was knocked down seemed to fit with the air of neglect and dispiritedness that pervaded the place and the family.

Emma began to dry the dishes. She received an appreciative nod from Mrs. Molloy. 'You'll find lots o' slow times, workin' in the shop.'

'Tomorrow I'll bring my sewing. Do you think he'd mind if I sewed when there were no customers? And I could sew while I kept Mrs. Freeman company.'

'Oh, he wouldn't mind that – at least, I don't *think* so. He ain't always easy to figure out.'

'He seems to get along all right with the customers.'

'Sure he does. But business ain't so good these days. Mrs. Freeman, now,' she went on with a conspiratorial jerk of the head towards the closed bedroom door, 'she had a nice way with 'er. When she was up and about there was more customers – people droppin' in, askin' her advice, just talkin' to her – maybe half an hour's talk for a spool o' thread. But it was good for business all the same.'

The doorbell rang. Emma was about to put down the dish-towel but Mrs. Molloy said, 'Don't worry. He'll look after it. The bell wakes him.'

So Emma, mindful of Mrs. McPhail's instructions, asked, 'What exactly did Mrs. Freeman do? I mean, how did she attract customers?'

Mrs. Molloy looked blank. 'I dunno. People liked talkin' to her. I'd hear them laughin' and ... sometimes they told her their troubles. She'd come out here and pour a cup o' tea for some poor lady who was cryin'.

And she fixed to have them two chairs in there. To sit 'n' talk.'

The words were skimpy, but they created a picture. 'Do they ever come and see her now that she's sick? They all ask after her, but do they visit her?'

'Sometimes. Her real friends do. Only it's not the same, havin' to come all the way through here, sittin' on a stool.... It's not like just poppin' in to buy two ounces o' tea. And I guess it's harder to talk about your own problems to someone who's sick herself.'

Then Mrs. Molloy told Emma about a daughter of hers who had been an invalid for all five years of her short life.

'A little saint she was! There ain't no other word for it. I made her a bed-jacket and she said, "Mother," she said, "give it to some poor child. I won't need no bed-jacket where I'm goin'." As though we ain't poor enough ourselves. But no! "Mother," she said....'

Without needing any encouragement, she talked on about this child and her other children. Eventually the door tinkled again, probably to let out the customer who had arrived earlier. Abner Freeman came to the kitchen.

'Okay, now you watch the shop for a while, Emma. I'll be in the shed out back or away seeing a fellow. You don't have to sit in there all the time, but keep an ear open for the bell.'

'Yes, Mr. Freeman.'

Mrs. Molloy left when she had finished the dish-washing. The last thing she did was to set Mrs. Freeman's bedroom door ajar. 'So's you kin hear if she calls,' she told Emma.

After that the house was very silent. From the yard came the sound of a hen cackling, and out on the road a cart creaked past. Once a flock of wild geese flew overhead honking.

Emma stood in the kitchen, wondering what to do. So far, since she had arrived that morning, there had been nothing but pressure and tension. She drew a deep breath ... and yawned ... and recalled that her night's sleep had been short and troubled by dreams. If Mr. Freeman could sleep in a chair and still wake up to attend to customers, why couldn't she?

She went to the shop and sat down. The chair was comfortable, made of wood but with a squashed cushion on the seat and a pad tied with tapes against the back. From where she sat, ready to doze off, Emma could see the whole range of shelves behind the counter. She let her eyes rove along them, then became curious. What was in all those bottles and jars and canisters?

Forgetting her tiredness, she went to the shelves and began reading the labels – cough mixture, liniment, metal polish of various kinds, food flavouring, tonic, dye, and remedies for every possible ailment. Quite a few claimed to be good for rheumatism and fever; no doubt they were in demand among the people who lived in this area near the marshes.

Before she went very far in her reading of labels, Emma noticed how dirty everything was. She had been half-aware of it all day but had pushed the fact aside so that she could concentrate on Mr. Freeman's instructions and the customers' requests.

Now she looked around and noticed that the counter top, though wiped, was greasy and that dust lay under the scales. The scales themselves needed polishing. The candlesticks were encrusted with old wax. All the bottles she had been studying were dirty, and so were the shelves. The floor had been roughly swept but there were dust-balls in the corners and under the chairs. The spots of blood that had dripped from the dead duck were not the only stains on the boards. There were spills near the tubs and barrels of merchandise; as Emma watched, a mouse crept forward, picked up a dropped raisin, and darted back out of sight. Emma was not afraid of mice – every house in York had them, whether or not there was a cat – but the appearance of this one, living on the spilled provisions, showed how necessary it was for someone to do some cleaning.

Furthermore, when she lifted a few of the bottles for close inspection, she saw that they were in disorder. The bottle at the front of the shelf did not always contain the same thing as those behind it. One bottle had lost its label. Another had neither label nor cork and the liquid inside had dried to a blackish, cracked sediment.

She could certainly do some tidying and cleaning. Squatting down, she began to remove objects from the shelf under the counter. She'd clean the shelf and then wash or dust the merchandise before putting it back.

Then she stopped. She ought to ask Mr. Freeman's permission first. And she didn't know where he was. What had he said? He'd be working in the shed and then going to see someone.

She went to the back door and looked out but there was no sign of him. She went to see if Mrs. Freeman was awake and could give permission for the cleaning, but she was still asleep.

It was a good plan, to clean the shop, and it might go a long way towards achieving Mrs. McPhail's goal of putting some heart into the place, but she'd have to wait until she had a chance to ask. Otherwise she might be accused of interfering, of taking too much onto herself. Tomorrow, to be prepared, she'd bring one of her big aprons from the hotel. In the meantime she'd better put the things back where they came from.

She had just finished doing that and was still squatting behind the counter when the doorbell tinkled. By the time she got to her feet the customer was in the shop.

This time it was a man. He had a valise with him, which he was lifting to set down on the counter. When Emma rose from behind the counter he looked surprised, perhaps startled by her sudden appearance. He held the valise in mid-air for an instant, then set it down as he had intended, at the same time using his other hand to remove his hat in courtesy.

His bearing and dress, including the fine leather gloves he wore, were those of a gentleman. Through the side window Emma could see a trim carriage standing by the edge of the road, the horse tethered to the unfinished fence.

'Yes, sir? May I help you?'

'I'd like to see Abner Freeman, please, miss.'

'He's not here just now.'

But at the same moment she heard heavy steps outside and Mr. Freeman burst in through the tinkling door, panting heavily and pressing his hand against his side.

'Saw you drive up,' he gasped, addressing the man. 'This ain't your usual day for calling.'

'I happened to be in the area.' He glanced at Emma, and Mr. Freeman jerked his head to order her out of the shop.

She went obediently but wondered what she ought

to have done if Abner had not come. It was another thing she would have to ask.

She went back to the kitchen, hoping to find Mrs. Freeman awake so that she could ask about her father. But the sick woman slept on. Emma stoked the fire. She filled the kettle from the water pail and hung it over the fire so that later she could make a pot of tea.

Before the kettle boiled, however, the customer left and Abner Freeman came to the kitchen.

'You kin go now, Emma,' he said abruptly.

'Go?'

'I'll be home the rest o' the day.'

'All right.' She got up from the bench on which she had been sitting. 'When I come tomorrow, would you like me to do some cleaning and tidying in the shop?' She smiled to show her willingness.

He stared at her with a return of his unfriendly and suspicious manner. Watching him, she was certain that he would refuse, though she could not understand why.

'Sure, if you want to.' He tried to make it sound like a matter of no importance, but clearly he had given it careful thought.

Emma persisted; she wanted to have a few things clear. 'Can I tidy the bottles so that all the ones that contain the same stuff are in the same row, one behind the other?'

'How d'you mean?'

'I'll show you.'

She led the way to the shop and pointed out to him the disorder she had found.

'Yeah, that's okay,' he said. 'But keep the front ones in front. New stock goes behind, see, and then gets moved forward when we sells the older stock. Always sell the front bottle first.'

'I'll do that. And can I dust and clean? It'll make everything nicer – for the customers and for you.' She tried to coax him into seeing the advantage of her plan.

'Sure, sure, clean as much as you like,' he said in an off-hand way.

As if he were doing her a favour, she muttered to herself while picking her way down the muddy walk to the lane and then to the Kingston Road. And why in heaven's name should he even consider refusing such a harmless and useful thing?

Chapter Four

As Emma walked back towards the hotel, she felt oddly disoriented. It seemed much more than just a few hours since she had come along here this morning. So much had happened to her! She almost felt like a different person, seeing things in a new way.

Perhaps because of that, she had a shock of surprise when she saw the familiar figure of John some distance ahead of her along King Street. He was carrying what might be a empty cloth bag over his shoulder and was talking to a lady in a bonnet whom Emma could not see clearly enough to recognize. As Emma watched they parted, the lady continuing along the street away from Emma, John touching his cap and then disappearing between two buildings.

There was really nothing unusual about this; John's work for Mr. Blackwood took him all over town. But most of his business would surely be with men, the principal users of the livery stable.

Of course he might have assisted the lady in some way – carried a parcel for her or returned a lost pet at some time. She might be the wife of one of Blackwood's patrons. Emma's imagination had no trouble inventing explanations.

When she reached the place where they had been, there was no sign of John. Emma had not expected him to linger, but somehow his complete disappearance added to the strangeness of everything.

Emma had arrived at the corner where she would turn north towards the hotel when she saw Mr. Blackwood coming out of a doorway just a few feet ahead of her. He was tucking something into his waistcoat pocket and looked so preoccupied that she thought he hadn't seen her. He was John's employer and, because of business connections with Mrs. McPhail, was often at the hotel. In fact, being unmarried, he frequently dined there.

But apparently he had noticed her.

'Hello, there, Emma!' he said in his big voice with the Yankee accent. He touched the brim of his tall hat.

'Hello, Mr. Blackwood,' she said, bobbing a little curtsey.

His public manner was always hearty and good-humoured. But Emma did not entirely trust him. She couldn't forget that he had bought her late father's farm and then, just a few weeks later, tried to sell it to the Heatheringtons at a very much higher price. Had he succeeded, he and Mrs. McPhail would have shared the profit.

All the same, she was always polite to him. She was afraid that if she angered him he would take it out on John.

Once she was back in the hotel, Emma lost her sense of disorientation. She was abruptly plunged into the familiar routine, setting the table for dinner, helping Mrs. Reynolds with her sick child, listening to Ruth's stories of what had happened during the day. But she noticed that John was late returning to the hotel and that when he did come in he said he had had dinner and was not interested in the dish of food which Emma had saved for him.

* * *

She was in the middle of a dream that night when she

was awakened by a thump. At first, as she lay blinking into the darkness, she thought that the noise was part of the dream, but then it came again. It seemed to be deliberate and to come from one of the guests' rooms on the floor below. Perhaps it was Mr. Vernon, an older gentleman who walked with a cane. It sounded like the sort of thump that might be made with a cane. Maybe he was calling for help. Emma got out of bed, slipped her bare feet into her boots but did not lace them up, and swung her outdoor cloak around her for warmth in the cold house. She did not take time to light a candle; she knew the house well enough to find her way in the dark.

As she opened the door at the bottom of the attic stairs, she saw a light coming up the staircase from the lobby. It was Mrs. McPhail with a candle. She gave Emma a glance and then went to Mr. Vernon's door, where she knocked softly.

'Mr. Vernon? Was that you summoning help?'

Emma heard no answer, but perhaps Mrs. McPhail did. At any rate, she opened the door and went in, just as the man in the bed made a retching sound and leaned over the edge of the bed.

'Emma! The basin! Quick!'

Emma seized the basin from the washstand and rushed to hand it to her aunt, but they were not in time for the first vomit. Mrs. McPhail held the basin to catch the rest.

'Wipe the floor, will you, Emma. But first get me a wet cloth and a towel for Mr. Vernon.'

Emma wetted a small hand towel in the water-jug on the washstand. This and a large dry towel she handed to Mrs. McPhail, who was supporting Mr. Vernon with her arm. Then she went across the hall to the closet to fetch a cloth for wiping up the vomit. She hated the smell of it and the airless room thick with the odours of an old person sleeping. But she was used to such things – however unpleasant, they were part of life, especially for a chambermaid in a hotel.

By now Mr. Vernon's attack seemed to be over.

'Sorry....' he said faintly. 'Maybe something I ate.'

It was meant as an apology, but it made Mrs. McPhail look very grave indeed. No doubt she, like Emma, remembered that Mr. Vernon had eaten dinner here in the hotel this past evening.

'Would you like a cup of tea, Mr. Vernon? Or shall we send for a physician?'

'Physician, perhaps. I don't feel at all well.'

'Certainly, Mr. Vernon.'

Mrs. McPhail drew Emma out into the hall. 'Run and fetch Dr. Ross, will you? Tell him it's urgent. Tell him what the trouble is – he may be able to bring some medicine with him. Hurry, now!'

Emma knew where Dr. Ross lived – down Yonge Street just beyond Blackwood's livery stable where John worked and then a few doors west on Newgate Street. She paused to tie the laces of her boots and then went to summon him.

The town was dark and quiet. She had no idea what time it was but there was only an occasional faint glimmer of light from a night candle behind a window. The starlight reflected in the puddles of water so that she could avoid stepping in most of them, but she did get her feet muddy. And, to judge by the uprush of smell, she stepped into several blobs of manure. She'd have to leave her boots on the back step when she returned, and wear her other pair tomorrow even though they were less comfortable.

But the night was not entirely quiet and dark. As she approached Blackwood's livery stable she heard subdued voices, a thud or two, and a horse snorting softly. The bare branches of a tree caught a gleam of light from a candle or lantern on the far side of the building.

Odd. But probably it was someone who had come very late to return a hired saddle horse or carriage. She knew from John that such things happened.

Without slowing down, she glanced again towards the light and the sounds. For an instant, through the gap between two outbuildings of the livery stable, she caught a glimpse of a cart and of two men, one in the cart and one on the ground, handling a cask. The man on the cart was wearing a white shirt, much whiter than anything that labourers usually wore, and his hair looked reddish in the dim light of the lantern. Then she lost sight of them.

Dr. Ross listened to her brief explanation and came back with her. He was a young man, new to York, said to be clever but rather modern in his ideas. Mrs. McPhail had called him in once before for a sick guest.

She was still with Mr. Vernon; she showed Dr. Ross into the room and then joined Emma in the hall. As she pulled the door shut, she glanced at the doors of the other four guest rooms.

Emma knew what she was thinking and put it into words. 'How can it have been the food, if no one else is sick? They all ate the same things, and so did you and I and Mrs. Jones and everybody.'

'Nevertheless it's bad for the hotel's reputation. People remember. Even if the food is proved blameless. And there's the Reynolds baby....'

'He was sick when they came!'

Mrs. McPhail shook her head. 'I'm afraid it makes

no difference. People will remember that he was sick here.'

Emma reflected that Mrs. McPhail was probably right. Abruptly she yawned.

Mrs. McPhail gave her a sharp look. 'You'd better go back to bed, child.'

'What time is it?'

'It was past one o'clock when Mr. Vernon pounded on the floor.'

'Oh, dear!' she murmured. Tomorrow was Sunday, but even so she'd have to be up at half past five. 'If you're sure it's all right.... Good night, then.'

***

The next day, because it was Sunday, Emma did not go to the store. But she did have her usual work in the hotel. While she was setting the table for breakfast, Mrs. McPhail said to her, 'Keep an eye on the guests, Emma. If any of them mentions being sick during the night, let me know at once.'

No one did, however, and a bit later Dr. Ross solved the problem of why only one guest had been sick. He visited his patient and then reported to Mrs. McPhail that Mr. Vernon had apparently made himself ill by treating a cough with a home-made remedy, antimonial wine.

'So we don't have to worry that it was the food,' Mrs. McPhail said to Emma. 'It was just a bilious attack.'

Emma spent the Sunday morning doing her usual work – the guests' bedrooms had to be done even though it was Sunday, and the lobby and dining parlour swept and dusted. In the afternoon she got permission to stay home from church. 'I have to do some mending and wash my hair,' she explained to Mrs. McPhail. 'Now that I'm working in the store I won't have any free time on weekday afternoons. Don't you think I could have this afternoon for myself?'

Mrs. McPhail granted the permission, and Emma spent the afternoon at the hotel washing her hair, mending her underskirt and a shirt of John's, and doing some work on a summer dress that she was sewing for herself.

It was not until she was on her way to the shop on Monday morning that she remembered what she had seen when passing the livery stable on Saturday night – a cask being unloaded from a cart into one of the sheds that opened away from the main courtyard of Blackwood's livery stable. Could it have been smuggled goods, contraband? Emma had heard that there was smuggling into Canada from the United States. Boats brought merchandise across Lake Ontario secretly, so as to avoid the duty that should, according to the law, have been paid on these imports, and landed it in small coves or at private docks. It was the customs officers' job to catch them, but there were not nearly enough officers to catch every smuggler.

It was one thing to be aware that such things went on. But if Mr. Blackwood were involved, that brought it much closer to home. Blackwood was John's employer.

John! Suddenly she remembered the money in her brother's breeches pockets. Perhaps John was involved, helping to distribute the contraband from the depot in Mr. Blackwood's shed. In a flash she saw it all – Blackwood's carts being used to bring the smuggled goods from the landing points along the lake,

Blackwood's shed to store the goods, Blackwood's employees to deliver them. And either Blackwood himself or the customers would pay John extra for such work.

Her brisk pace slowed while she brooded over this. One part of her was struck by the neatness of it – she couldn't imagine a better cover for smuggling than a livery stable – but much the larger part was worried and angry. It was wrong of Blackwood to take advantage of John like that. John might not even know how wrong it was.

But there she corrected herself immediately. John *would* know. He was at least as well-informed as she was. He would know about smuggling.

Smuggling was illegal and therefore dangerous. If smugglers were caught...? She didn't know what the punishment was. A fine? Imprisonment? Public flogging in the market place?

The jail was just along here, an imposing building next to the court house. She had passed it often but had never thought that it might have any relevance to herself. If John were involved in smuggling, though, and were caught....

With her mind on this, she nearly bumped into two men standing talking. As she passed, she noticed that one was Mr. Michaels-Harbottle and the other was the man with the gloves and the valise who had come to see Mr. Freeman at the shop on Saturday. She heard him say, 'That's all right, then. When do you expect to hear from Miller?' and Mr. Michaels-Harbottle's gravelly voice mumble something in reply.

At another time she would have been interested in this glimpse into a larger world and a wider network of people than the one she inhabited. Now, with her mind full of anxiety about John, she merely continued on her way.

As she came within sight of the Freeman store she remembered that she wanted to find an opportunity to talk privately to Rose Freeman about Martin Anderson. She had decided that, for this talk, she wanted to be alone with Mrs. Freeman, without constant interruptions. That meant that she'd have to do it in the afternoon, when Mrs. Molloy was gone. Now, this morning, she'd start cleaning the shop.

She got a cleaning cloth and a bucket of soapy water from Mrs. Molloy and was about to start taking things off the shelves when she paused. This job might take her several days, and during that time she would still have to be able to serve the customers, to find what they wanted. Besides, Mr. Freeman had told her to keep the bottles in order, with the newest stock at the back. She thought about it for a few moments and then went out to the back yard where Mr. Freeman was working.

'Can I borrow a board from you – about so long?' With her hands she measured a distance that was somewhat longer than the length of each of the shop shelves.

'What for?'

'The cleaning I'm going to do in the shop. I want it to put things on while I'm cleaning each shelf.'

Without a word he went to one of the sheds and came back with a suitable board, dusting it off with his hand as he walked.

'This do?'

'Yes, just right. Thank you.'

She took the board back to the shop and began removing things from the first shelf, the one at the top right-hand side. She dusted each object as she moved it. Then she wiped the empty shelf before returning the merchandise to it in tidy rows. Some shelves were caked with dirt, and at the back of one she found a tonic bottle that had fallen over and lost its cork, so that the tonic had spilled along the shelf and down to the one below.

Two customers came in during the morning; she served them because Mr. Freeman was out. He came home for dinner and afterwards went away again, this time having donned a hat and coat.

When she had washed the dishes, Mrs. Molloy came to the shop.

'I'll be on my way now, dearie,' she said, arranging her shawl over her head. 'Mrs. Freeman's asleep. She's not so good today, I don't think, but she hasn't asked for her special medicine.'

'What do I do if she's worse?'

'She don't get worse all at once. And Charlie's supposed to come home sometime during the afternoon. He's not workin' a full day today. He knows about the medicine. But don't worry, she's asleep now. If she starts feelin' worse she'll wake up and she'll tell ya what to do. It happened once before when I was here alone. Don't get scared – she'll ask for help when she needs it.'

Emma accepted Mrs. Molloy's assurances; at this moment there was nothing else she could do.

'All right, Mrs. Molloy. See you tomorrow.'

Mrs. Molloy had not been gone long before a customer arrived, a large-bosomed woman with a prosperous and self-important air. She had two little girls with her, and out on the road stood a wagon driven by someone who might be a hired man but could also be an extremely meek husband.

'Good afternoon, ma'am,' Emma said, getting down

from the stool on which she had been standing to reach a high shelf.

'Where's Abner Freeman?' the woman demanded.

Emma bristled at the abrupt and arrogant words but, having some experience of women like this at the hotel, controlled her irritation and drew a protective shell around herself.

'He's just out on business, ma'am. I'm his assistant. Can I help you?'

The woman surveyed Emma coolly, then shrugged. 'I suppose you can do the job or he wouldn't have left you in charge.' She appraised the contents of the store in a lordly way.

'I'd like whiskey, please. The best that Abner's got.' She lifted a gallon jug and set it on the counter. 'You can fill this.'

'Excuse me, ma'am, but may I enquire about payment? Will you be asking for credit or paying cash?'

The woman stared at Emma. Her eyes were pale blue and set in shallow sockets. She wore a fashionable bonnet which did not suit her large, squarish face. 'Put it on my account. Abner always gives me credit.'

'In that case I'm afraid I will only be able to let you have staple items. Whiskey is not a staple item; it's not basic food or medicine.'

'What's all this?'

Emma flushed. 'Mr. Freeman's policy about credit, ma'am, which he explained to me just last week.'

'This is outrageous! I have been a good customer of Abner Freeman's for years and have never encountered nonsense like this. Ask Mrs. Freeman. She knows me.'

'She's asleep, ma'am, and not feeling well today. Shall we continue with your list of staple items?'

'When will Abner be back?'

'I have no idea.'

The woman glared at Emma but clearly her mind was working. 'We will go though my complete list. Perhaps by the time I finish you will have a more accurate idea of the kind of customer I am and of the appropriate way to serve me.'

Emma bowed her head slightly and briefly. 'Very well, ma'am.'

'Whiskey, as I said. You fill the jug and my man will come and carry it.'

'Shall we leave the whiskey to the end, ma'am? Perhaps Mr. Freeman will return in time to decide about it.'

The woman paused for a moment. Emma was afraid that she would begin arguing again but in the end she said, 'Bootlaces, then. Black. The longest you've got.'

Emma fetched the box of bootlaces from the shelf under the counter and searched through it until she found the longest pair.

'Yes, ma'am?'

'Six cakes of soap.' She pointed to a drawer behind Emma in which the soap was kept.

'Three pounds of candles.' She watched narrowly while Emma weighed them.

'One bottle of cough mixture.'

Emma reached up to the shelf. 'This kind, ma'am?'

'It's the only kind that Abner carries, isn't it? It will have to do.'

'I believe it's generally considered very effective.'

The customer did not reply to this. Instead she said, 'Two pounds of raisins – the large ones.' She took a tin canister from her basket and set it on the counter.

Emma weighed the raisins and put them in the canister.

'An ounce of peppercorns. Abner always wraps them in a twist of paper for me.'

Emma measured out the right amount of peppercorns and put them on a portion of a sheet of old newspaper. She folded the two sides of the sheet together to make a tube and twisted the ends of the tube closed. This was what she had seen other shopkeepers do; it had looked easy but it wasn't, and the final product was not as neat as she had hoped. However, it held together well enough.

'Two of those candy sticks for the children.'

Emma laid the candy beside the other things. 'Anything else, ma'am?'

'Oh, yes, I'm not finished yet. Half a dozen cinnamon sticks.'

Emma counted them out.

'Four pair of those small metal plates for tacking under the heels of boots.'

Emma got them out of one of the drawers.

'That will be all for today.' The woman's tone suggested that this might be the last time she ever came to Freeman's.

They had reached the end of the list without Abner Freeman returning, and now the customer looked challengingly at Emma. 'Well, girl, have you bethought yourself? Are you going to give me credit?'

'For the staple items I will gladly give you credit, as Mr. Freeman instructed.'

'I insist upon having credit for everything. My wagon is outside, and it's convenient for me to take everything now. I live some way beyond the Don River and do not come to town daily. And I *won't* bow to your foolish arrogance.'

'Mr. Freeman's policy....'

'He never had such a policy before. It's ridiculous.'

'If you would tell me your name, ma'am, I'll check in the book.'

'I'm Mrs. Ferguson. Mrs. Roderick Ferguson.'

Mr. Freeman usually spread the book open on the counter, but Emma wanted to consult it without Mrs. Ferguson being able to see the pages. So she held it near the window behind the counter, on the pretence of needing more light, though at the same time she kept one eye on Mrs. Ferguson to make sure that she did not slip anything into her roomy basket.

The name 'Ferguson' did indeed appear in the ledger every week or two. Luxury items were included in the lists. So far as Emma could tell, however, the account had not been paid for nearly six months. Yet Mrs. Ferguson did not look like a poor woman. But if Emma gave her credit, and Mr. Freeman disapproved.... She knew that employees often had to pay out of their own pockets for any mistakes they made. She could not afford to make such an expensive error.

'I'm sorry, Mrs. Ferguson, but I must follow the policy laid down for me. Would you like me to put the staple items on your account, so that you can take them with you, or would you prefer to wait for Mr. Freeman?'

Mrs. Ferguson fumed, the ribbons on her bonnet trembling with her rage, but finally decided to take the staple merchandise.

Emma opened the book to a clean page and began listing it. As she wrote each item down, she moved it to a different area of the counter. She paused a moment when she came to the raisins and the cough mixture but Mrs. Ferguson, watching her every move and apparently reading her mind, settled the matter. 'The cough syrup is needed for one of the servants,' she said. 'The raisins are essential for some baking which I must do this afternoon.'

The candy, the peppercorns, the cinnamon, the metal plates for boot-heels, and the whiskey were not basic food or medicine and Emma was firm about them. She handed Mrs. Ferguson her empty whiskey jug, put the luxury items aside, and said, 'Now, if you would be so good as to sign the ledger....' She turned the book around and handed Mrs. Ferguson the quill.

Mrs. Ferguson firmly wrote the signature that Emma recognized from earlier pages in the ledger and then packed her purchases in her basket.

'Good day, Mrs. Ferguson,' Emma said.

Mrs. Ferguson said nothing as she strode out, the two little girls trotting to keep up.

Emma was about to put the non-staple items back where they came from but after a moment's reflection decided to leave them on the counter until the dreaded time when she would have to explain the matter to Mr. Freeman. She sighed; it had not been a pleasant experience. At the hotel, Mrs. McPhail usually handled people like this; Emma realized how much firmness, patience, and self-control it required. No wonder her aunt had become the sort of person she was; the qualities required to make a successful hotel-keeper had spread through her whole personality.

Or maybe they had been there all along.

Chapter Five

Although she might be said to have won the battle with Mrs. Ferguson, Emma was not at all sure that she had done the right thing. Mrs. Ferguson had had luxury items on credit before. But Mr. Freeman had said.... And Mrs. Ferguson hadn't paid her account in nearly six months....

Her mind went round and round. She longed for Mr. Freeman to come home so that she could explain the matter and have him make a decision, even if it led to a scolding. Anxious and restless, and not ready to return to the job of cleaning the shelves, she went to see if Mrs. Freeman was awake and ask her whether she had acted correctly.

But while walking from the shop to the kitchen she rejected that idea. She had made her decision and acted on it; it was Abner Freeman with whom she had to talk it over. Rose Freeman might have helped her earlier, but Emma hadn't consulted her.

Now, pausing in the kitchen doorway for a moment, Emma realized that she had been wrong not to consult Rose. Mr. Freeman had said that she could do so, and that was what she should have done.

But Rose had been asleep. Well, of course she might have been awake by then. Emma could have looked. Rose was not feeling well today. She would, however, have been able to answer a simple question about a customer – an *important* question, having to do with the good-will and reputation of the store. Emma had been sent here to try to help the business, not damage it.

She should *certainly* have asked Rose Freeman about

giving Mrs. Ferguson credit for her luxury items. If Rose was asleep, she should have wakened her.

For a minute or two Emma stood still, staring blindly ahead of her. She felt cold all over at the realization of how wrong she had been.

But Mr. Freeman could have prepared her better, or not have left her alone.

He had told her to ask Rose, and that was what Emma ought to have done.

At what point should she have gone to Rose?

As she asked the question, she remembered the scene in the shop, remembered her reluctance even to take her eyes off Mrs. Ferguson. Perhaps Mrs. Ferguson could have been trusted not to steal; she might consider it beneath her dignity. But it had not been beneath her dignity to bully Emma.

It had been a clash of wills. To Emma it had felt as though Mrs. Ferguson was bullying her personally, not in her role as shop assistant. It was more a conflict of individual people than of a customer and a sales clerk. Emma might have gone to Rose if the matter had been purely one of business, but as a person she had to fight the battle herself.

She stood for a moment longer, trying to calm down. She didn't feel cold now but was angry and gloomy, and she dreaded the moment when she would have to tell Abner Freeman what had happened.

In the meantime there were other things she had to do. She put wood on the fire and hung over it a kettle of water for tea. She peeked into Rose Freeman's room through the half-open door and found her awake.

Rose, seeing her, asked how she was progressing with the cleaning of the shop.

'Pretty well,' Emma said, going in and sitting down

on the stool. In spite of her resolution, she nearly spilled out the story of Mrs. Ferguson, but she held it back. It would be best to talk first to Abner.

This was, however, a good opportunity to ask about her father. Worrying about the Ferguson affair wiped out a good deal of Emma's pleasure in the prospect of talking about him, but it was a useful subject of conversation.

'You said on Saturday,' she began, 'that when you were young you knew my father, Martin Anderson.'

'I don't know whether I really *knew* him, Emma. I was just a servant, and he wasn't living with his parents for most of the time that I worked there.'

'Tell me what you do know about him, please. When he died I was too young to see him as a person. I've been trying since then to find out what he and my mother were like. It seems ... it seems important.'

'Well, I'll have to go back a bit. When I came here from England with my sister and her husband, I got a job working for your grandpa and grandma. No, I guess she wasn't your grandma, because she was your dad's stepmother. Isn't that right?'

'Yes. She was Mrs. McPhail's mother.'

'That's what I thought. Well, at first Martin was still away east of here – Cornwall or Kingston or somewhere. Then he came here to York and signed up for the army – the regular British army, I think it was, not the militia. He lived at the fort then, so he just visited his dad and stepmother. When the war came – that's the war with the Americans in 1812 – he fought and was wounded at Queenston. He came back here to York to recover. That's when he lived with us. Of course the next year we had the Americans here sacking and looting, and your dad did what he could helping people hide their belongings and fighting fires and things like that. His arm, the one that had been wounded, wasn't much use and he didn't take part in the later battles, I don't think. From the time he was hurt he lived with us. He got along all right with his dad but not with his stepmother. And no wonder, 'cause she was a hard woman. I didn't like her myself but.... Well, I worked there till I married Abner and then stayed on part-time. Your dad, he was out of the house most of the day, when he wasn't in the attic reading.'

'What was he like as a person?'

'A nice young man. Good-natured most of the time. But obstinate! He'd be going along easy as you please, and then someone would get across him or contradict him and bang! Martin would get all stubborn and dig in his heels.'

'Did you know my mother?'

'Only to see. She was at the house just once. The first time Martin brought her home to meet the family, his stepmother really insulted her. Your mom worked in a pub then, and Mrs. Anderson thought she was no good ... well, you can imagine. Girls who worked in pubs! That's one of the times your dad got stubborn. He carried right on planning to marry your mom and start a farm – he just never talked about it to Mrs. Anderson.'

By then the tea-kettle was making a rustling noise. Emma got to her feet.

Mrs. Freeman was still reminiscing. 'Stubborn he was, and independent. He liked to rely on himself, not other people. He wanted to do things his own way. I always wondered what sort of life he'd give your mother, 'cause men like that ... they can be real hard to live with.'

Emma, pausing in the doorway, saw in her mind's eye the point where Rose Freeman's story merged with what she herself remembered about her parents. 'I think maybe ... maybe he drew my mother in and they became self-reliant together. Not against each other, but together against the rest of the world. They grew into one strong "person", like the tree you see in the bush sometimes, which was two separate trees when they were small but have sort of blended to make one tree.'

Mrs. Freeman had been following her own thoughts. 'It would take a special woman to live with a man like that.'

'She *was* special. They both were.'

But what Emma reflected on as she made the tea was her father's obstinacy and independence. John had it – and so, perhaps, did she. This very afternoon, tackling Mrs. Ferguson herself, she had preferred to make her own mistakes and not ask Rose for help.

The incident showed, however, that obstinate self-reliance could have unpleasant and even dangerous consequences.

***

While waiting for the tea to steep, Emma went to the bedroom to ask Mrs. Freeman whether she liked milk and sugar in it.

'Just sugar, please, Emma.'

As she spoke, the doorbell tinkled. Heavy boots stumbled over the sill and Abner's voice could be heard cursing in a slurred way and going into the shop.

Drunk! thought Emma. She exchanged a quick glance with Mrs. Freeman. She poured Mrs.

Freeman's tea and took it to her, then went to the shop. It would be bad enough having to report on her encounter with Mrs. Ferguson, but she was dismayed at having to do so to a man who was drunk and already in a bad mood.

Abner Freeman was standing with his hands in his pockets, glowering at nothing. Emma had intended to begin by offering him a cup of tea, but when he saw her he demanded, 'Well? What's been going on?'

At first she thought that he must somehow have heard already of her confrontation with Mrs. Ferguson, but then she realized that he was just asking in a bad-tempered way how she had managed in his absence.

Emma drew a deep breath and gathered all her resoluteness.

'Mrs. Ferguson was here. She wanted a lot of things – on credit. But I remembered what you said and let her have only the staple items on credit, not the luxury ones. Those,' she said, pointing to the things on the counter, 'those, and a gallon of whiskey, were luxury items.'

'Mrs. Ferguson,' he muttered. 'Oh, hell!' He rubbed one hand over his face. 'Was she mad at you?'

'I'm afraid she was. We had a sort of argument. I looked in your book and saw that you had given her credit before, even for luxury items, but that she's not very good at paying her account. It was hard making up my mind but I remembered what you said on Saturday about giving credit only for staple or basic items.'

He had begun to wander around the shop, randomly, not meeting Emma's eyes. But Emma watched him closely for any reactions. Though she had done the wrong thing, she still felt that she had followed his instructions. Now it was up to him to decide what to do.

He seemed to be taking a long time. He looked grumpy, and he walked in a slouching way, dragging his feet, occasionally pausing to stare at something. Again she wondered why he had become a shopkeeper.

However reluctant he was, he would have to make a ruling, so that she would be prepared for the future.

'I know you'd probably have done something different,' she said. And when he still didn't speak, she added, 'Shall I put these things back on the shelves and in the drawers?'

'No, no, we got to deliver them to her.'

'Deliver them?'

He gave an enormous sigh. 'We can't let Mrs. Ferguson be mad at us. You'll have to deliver the stuff and apologize.'

'Apologize? For what?'

He shrugged. 'It don't matter how you do it. Blame me if you like. Just make it right with Mrs. Ferguson.'

'I followed your orders. I did exactly what you said. And I was reasonable and didn't lose my temper.'

He gave her a brief, sour glance. 'I said you kin blame me.'

'She doesn't even pay you regularly.'

'She pays in the end. If I offend Mrs. Ferguson....'

There was a heavy footstep behind Emma, who was still standing in the doorway between the passage and the shop. It was Charlie.

'Hello,' she said, glad of the interruption. She stepped aside to let him into the shop.

He gave her a grin as he passed, but when he had lounged in and was leaning against the wall he spoke to his father.

'Are we going to offend Mrs. Ferguson?'

'No, o'course not. This girl ... Emma, here ... refused her credit....'

'Only on luxury goods,' Emma said. 'Following *your* policy.'

'I'm sending her to apologize.' He glanced at his son. 'You go with her, show her where Mrs. Ferguson lives. Carry the jug o' whiskey that she asked for.'

There was so much careless contempt in Abner Freeman's voice that Emma expected Charlie to refuse, or to explode in anger. But he only said, 'Okay. Now?'

'Yeah, now. Fetch a basket for this stuff. You, Emma, write it down in the book.'

Not happy with what she had to do, but seeing that it was unavoidable, she went behind the counter and began adding the luxury items to Mrs. Ferguson's list. After writing down the first item, she looked up.

'Does this mean that Mrs. Ferguson always gets credit for everything? I have to know.'

'Yeah. She does.'

'Anyone else?'

He glared at her. 'I'll have to think about that.' He took an empty gallon jug from under the counter and began filling it from the barrel against the wall, gloomily watching the liquid flow from the spigot. When Charlie returned with a basket, he handed the jug to him.

A minute later, Charlie and Emma were out on the road, walking east towards the bridge over the Don River.

For the first few minutes they walked in silence. They passed the muddy lane leading to the windmill, and another couple of lanes to either side. There were a few houses on their left; on the right were the marshes.

The water was high because of the spring thaw, and in places it covered part of the roadway. At one point Emma noticed an island, some way into the swamp, on which were a couple of squatters' shacks with a footpath leading to them, and a makeshift bridge. A dog sat at the door of one of them scratching its fleas, and two children were rooting among the rushes and mud at the edge of the island. A bit further, where there was a larger pool of water, ducks and geese swam and wading birds skittered and dipped along the edge. There were other birds as well, a robin hopping on the road ahead of them, swallows and gulls flying overhead. An invisible flicker chattered among the trees with their thickening haze of spring green. Black flies darted at Emma and she got several bites on her face.

Gradually they left the marshes behind. At the point where the bridge crossed it, the Don River had a recognizable shape and banks high and firm enough to support a bridge.

Only a portion of Emma's mind was on her surroundings. She rebelled at the prospect of having to apologize to Mrs. Ferguson; she admitted that she had been wrong, but the mistake for which she blamed herself was not the same as the action for which she had to apologize.

When explaining the matter to Abner Freeman just now, she had realized something else. Refusing customers credit on luxury goods might be his policy but he did not necessarily follow it. Hadn't he said that he had never before put into words the rules which he and Rose had worked out for themselves? In practice, he would bend the policy to suit the customer. He would certainly bend it to suit an arrogant and overbearing person like Mrs. Ferguson. He hadn't the will or the strength to stand up to her, and perhaps he saw no need to.

But Emma still considered that she had been right to follow his instructions, and she thought he should have admitted that those instructions had been inadequate.

It was partly to distract herself from such thoughts that she began looking for something to talk about with Charlie.

'Is it far to the Fergusons?' she asked.

'Couple o' miles. They live on the lake beyond the marshes. Big farm – they just bought out one o' their neighbours who couldn't make it. Got hired help in the house and on the farm.'

That fitted; Emma remembered Mrs. Ferguson's air of arrogant prosperity and the hired man sitting on the seat of the wagon.

'Is that why she's important to your father – because she's rich?'

Charlie laughed, and the sound was so surprising and so cheering that Emma smiled in response. He had thrown his head back and the breeze lifted his hair in tufts. He looked even bigger than he had done earlier, and strong and carefree, quite different from the way he looked at home. As with the private, friendly smile he had given her on Saturday, Emma felt as though she had discovered something valuable.

He looked at her, his eyes still full of laughter. 'O'course! Any shopkeeper likes rich customers. He doesn't make a living selling someone two ounces o' tea.'

'But if Mrs. Ferguson doesn't pay her bills....'

'Like Dad said, she pays in the end. Or rather, her husband does. Every now and then he and Dad shut themselves up together in the parlour with some whiskey and settle everything.'

'Well, I think your dad should have told me. And I don't think I should have to apologize. What am I going to say?'

She looked up at him, genuinely in search of advice. But his face took on a vague, closed look.

'I dunno.'

'Mrs. Ferguson won't make it easy for me.'

'No.'

'Your dad said that I could blame him – anything so long as I put it right again. Do you think he really meant that?'

Charlie said nothing, so she was forced to answer her own question. 'I guess I'd better not blame him – not really. I could ... I could say that I hadn't understood when he explained his policy. That there was so much to learn all at once....' She frowned at the muddy ruts in front of her. It sounded lame and weak. It might have worked with a kind-hearted person who was prepared to accept the spirit rather than the words of the apology. But Mrs. Ferguson was not kind-hearted – and, Emma had to admit, she herself was not really apologizing.

Just to the left of them now was a jumbled pile of logs overgrown with brush and weeds.

'Somebody's log cabin collapsed,' Emma remarked.

'No, it was a ... a kind of fort. In the war with the Americans.'

'A kind of fort?'

'Yeah, to defend the bridge, I guess. An old guy told me once. He'd been in the militia.'

'Oh, a blockhouse! No,' she amended, observing the pile more carefully, 'it can't have been a blockhouse.

There's not enough logs. Maybe one of those bits of wall that they built to give the soldiers something to shelter behind.'

Ahead of them now was the bridge, a covered bridge spanning the rather narrow ravine which the river had made for itself at this point. Their steps, as they walked through the tunnel-like structure, sounded hollow. Through the openings along the sides they could see that the river was high with the spring run-off and the rain up-country. The stream had flooded its usual banks and spread on either side towards the walls of the ravine. The current was strong; as Emma watched, a huge stump was swept down towards them and out of sight under the bridge.

When they emerged, they had to move aside to make way for a wagon loaded with lumber coming out of Mill Road and turning towards the bridge. As was often done when heavy loads had to be moved through the deep mud of the spring roads, oxen instead of horses had been hitched to the wagon. They made a sound like thunder in the bridge.

The sight of the team and wagon reminded Emma of another topic of conversation.

'Do you like your work?' she asked Charlie. 'Being a driver for Doel's brewery?'

She looked at him, waiting for his answer. As she watched, the vague look disappeared and his eyes became bright again.

'Oh, yeah, I like it a lot. Working with horses, talking to people....'

'You must know just about everybody in town.' Beer, she knew, was delivered to all the taverns and hotels, to the big houses for the servants, to the fort for the soldiers. Captains of ships bought beer for their crews, and farmers bought it for their families and the hired help.

'Yeah, I know quite a few. Only Doel's customers, o'course. There's other breweries too, with their own customers.'

'Do you deliver to my aunt's hotel?'

'No, she buys from Joseph Bloor. But I know your aunt from when she's been to see my mother 'n' dad, and I know your brother to see.'

'He knows you too.' As she spoke, her worries about John came to life again, but she pushed them down. She asked, with an attempt at light-heartedness, 'What do you do while you're just sitting on the wagon? You don't have to drive horses every second of the time.' She had heard that some long-distance teamsters knitted socks, but somehow she couldn't picture Charlie doing that.

'I ... I whittle.'

He mumbled the word so that she couldn't catch it.

'You...? Pardon me?'

He glanced up but did not quite meet her eyes. 'I whittle. Carve wood.'

'Do you really? What sorts of things do you carve?'

He stopped, set down the jug, and burrowed in his pockets. Out of one he drew a jack knife and a small carving of a swimming duck, its head cocked alertly. Out of the other came an unfinished carving of a lap-dog with a wrinkled, up-turned nose, which he must have seen in the possession of one of the ladies in town, or in the care of a servant. The snooty little face, together with the chin and ears, was the only part finished; the rest was still a roughly chopped piece of whitish wood.

Emma laughed aloud at the little portrait. 'Oh, I like

that very much! I hope you're going to finish it.'

'I ... I don't know. I think mebbe it is finished. The rest don't matter. It was the face I wanted.'

'I see what you mean.'

He returned the things to his pocket and picked up the jug.

'Have you done lots of them?' she asked as they walked on.

'Mebbe a dozen.'

'Do you do only birds and animals? Not people?'

'Mostly animals. I did one of the lighthouse at Gibraltar Point but that ain't interesting. I tried to do Mother once but somehow.... It doesn't seem to work when it's ... you know ... serious. There has to be something funny about it.'

'Something funny ... yes. The duck is all right, but the little dog is really good. It says something.'

***

The Ferguson house, when they reached it, surprised her. From Mrs. Ferguson's airs, and from the Freemans' attitude towards her, Emma had expected it to be rather grand. But it was just a log house like so many others, ground floor plus attic and a rather long back wing. A barn and several sheds clustered to one side. Everything was in good repair but there was no sign of unusual wealth.

Now that they were here, Emma had no thought to spare for anything except the humiliation of having to apologize to Mrs. Ferguson. She followed as Charlie led the way around to the back of the house and up two steps to a veranda. She let him knock on the door but, remembering that it was she and not Charlie who had to apologize, she moved to stand beside him.

The door was opened by a girl of about thirteen with a kitchen knife in her hand. When she saw strangers, she made a little curtsey.

'Is Mrs. Ferguson at home?' Emma asked.

The girl looked over her shoulder. 'Yes, miss.'

'May we see her for a moment, please?'

Mrs. Ferguson's voice came out at them. 'Don't hang about, Nellie. If it's for me, show them in. If it's for Mr. Ferguson, tell them that he's out back somewhere.' The voice had the same overbearing tone that had made Emma bristle earlier that afternoon.

The girl and Emma exchanged looks which, though carefully expressionless, conveyed understanding and sympathy. Nellie opened the door wider, and Emma and Charlie went in.

The kitchen was big and comfortable. Mrs. Ferguson was working at the main table rolling out pastry for pies and supervising her two little girls who were learning to knit. Two smaller children were sitting in a play-pen nearby. The girl who had let them in returned to her work, which seemed to be the cutting up of potatoes for stew.

When she saw Emma, Mrs. Ferguson reached for a cloth and wiped her hands. She raised her eyebrows as though asking the reason for this visit, although Emma knew that she had noticed the jug and basket and had already drawn her conclusions.

Emma kept it as short as possible.

'Here are your other purchases, Mrs. Ferguson. Mr. Freeman says you're to have them, and I've written them down in the book. I ... I guess I hadn't quite understood what he meant when he explained his policy about credit.'

It disgusted her to have to tell a lie; she knew very well that she had followed the rule which Mr. Freeman had laid down. As for what she considered her real mistake – not consulting Rose Freeman, wanting to deal with Mrs. Ferguson her own way – she considered that to be separate and not something for which she had to apologize.

'Oh, so you admit that you were wrong!'

'Not really, ma'am. I did what he told me – what I thought he told me. But I guess I didn't understand, or he didn't say exactly what he meant. Anyway, here are the rest of your things.'

'I trust it won't happen again.'

'Oh, no, ma'am, certainly not.' One humiliation like this was enough, Emma thought.

'Very well, then. You may unload the basket on that table, and set the whiskey on the floor in that corner. I'll return the jug when it's empty.'

Silently Emma and Charlie did as they were told. Then they went to the door.

'Good day to you, ma'am,' Emma said.

'Good day.'

They said nothing until they reached the road and had turned towards York again.

'Horrid woman,' Emma muttered.

'She sure is.'

'And I'm not free of her, because I gather she comes into the shop fairly regularly.'

'Oh, not all that often. You might be gone by the time she comes again. How long're you gonna stay?'

'I don't know. A few weeks maybe. My aunt will tell me. I guess she and your dad will decide.'

'Why've you come?'

'To help your dad, now that your mother's sick.' She

wasn't going to mention Mrs. McPhail's instructions that she put some heart into the business. 'I guess your dad will have to find someone permanent soon, but for now I'm to help out.'

'Who's doing your work at the hotel?'

'I do some, mornings and evenings, and there's another girl.'

'You got any family besides John?'

'No, they died in a fire, two years ago. John and I got out but the others were killed. Mother and Father and two baby girls.' She kept her voice steady but inwardly she trembled again at the memory of that awful night, her father with his clothes on fire, the flaming roof collapsing into the house, the smoking ruins the next morning, the four sheeted bodies on makeshift stretchers in the shanty with its ice-cold air heavy with the smell of burned flesh and of the evergreen boughs that she had brought to lay on them.

'That's bad,' he said gently. 'And there's your aunt, o'course.'

'She came to fetch us. But she's not ... not like a mother.'

Charlie said nothing.

They walked on in silence. As they reached the bridge they met a horse and cart driven by a man in labourer's clothes. The driver and Charlie nodded to each other.

'Who's that?' she asked.

'Blackwood's hired man, Ralph. Works with your brother.'

'The one who replaced Fred Baker?' Fred Baker had been employed by Blackwood when John had started working there. He had been a dependable, cheerful man who had kept an eye on John. Emma had been sorry when he left a few months ago. 'What's this new man like?'

'Dunno. Never talked to him.'

After reporting to Mr. Freeman, Emma was allowed to go home. As she walked back to the hotel, she thought about Charlie. He might be clumsy and unsure of himself because of his bad relations with his father, but during this afternoon he had shown several other sides of his personality. That carving of the little dog was very good. She wondered whether she could ask to see the rest of his carvings – whether he would be embarrassed or pleased by such a request.

Perhaps it would be best to wait until they knew each other better.

Chapter Six

That evening again John was late coming home from work. There was a blustery wind blowing rain in gusts against the windows and making the smoke from the fireplace in the hotel kitchen puff out into the room. The weather made Emma restless, and John's lateness worried her. Instead of going upstairs to her room in the attic after her work was finished, she lingered in the kitchen, huddled near the fire or abruptly getting up and prowling around. Mrs. Jones, the cook, was there mending one of her black stockings. Beside her on the stone apron of the hearth stood a pot of tea keeping warm, the pot on a trivet with hot coals beneath.

'You worryin' about John?' she asked Emma.

'I don't like it when he's as late as this.'

'Just kept behind at Blackwood's, I expect.'

That was what Emma expected too – and feared. In the past he had sometimes had to clean a carriage that was returned late and would be needed early the next morning. But now she was afraid that he was being detained for other work such as unloading and delivering smuggled goods. She remembered the empty sack he had been carrying the other day – and that had been in daylight. How much more likely that he would be sent out on such business after dark!

'Like a cup o' tea?' Mrs. Jones asked.

Emma nearly refused, afraid that the tea might keep her awake, but she changed her mind. A cup of tea would be a comfort, and it would give her an excuse to stay in the kitchen a little longer.

The tea was good and hot; Mrs. Jones was always

particular about that. Emma wrapped her hands around the cup and leaned closer to the fire.

'You cold?' Mrs. Jones asked. 'Not sickening with something, are you?'

'I hope not. I haven't the time to be sick.'

'That's what my husband used to say – though it's not work that took up his time so much as enjoying hisself. Once when we lived in Kingston he broke his leg right when the pigeons were migrating, and he made a pair of crutches so's he could go out and stand somewhere and shoot them.' Mrs. Jones chuckled; she was tolerant now of the failings of her long-dead husband. 'He'd never have gone to that trouble just to go to work.'

'Did he ever have a regular job?'

'Back in England he was an under-gardener. You know, assistant to a gardener on a big estate. But there wasn't much demand for gardeners here so he worked at one thing or another, or didn't work at all. When we was in Kingston he mostly worked down by the harbour, with the boats. He liked that better'n most other jobs.'

'What sort of work did he do on the boats?'

'Oh, nothing special. Loading and unloading. And I don't suppose it was all legal stuff either. Sometimes he was away half the night and would come back with more cash'n usual. The end o' the lake's handy for smuggling, close to the American States like that. Lots o' handy little landing places just outside Kingston.'

Emma's attention had sharpened at the mention of smuggling, but she tried to keep her voice casual. 'Is there a lot of smuggling into York too?'

'Oh, sure, bound to be. Comes in by boats along the lake.'

'When you shop, do you know what's smuggled?'

'Sometimes I can guess.' Mrs. Jones gave Emma a quick and furtive glance. 'Mrs. McPhail, she don't like the hotel to use smuggled goods. Not respectable. And it's against the law. Not all smugglers are caught, but the preventive men are out there looking for them.'

'What happens to those who are caught?'

'The boat or wagon or whatever's being used is taken by the customs.'

'The whole thing? The whole wagon or boat?'

'That's right. And everything in it. It's sold at auction. The officer who caught the smuggler gets some of the money, and so does the informer, if there was one. There's profit in reporting smugglers. O'course there's also profit in *not* reporting them. They might bribe you with free brandy, if you handle it right.'

In spite of Mrs. Jones's attempt at a joke, Emma felt uneasy at the picture thus painted for her. She would have liked to ask what the punishment would be for someone like John, delivering smuggled goods, or for Mrs. McPhail if her hotel were caught using them.

'So people continue smuggling,' she said. 'And other people continue to buy things that have been smuggled in.'

'Sometimes the smuggled stuff's cheaper, or it's all there is.'

Mrs. Jones abruptly stopped speaking and began rooting for something in the sewing basket beside her. Perhaps she didn't want to talk about smuggling any longer. From what she had said, Emma concluded that sometimes she did buy contraband merchandise, knowing that she did so but keeping quiet because of Mrs. McPhail's disapproval.

Emma was sorry to have the subject closed; she

would have liked to ask what was smuggled and how it was done, how and where the goods were sold, who did the work. But even if the subject had not been so firmly closed she would not have dared to ask. Showing too much interest might not be a good idea, and if Mrs. McPhail was opposed to smuggling she might be extremely angry at the possibility of John being involved in it.

John arrived just as Emma drank the last of her tea.

'Had to take a bridle to the harness man to be mended and wait to bring it back,' he said.

It was a reasonable explanation, and it might well be true. But as she followed him up the stairs to the attic she heard coins softly clinking in his pocket.

* * *

During the following days, Emma's routine changed slightly. It was decided that she need not arrive at the store until about ten o'clock. During the morning, Mr. Freeman was at home to serve the customers, and both he and Mrs. Molloy were there to look after Mrs. Freeman. But Abner liked to go out in the afternoon, so he asked Emma to come at ten o'clock and stay through the afternoon until he returned home.

As the work at the store became, in this way, a part of her daily routine, so it wove itself into her thoughts and feelings. At the hotel, on the Thursday morning of that week, she found some newspapers left by a departed guest. Remembering that Abner had asked her to bring along old newspapers for wrapping customers' purchases, she laid them ready to take with her. On the Friday, while walking to the store, she picked a bunch of marsh marigolds to brighten Rose

Freeman's tiny and fusty-smelling room.

When she arrived for work on the Wednesday of the week after that, Mr. Freeman pointed to a newspaper-wrapped parcel lying on the counter.

'End o' the afternoon, on your way home, kin you take that to Miz Morgan at the school? It's her regular supply of tea. Not out o' your way, is it?'

Actually it was a block or so out of Emma's way, but she didn't mind. Miss Morgan was a friend of hers, an American woman who had stayed at the hotel while looking for a suitable building in which to set up a school. Emma had helped her sew curtains in return for being allowed to borrow books, and Miss Morgan had once taken her to a concert of music performed by two visiting singers and the band of the British army detachment stationed at the fort.

'Meantime,' he added, 'carry on with the cleaning.'

By now Emma had finished all the open shelves and the drawers. That left the cupboards below them. She put on her apron and began.

Some of these cupboards had doors, so the contents were not quite as dirty as the merchandise on the open shelves had been. But the first cupboard, when she opened it, smelled stale and there were lots of mouse droppings. She began emptying it. Out came jugs of different sizes, and the small crockery gallipots in which women put their home-made cosmetics and medications. Out came several new but dusty tea-caddies, candle-snuffing tongs, and the cylindrical metal containers used for storing candles so that the mice couldn't eat them. Out came two tinderboxes. Behind them was a paper of pins, so rusted that the pins were useless. It must be a very long time since anyone had cleaned this cupboard out entirely.

Kneeling and bending down until she could see right to the back of the cupboard, she spotted a pale blob in the dimness. She reached and brought it out. It was a package of writing paper held together by a strip of paper wrapped around and with its ends glued. Two corners of the package had been nibbled by mice, and the bottom sheets were warped from having got wet at some time, though now they were dry.

Emma wondered why the paper had been put there. The rest of the shop's stock of writing paper was in one of the drawers; none was kept in these lower cupboards, especially so far at the back. It looked as though someone had pushed it there to get it out of sight. Perhaps Mrs. Molloy had caused the water damage and shoved the paper out of the way so that she wouldn't be blamed. If one of the Freemans had done it, surely they would have used the unspoiled sheets. The mouse damage had probably happened after the paper had been put away in this low cupboard, where there was abundant evidence of mice.

Emma, sitting back on her heels, decided that she would ask Mr. Freeman if she might have the damaged sheets. She had been wanting to write to the Heatheringtons.

As she went on with the cleaning, she thought about Major and Mrs. Heatherington. Like Miss Morgan, they had been at the hotel when Emma and John had arrived there a year and a half ago. It was the Heatheringtons who had bought Emma's parents' farm – who would, if Emma had not helped them, have paid Mr. Blackwood an inflated price for it. When they left the hotel to move to the farm, they had given Emma, by way of parting gift, a little bottle of ink, a quill pen, and some sheets of writing paper. Emma had used all the paper writing to them; she enjoyed writing letters, finding satisfaction in trying to put her thoughts and experiences into words that would be read by someone else.

When Mr. Freeman came in, she showed him the paper and asked if she might have the damaged sheets. He didn't answer at once but turned the package over and over. Then he pointed to the water damage.

'That was Mrs. Ferguson's fault. She bought the paper – last winter, I guess it was, and then when she was packing the stuff in her basket she set the paper down on the windowsill. The sill was wet with water from the ice melting off the windows, and she insisted on having another bunch o' paper. Said the damage was my fault 'cause I hadn't wiped up the water. I was so mad at her I just shoved the paper out o' sight.'

'May I have the damaged sheets, Mr. Freeman? You can't sell them, can you?'

He thumbed through the bundle to see how far the water damage went, and turned it in all directions again, apparently to examine the mouse nibbles. Then he handed her the bundle.

'Here, take the lot. See, it says "one quire" and if I give you some sheets it won't be a quire no more. A quire is twenty-four sheets.'

'Oh, thank you, Mr. Freeman!'

'What'll you do with it? Write po'try?' It wasn't clear whether he was joking or really thought that she might secretly be a poet.

'Write letters. I have friends in the country whom I don't see very often. I write to them whenever I have some paper.'

He gave her a sardonic glance. 'You kin write a lot o' letters on that. Rather you than me, lass.'

***

When Emma reached the school she found Miss Morgan alone – it was late afternoon and the students had gone home. She was in the schoolroom, sitting at the table that served as a desk. Beside her was a pile of slates; she was checking what the younger pupils had written. When Emma came in she leaned back and stretched her arms over her head.

'Hello there, Emma.'

Even when relaxing, Miss Morgan looked energetic. She was in her early thirties, thin and vigorous. Her dark brown hair was gathered in a bun which always looked loose but never seemed to fall down.

Emma sat down on one of the seats that the students used, long benches standing alongside a big table with ink stains on it. The table was bare now; one of the last tasks of the school day was to collect books, ink bottles, pens, slates, and other equipment and put it all neatly on a shelf running along one of the walls.

Emma set the parcel of tea on the ink-stained table where Miss Morgan could see it.

'Hello, Miss Morgan. I brought you your tea.' Then, seeing a puzzled look on the schoolmistress's face, she explained. 'I'm working at Freeman's for a few weeks, helping out in the shop. Mrs. McPhail arranged it.'

'Well, well, that's a change. Are you enjoying it?'

'I ... yes, in some ways I am.' She was surprised at the discovery and realized that it was true. 'At first I thought Mr. Freeman resented my being there, but he seems to be used to it now. I'm very much in the family, not just out front in the shop. I also help look after Mrs. Freeman. She's bed-ridden, and the cleaning woman is there only in the mornings. So in the afternoons I make tea for Mrs. Freeman and talk to her for a few minutes now and then. She told me something about my father – she used to be a servant in my grandfather's house – but she couldn't tell me much. Perhaps she ... perhaps some people are not very observant. I think I might have noticed a little more. Servants have such a lot of opportunities.'

'You should know, Emma!'

'I do!' Then, realizing that Miss Morgan was teasing her in a friendly way, she gave a little laugh. 'Well, it's not my fault if people talk all around me as though I didn't exist. I don't deliberately eavesdrop.' Well, maybe once I did, she added silently to herself, remembering a Sunday afternoon when she had overheard Mrs. McPhail and Mr. Blackwood talking about the sale of the farm to the Heatheringtons. Afraid of blushing self-consciously, she looked around for something else to talk about. 'But Charlie is observant. He's the son – he drives a dray for Doel's brewery.'

'Yes, I've met Charlie. He's brought me my tea a few times.'

'Well, when he's out with the dray, driving all those miles, he does little wood-carvings.' For a moment she wondered whether she was betraying a confidence, but then she realized that if he did the carving out in public, sitting up there on the seat of the big brewer's wagon, it couldn't be very much of a secret. 'He showed them to me. One was delightful – a little lap-dog, the pug-nosed kind, terribly snooty. I was surprised because he doesn't look....'

She stopped short. She had been about to say that Charlie didn't look artistic, but realized how awful that would sound.

Miss Morgan gave her a keen look. 'People are surprising, aren't they? Do you get along well with Charlie?'

'I hardly ever see him. He's out most of the day.'

'What does this extra job do to your daily routine?' Miss Morgan, having lived in the hotel for several months when she first came to York, knew how hard Emma worked.

'I'm busier than ever. I hardly have any time to myself now, because usually I'm at the store all afternoon and then, when I get back to the hotel, I have to help with the guests' dinner.'

'I've wondered sometimes whether you wouldn't enjoy doing something artistic yourself, something that wasn't strictly necessary and useful.'

'I read the books you lend me – for half an hour a week, if I'm lucky. For months I've been sewing a summer dress and it's not nearly finished. I don't have time for anything I'd really like to do.' She caught the complaining tone in her own voice and quickly changed the subject again. 'But I've found a little benefit in working at the store. Mr. Freeman collects old newspapers for wrapping things in. Like your tea,' she said, tapping the parcel in front of her. 'Whenever I have a moment I can read those papers. They're old but there are some interesting things in them – reports of events in England or New York, or advertisements for new merchandise that the stores here have received. Sometimes I read things aloud to Mrs. Freeman when we're alone in the afternoon having a cup of tea. It's like ... like being connected to the rest of the world.'

'I'm glad you have those moments of relaxation.'

'Being company for Mrs. Freeman is part of the job. But I know what you mean. And after all, some of the work at the store is less heavy than the scrubbing and carrying that I do at the hotel. Weighing tea or raisins is almost lady-like!'

That reminded Emma that she had only dropped in to deliver the tea. She got up and carried the package to Miss Morgan's desk, where she put it beside the pile of slates.

Miss Morgan also got to her feet. She shook out the serviceable grey skirt which, when teaching, she always wore with a grey or blue blouse.

'Keep me up to date, Emma, about yourself and about the Freemans. I hope they manage to keep the store going. I'd be sorry to lose my supply of economical tea.'

'Is that why you buy it there?'

'Yes. It's a struggle sometimes, making the money go far enough.' Miss Morgan had inherited a little money from her parents but for the most part depended on fees from her students, which were often paid late and which might come in the form of firewood, unground wheat, or dead poultry. One payment had been in live poultry. Miss Morgan had borrowed a portable chicken coop, given the hens the run of the yard and street, and enjoyed the fresh eggs until the last hen had ended up in a soup.

***

Emma's route from the school to the hotel led past Blackwood's livery stable, where John worked. Just before she got there, she heard shouting and an angry cry. When she rounded a corner she saw a man strike John on the side of the head. The man held John by the shoulder and was raising his free hand to hit him again when John broke loose. All this happened as Emma ran up to help. She drew breath to shout, but the man had already turned and was making off.

'Who was that?' she demanded of John. 'Why was he hitting you? Did he hurt you?'

John evaded her attempt to inspect his face. 'Oh, it's just Ralph's brother. He and Ralph don't like me.'

'Ralph who works for Mr. Blackwood? Why doesn't he like you?' Anxiety made her more abrupt than she had intended. Seeing John mistreated had revived all her worries about him.

He gave her a mulish look. 'I dunno. People are funny.'

It was such a pointless remark that she nearly asked him what he meant. But the look on his face stopped her. It was not only obstinate but resentful as well. She couldn't bear the thought that John should resent her. Since their parents' death two years earlier, she and John had been friends and allies. They did not tell each other everything but they were always together against whatever threatened either of them. If John turned against her it would be like losing her family all over again.

She was the elder, and she would have to reach across before a real gulf opened between them.

'I'm sorry, John. I was just angry at seeing that big bully hit you.' She grinned. 'Next time, pick on some-one your own size.'

He gave her a sidelong look. 'He picked on me.' But, although he refused to respond to the joke, he no longer seemed resentful. He shook himself to settle his rumpled clothes, and touched an exploratory hand to his cheek. 'No blood.'

'You'll probably have a bruise. Do you have to go

back to the livery stable or are you finished for today?'

'I'm finished. You going home too?'

'Yes.'

In order to put the near-quarrel firmly behind them, she told the story of the damaged writing paper. By the time they reached the hotel, relations seemed to be comfortable again. But Emma did not forget the beating John had received and continued to wonder what lay behind it. Either John had done something wrong and been punished, or he had encountered an undesirable couple of men.

Chapter Seven

The next few days passed uneventfully. The weather continued to warm up and the black flies were plentiful. Mosquitoes emerged, and in the evenings swallows and bats scooped over the land feeding on the insects. Mornings were damp and cool; the mists which formed over the marsh at night were often not quite gone when Emma arrived at the store. The leaves on trees and bushes were almost fully out.

At the hotel, as usual, guests came and went. Mr. Michaels-Harbottle was away for two days – John, at the docks on business for Mr. Blackwood, saw him returning on the Niagara boat. Mr. and Mrs. Reynolds and their ailing baby left, after giving Emma a generous tip for her help in looking after the child.

At the store, Emma finished cleaning the shelves and the merchandise on them. She washed the counter tops, the floor, and the windows. She took the scoops one day to Mrs. Molloy to be done with the dishwashing. Most satisfying of all, she cleaned and polished the scales until the brass shone like gold and seemed to light up the shop with their brightness. All this cleaning was a real improvement; she felt that she was making good headway with the assignment that Mrs. McPhail had given her. In addition, she was becoming acquainted with the customers and finding tactful ways to discover what they would like to have available in the store. This information she passed on to Mr. Freeman.

When she finished cleaning, she began to take her sewing to the store, so that she might make use of her spare time. Reading old newspapers in the odd free moment between customers and cleaning was fun, but there were more important things to do.

One day she arrived at the store to find Mr. Freeman's horse standing saddled by the front door. She encountered him just inside the tinkling door; he said that he would probably be back late but that Charlie would be home by the end of the afternoon. Then he put on his hat, mounted, and rode eastwards in the direction of the bridge over the Don River.

Business was slow that day. After lunch, while Mrs. Freeman had her nap, Emma sat in the shop sewing. As she stitched one long seam of her summer dress, she heard her mother's voice telling her how important it was to make the stitches small and to keep the line of stitching straight. The memory of her mother led to the thought of Mrs. Heatherington, to whom she had written a letter yesterday afternoon – Sunday afternoon – while her hair was drying. It was almost the letter that she might have written to her parents had they been alive – almost but not quite. With the Heatheringtons she found herself being a little reserved. She could not pour out everything. For instance, she had not told them her fears that John might be involved in something illegal. Major Heatherington was a retired army officer and was acquainted with the Lieutenant-Governor, Sir John Colborne, and with other officials in York. He would surely be on the right side of the law and might feel obliged to report anything illegal that he heard about. Emma could not take the chance. Yet she would very much have liked to share her anxiety about John with the Heatheringtons.

She made the last few stitches with the thread that was in her needle and bit off the tiny end that was too short to work with. 'Don't waste thread,' her mother had always said; besides, Emma liked to see how close she could go to the end.

As she unwound a new portion from the spool, the bell of St. James' Church began to toll the slow, heavy strokes that signified a funeral. Someone was being buried – maybe the sailor who, a couple of days ago, had been crushed between a ship and the wharf. Or an old person, or one of the many babies who did not live to grow up. York was a big enough town to contain great numbers of people about whom she knew nothing.

Then, while she was still listening to the funeral bell and gazing out of the window in a brief tribute to whoever had died, she saw a robin land on the fence and perkily look around as though it owned the world. A moment later it hopped to the ground and began to look for worms. People might die, she thought – they *would* die – but there would always be robins.

* * *

While Emma and Mrs. Freeman were drinking tea later, Mrs. Freeman remarked that Charlie might be late tonight.

'Are you sure?' Emma asked. 'Your husband said that Charlie would be home by the end of the afternoon.'

The time of Charlie's return mattered to Emma. The shop stayed open until about six o'clock; if Abner Freeman arrived home before that, he dismissed her. Today, because he had said that he would be late, she knew that she would have to stay until six to attend to the store. After that she would stay to look after Mrs.

Freeman until Charlie came home.

If she left the store at six o'clock, she had to go straight back to the hotel to help with the guests' dinner. If she could leave the store earlier, she could have the extra time – anything from a few minutes to an hour or more – to herself.

These arrangements, so important to Emma, were treated very casually by the Freemans. There was no sign that Abner Freeman ever made a point of coming home earlier in the afternoon for Emma's sake, or that Charlie was aware that his comings and goings had any connection with hers. They seemed to think that she was completely at their service and had no obligations elsewhere.

Mrs. Freeman apparently didn't notice the slight reproach in Emma's words. 'He's often late at this time of year. It's spring – the muddy roads slow him down, and sometimes there's a bridge washed out. Actually it's a good sign. Mr. Doel is sending him out on longer trips, now that he's seen that Charlie is dependable. I guess some people, when they first meet Charlie, think he's a bit ... a bit simple.' She gave Emma a worried glance.

'Maybe his manner is a little misleading,' Emma offered hesitantly. She had seen Charlie last week driving the dray and staring ahead of him in a slack-jawed way that indeed made him look almost half-witted.

'He's shy, that's what it is.'

'I expect you're right,' Emma said. Obviously Rose Freeman worried about her son, and Emma was afraid of saying something tactless or hurtful.

When Charlie did not return by supper-time, Emma heated a pot of soup left ready by Mrs. Molloy and served some to Mrs. Freeman and herself. Then she helped Mrs. Freeman wash, put on a clean nightgown, and tidy her hair.

'I think I'll go to sleep, Emma. I won't need a candle, but you can leave the door open a crack.'

So Emma sat in the kitchen waiting for Charlie or Abner Freeman to arrive. While sewing doggedly, she reflected that one of the neighbours might have been asked to come and sit with Mrs. Freeman, or that perhaps she could have been left alone for an hour or two if there were no candles burning and the fire was safely banked. However, it was not up to her to arrange such things.

Eventually she found it impossible to sew any longer by the light of one candle so she bundled her sewing up ready to take home with her. She crossed her arms on the table, leaned her head on them, and simply waited.

Charlie's arrival wakened her out of a doze. He mumbled something about trouble with the wagon but seemed to see nothing unusual in her still being there. He did, however, give a thought to her walking home in the dark. 'Better take the lantern,' he said, lifting it down from a hook near the back door and lighting the candle inside it. 'See you tomorrow.'

She was glad of the lantern, even though it threw only a very feeble glimmer. There were a few lights here and there but many of the houses were dark. Everything was so silent that she could hear a cat drop softly down from a fence, a dog in the road scratch itself, a distant owl give a cry.

The hotel was not quite dark. There was a light in one of the guests' bedrooms, and in the kitchen Mrs. Jones was just preparing to go up to bed.

Emma blew out the candle in the lantern and set it down by the back door. 'I must remember to take that back tomorrow,' she said to Mrs. Jones. 'How is everything here?'

'Same as always. I didn't see John come home but then I was out for a while. That Joe Tubb is in trouble again – someone came to complain to Mrs. McPhail but I didn't hear what he's supposed to have done. We had a full house for dinner – all the guests and some people from the garrison. Ruth did the serving real neat.'

Emma filled a jug of water from the big kettle kept warm near the fire, and lit her bedroom candle. Then she followed Mrs. Jones.

In the attic she glanced at the far end where John slept on a pallet on the floor. By the dim candlelight she saw the usual lump of covers. She went into her own tiny room, meeting her reflection in the quarter-pie window, and yawned as she set down the candle and the jug of warm water.

Only then did she notice a scrap of paper on the pillow. She picked it up; it was a corner torn from a discarded newspaper.

> Gone to Kingston on business
> for Mr. B. – back in a few days.
> J.

The note jolted her awake. She was surprised and alarmed; in a flash she saw John talking to smugglers, carrying contraband, being caught and jailed and flogged in the market square.

When she had gathered her wits she took her candle and went to look at his pallet. What she had taken for John's sleeping form was a mound of covers, apparently not even meant to deceive her. It was certainly not John.

She tiptoed back to her room so as not to catch the attention of Mrs. Jones, who would be getting ready for bed in her own small bedchamber next to Emma's.

Of course she had to go after him. Her first vision of public flogging might be an extreme one but all the same she had to make sure that he did not get into trouble with the law, or to get him out of trouble if he was already in any. She had no doubt that the business taking him to Kingston was dangerous or illegal. It might be smuggling, or it might be something else. Emma didn't trust Mr. Blackwood; he had tried to cheat Emma, John, and the Heatheringtons in the deal about the farm. If that was his way of doing business, he might be involved in other dishonest practices. Emma knew that he bought and sold horses – every livery-stable owner did so – and horse-dealing was a notoriously corrupt occupation.

If the errand was an honest one, wouldn't John have said in a few words what it was?

John was only thirteen, and the last words Martin Anderson, their father, had said to Emma before he died were 'Look after John!'

So she set her mind to work on the problem of how to get to Kingston.

Steamboats went to Kingston several times a week, almost daily – or so she understood. John would have taken today's boat, and she would take tomorrow's, if there was one. The boat trip would cost money, and she'd have to buy food. She got out her savings. She had no idea whether she'd have enough; the little pile of coins looked pathetically inadequate. John had sometimes lent her money; she'd have to borrow some now. She went to his corner of the attic and began hunting for his hiding place. Eventually she found it, the money wrapped in a piece of cloth and tucked into the space between rafter and floor. Normally she would not have invaded his privacy but this was a crisis.

She took his bundle back to her room and opened it. It was quite a lot bigger than hers – and even so he must have taken some to Kingston with him. She counted out what she thought she might need and, on a scrap of paper torn from one of the mouse-nibbled sheets, wrote the amount and 'Borrowed by Emma'. This she put with the money, tied the cloth around it, and returned it to the hiding place.

What next? She'd be away for a few nights at least, longer if she had difficulty finding John or encountered other delays. She spread out the cloth in which she carried her apron and sewing to and from Freeman's; on it she laid her one spare set of underclothing and her comb.

She would have to leave the hotel very early, before anyone was up, or she would certainly be prevented from going. But she would write notes for Mrs. McPhail and Mr. Freeman. Both of them would be furious, but it couldn't be helped. The note to her aunt she could leave on the front counter of the hotel; the other she would attach to the lantern which, before dawn, she'd take back to the store and leave on the step.

The wording of the notes gave her some trouble. She wanted to say that she had gone after John but could not find a way of doing it without hinting that he might be in trouble. In the end she pinned John's note to a piece of paper and, addressing Mrs. McPhail, wrote: 'Anxious about John and have followed him. Back soon.' To Mr. Freeman she merely wrote, 'Away for a few days. Back soon.' If he wanted more information, he could talk to Mrs. McPhail. Emma had a vision of them with their heads together, raging at her and devising punishment. It was not an amusing picture.

By the time she had done all this, a portion of the night had passed. She was far too anxious to sleep, and in any case she had to be up even earlier than the usual five o'clock if she wanted to be out of the hotel before anyone else was up. So she undressed and washed, then dressed again. She undid the one long braid of her hair, combed it, and braided it neatly. She cleaned her teeth with the corner of a handkerchief. Then she blew out the candle – it would be wasteful to keep it burning – and set the door slightly ajar so that she could hear the clock in the lobby chiming. After all this, she lay down on the bed to wait but kept her eyes open and made more plans. When she went downstairs she should pick up some food in the larder to eat on the trip. She would have to be very quiet. Striking a light made too much noise so she would have to find her way by moonlight.

That reminded her of something else. From the shelf above her bed she took her tinderbox and added it to the contents of her bundle. It was the one legacy she had of her parents. Maybe it would bring her good luck. She would need all the luck there was. She had no idea how she might find John in a town the size of Kingston. The note left it unclear whether he had gone by himself or with Blackwood. She would have to ask and ask and ask. But it had to be done.

***

Later that morning, Emma was on a ship sailing out of the bay, between the town and the peninsula. The town lay to the north, stretched along the low shore with the fort at the west and the uncompleted windmill at the east. The peninsula was low-lying but had trees growing on it, and as the ship rounded the western end she saw the lighthouse on Gibraltar Point.

The schooner had been heeling slightly to the left, under the pressure of the north-west wind; when it rounded the end of the islands and passed the lighthouse it straightened and then, turning towards Kingston, it heeled in the other direction. Emma was surrounded by the rush of air and the creak of rigging.

She had not expected to take a sailing ship, because most people now travelled on the more reliable steamships. But when she reached the harbour early that morning she had been told that the next steamship to Kingston was not scheduled to leave until tomorrow. However, a schooner carrying freight was leaving in about an hour – the man pointed to where it lay, being loaded – and would probably take her.

She found the master of the ship supervising the loading. Yes, he was going straight to Kingston. They ought to be there tomorrow morning, with such steady weather and the wind behind them. She could make the trip for a dollar and bring her own food – he wasn't really in the passenger business – and be sure to stay out of the way of the men. No, she couldn't come on board until they had finished loading. She could wait on the wharf or somewhere close by where she could hear them blowing the horn when the ship was ready to leave.

The customs house was located at the point where the wharf joined the shore. She found a quiet nook against the building; here she could sit down and keep watch. To one side was the ship being loaded, to the other side the town. It was important to be able to watch out for anyone looking for her; if she spotted someone – old Joseph Tubb, perhaps, or even Mrs. McPhail herself – she could slip further along the wharf among the sheds and the piles of cordwood for the steamships.

One of the things that worried her was travelling alone, not because she was afraid but because it didn't look right for a girl to travel by herself, especially on a schooner with a crew of rough sailors. At the very least she hoped for other passengers, preferably including women.

This problem was solved for her. Some time later, as Emma idly watched the loading, she saw the captain being approached by an elderly man and wife, clearly not very well off, each carrying a cloth bundle like Emma's. Though their voices were inaudible, it seemed that they also asked for passage and that the captain gave them the same reply as he had given Emma, because the two old people turned aside and sat down on a pile of cordwood to wait.

So Emma watched the loading of the ship and the early-morning bustle of the town. She saw Mr. William Lyon Mackenzie with his fiery red wig hurrying into his printing shop almost across from the customs house and, a little later, a messenger boy coming out with a parcel to deliver. She saw a sailing ship come into the harbour and lower its sails to wait for a tide-waiter to come out to it. Tide-waiters were the customs officials whose job it was to go out to meet incoming ships from the American side of the lake and to check the cargo before any of it was unloaded. A few minutes later she saw the tide-waiter get into his dinghy and begin rowing out to the ship.

A few minutes later, watching the town, she had a

scare when she saw young Joe Tubb walking along. Had he been sent to fetch her back? He was an unlikely person for Mrs. McPhail to send, but all the same she watched him closely.

However, he was apparently not looking for her. He was simply loafing along, throwing a stone at a gull perched on a low post, staring vacantly at the incoming ship which was now being boarded by the tide-waiter, picking up some small object off the ground and putting it in his pocket.

At length one of the crew on the schooner that Emma would take blew a blast on a long tin horn to announce that the ship was about to leave. The captain gestured to the elderly couple sitting on the pile of logs and looked around for Emma. She got up and went along the wharf towards him.

So now she was out on the lake, heading for Kingston.

The elderly couple, to whom she had introduced herself, were a Mr. and Mrs. McIntosh, who were going to see their son and daughter-in-law in Kingston. Having explained her own journey in a few words, Emma moved far enough away to allow them their privacy while being still more or less in their company. When the ship was out on the lake and heading east, she found a quiet corner on deck. There she sat down to watch the Canadian shore pass, and promptly fell asleep.

It was the sound of men shouting that woke her. At the moment of waking she was alarmed, but there was no need for fear. The sailors were simply shouting to each other as they made a change in the sails. She watched entranced as they furled a sail high up on a yard.

The atmosphere of the ship was wonderfully tranquil. Emma's sense of anxiety about John and of urgency to reach him fell away from her. She was travelling to Kingston as fast as she could and, in a sudden burst, felt buoyantly, gloriously happy to be on a ship on the lake, away from the store and the hotel.

Later in the day some clouds came up and the wind strengthened. This increased the noise of wind in the rigging and water rushing along the hull and made the ship seem almost to fly over the lake. Emma opened her bundle and ate one of the crusts of bread and a bit of the cheese which she had taken from Mrs. Jones's larder.

As she ate her bread and cheese, she realized that she had forgotten to bring anything to drink. She set out to look for Mr. and Mrs. McIntosh, hoping that they might have a mouthful of something to spare, but when she found them in the cabin they were asleep. Also in the cabin, however, was a barrel with a spigot. She waited near it until one of the sailors came to fill a cup of beer for himself.

'May I have a little to drink?' she asked. 'Just a sip?'

'Sure, miss.' He refilled the cup and handed it to her.

She and the McIntoshes, and those sailors who were not on watch, slept in the cabin that night, lying on the few benches or on the floor. Emma was glad that she had brought her cloak. She had not worn it in town for the last few days because the weather was too warm, but she had almost instinctively taken it with her on this trip. Therefore she was warm enough, but she slept restlessly on the hard surface among the unfamiliar noises of the schooner.

About the middle of the next morning the ship

reached Kingston. Emma took her leave of Mr. and Mrs. McIntosh and set off to find John.

***

She had been working out in her mind how best to do this. If John was alone and not with Mr. Blackwood, he would be very difficult to find; no one would notice a boy of thirteen with nothing to distinguish him from others. He might not be staying in a hotel or inn; it was not unusual for poor people, at this time of year, to sleep out in the open or in someone's shed. Emma herself, on a trip she made to Dundas two years ago, had spent the night under some boards leaning at an angle against the side of a barn.

Or John might be staying with friends of Blackwood's. Or he might not even have remained in Kingston but have travelled inland.

Trying to find him was such a discouraging prospect that Emma had decided to try the easier route first. It was, after all, just as likely – perhaps more likely – that he was travelling with Mr. Blackwood, as his servant. And Blackwood might be known; he travelled often and seemed to go everywhere. If he were not visiting friends he would certainly stay at a hotel, probably the best one in town, and would be much easier to find.

When she had disembarked from the schooner, therefore, she approached a woman with a shopping basket.

'Excuse me, ma'am, but can you tell me which is the best hotel in town and how I can find it?'

The woman gave her a suspicious look. Emma knew very well that people would be mistrustful of girls asking about hotels but hoped that her appearance and manner were reassuringly respectable.

'Why, lass, there's the Old King's Head, or the Kingston Hotel, or Bamford's Steamboat Hotel ... there's lots of good hotels! Bamford's is real nice. My neighbour's boy worked there as a 'ostler, and he always said it was the best....'

Emma asked the way to Bamford's. She had to begin somewhere.

'Oh, it's just up here. You go along the market and up ... or o'course you can cross the market, in behind the Market House there ... no, I guess you better go along the street and up, and you'll see the sign for Bamford's Steamboat Hotel.'

Emma repeated the name and thanked the woman. The directions had not been entirely clear but the woman's finger had pointed steadily up the street that ran alongside the harbour and perhaps a little to the left, inland.

Emma followed the street. The lake was on her right, with a wharf or two, some warehouses and other buildings, a short stretch of muddy shore, and an island some distance out. On her left was the market place with a building on it, just like the market place in York. It didn't seem to be market day but there were a few wagons standing about, a couple of men arguing about a horse, people using the square as a shortcut from street to street.

When she got to the end of the block, she found that there were two streets which might be described as 'up', one roughly straight ahead and one going more to the left. On neither one could she see the hotel. Hesitantly, she went straight ahead but, remembering that the woman's finger had gestured a bit leftwards, took the first turn left.

Unexpectedly she found herself in an alley which was nothing more than a garbage dump. The stench was sickening. Two men with shovels were half-heartedly loading the reeking refuse into a cart; they had handkerchiefs tied over their noses and mouths but, as Emma watched, one of them pushed down the handkerchief and went to take a deep drink out of a tankard which stood against a building. The horse between the shafts of the cart stamped and shook its head and swished its tail against the hordes of flies humming in the air.

Emma put her hand over her nose and retreated. For a moment she wondered why the garbage was being moved after clearly having lain there for ages, but then her attention returned to her own mission.

When she stood again in the street which had led her up from the harbour, she reminded herself of what the woman had said: '... go along here *up*....' She went along the street in her original direction and then, remembering the leftward tendency of the woman's finger, took the next street left.

Here there was actually a sign reading 'HOTEL' right ahead of her. She went in and found herself in a bar-room. Several men drinking at the bar gave her brief glances; most of them turned back to their beer but one of them stared and stared at her. Trying to ignore him, she went to the bar and asked a hunch-backed bartender whether Mr. Blackwood from York was staying there.

'Ain't got no rooms,' the man said.

'But your sign says "Hotel"!'

He shrugged and turned away.

When she was out on the street again, she had lost her sense of direction. She walked the few steps to the nearest corner and looked for the water of the harbour but was bewildered to find glittering water in two directions. The sun was beating down on her, and she realized that she could have used it to help regain her sense of direction if only she had noticed its position at the beginning of her search. But she couldn't be sure that she remembered its position correctly. Confused and discouraged, tired after one sleepless night and one restless one, hungry because she had eaten nothing more than a bit of bread and cheese in a day and a half, she became dizzy and found herself leaning against the wall of the hotel-without-rooms.

It took her a few minutes to gather her courage and put her weight on her own two feet again. When she did so, she tried to think how she should resume her search.

Everything around her was strange now except the hotel-without-rooms. She couldn't remember the woman's directions. She could hardly remember why it had seemed so important to come to Kingston.

She looked around for someone of whom to ask help again. There were enough people on the street – hurrying pedestrians, an old man with a cane, a man pushing a wheel-barrow, another one unloading crates from a wagon – but all of them were busy or unappealing. Then a girl of Emma's own age came out of a doorway and turned towards her.

Emma had a moment's panic when it seemed as though she had even forgotten the name of the hotel she was looking for. But then she remembered it and asked the girl how to find it.

'Bamford's? Why, it's just round the corner, to your left, on the other street.'

Emma thanked the girl and followed the directions.

This time she did indeed see its sign. When she reached Bamford's, she went in.

It was small but respectable. The only person in sight was a woman in an apron dusting a coat rack. Emma asked her if Mr. Blackwood from York was staying there.

'Blackwood? Don't think so.'

'May I have at look at the register?' She had noticed the volume lying open on the counter.

'I guess so.'

Emma turned the register to face her and read the last few names. But indeed Mr. Blackwood's was not among them. She felt her courage sink again.

'No, he's ... he's not here. Can you suggest another hotel where I might try?'

'Well, there's several. You lookin' for a big fancy hotel or a small cheap one?'

'Big and fancy,' Emma said without hesitation.

'Then if I was you I'd try the Kingston.'

'Where is it, please?'

'Here, I'll show you.' She led Emma out onto the street and pointed. 'Up here to the corner, then left along King Street for a couple o' blocks. Handsome stone building.'

There was something clear and decisive in the woman's manner that heartened Emma.

'Thank you very much indeed, ma'am.'

'Sure, lass, that's okay. Hope you find the genelman.'

She found the Kingston Hotel easily enough. It was a substantial two-storey stone building in what was clearly a better part of town than the area where she had first gone.

The lobby was more ornate than the one in her aunt's hotel but nevertheless looked familiar. As she approached the counter, a tubby man came out of a door behind it. He gave her a very sharp look which Emma, used to the ways of hotels, could easily interpret. He was sizing her up: if she was a servant, she'd be sent around to the back door; if she was a prostitute, she'd be scolded away from the place altogether; only if she looked like a respectable person would she be given a civil reception at this counter.

'Yes, miss?' he said cautiously. It sounded as though his verdict on her was not a very confident one but he was giving her the benefit of the doubt.

'Is Mr. Blackwood, from York, staying here?' She tried to put some assurance and even authority into her voice, knowing that otherwise she would certainly not receive an answer.

'May I ask why you wish to know?'

Emma's heart gave a hopeful jump.

'I come from York. I have an urgent message for Mr. Blackwood.' She had no difficulty now in sounding confident. After all, this tubby little man was only a servant himself. 'Do I understand that he is here?'

'He's not in at the moment, miss, but he'll be back for luncheon.'

Both Emma and the clerk looked at the tall clock whose ticking filled the lobby. It was a quarter to twelve.

'You are sure that he will be lunching here?'

'Oh, yes, miss,' said the man with an offensive smirk. 'It's all arranged.'

Now that Emma was so close to finding Mr. Blackwood, she refused to be offended by the clerk's manner. She smiled to suggest that she shared whatever the clerk seemed to be gloating over. 'I presume,' she said, 'that he brought a servant with him on this trip?'

'Just a young fellow, his valet.'

That must be John! Emma gathered her wits to extract one more piece of information.

'They will be back very soon, I imagine,' she said with another glance at the clock. 'If you would be so kind as to tell me in which direction they went, I could walk along to meet them.'

The man looked uneasy for a second, but self-satisfaction overcame him again. 'Well, miss, if you was to walk along King Street here for a few steps towards the church, you might meet Mr. Blackwood and his party.'

The reference to a 'party' puzzled Emma but she was not going to be deflected now. 'That church?' she asked, pointing to the one she had noticed earlier, located nearly opposite the hotel.

'Yes, miss.'

'Thank you very much.'

When she was out on the street, she realized that the sort of person she had pretended to be would have tipped the man. But it was too late now, and she couldn't really afford to tip other servants. Anyway, he was not even aware of how much information he had actually given her. If she were to tip him, might he not become suspicious? So she put the matter out of her mind.

She crossed the street towards the church. Three carriages stood in front of it, and several poor people and children were gathered near the walk that led from the street to the building. As Emma approached, the front doors opened and a wedding party emerged.

Emma barely noticed them; she was looking for John or Mr. Blackwood among the vehicles and people on the street. But her searching eye glanced at the bridal couple ... and then looked again. The groom was Mr. Blackwood! And a few feet to one side stood John, in a new suit of clothes! Clustered closer to Mr. Blackwood and his bride were a few other ladies and gentlemen, two of the latter in military uniform.

So *that* was what all the secrecy had been about!

Emma stayed well back. Part of her problem was solved, and she preferred to remain out of sight until she could talk to John.

The crowd thickened, and someone started a 'Hip, hip, hurray!' One of the men in Blackwood's party distributed tips to the bystanders. The wedding group moved towards the carriages.

But Emma stiffened when she saw, hanging back from the edge of the crowd, the man whom she had seen beating John recently. He had his hat pulled low and did not come close enough to be included in the tipping.

If he was not looking for a handout, why was he here?

Chapter Eight

When the ladies and gentlemen had climbed into the carriages and the crowd dispersed, John accosted Emma.

'What are you doing here?' he demanded.

'I could ask you the same – only I can guess some of it. I like your new clothes.'

'Wedding finery,' he said, looking embarrassed. 'As you see, we're here because of Mr. Blackwood getting married.'

'Why *here?* Isn't the lady from York too? I've seen her there but I don't know her name.'

'Florence Smith. They came here because they're sort of eloping. Miss Smith has a brother who didn't think she should marry Mr. Blackwood. So it had to be a secret.'

'And you were in the secret.'

'They needed someone to carry messages.'

And they paid you extra, she thought. It fitted. Those clinking coins – some of them, at least – had come from this, an activity which was secret but not illegal.

'Why didn't the brother want her to marry Blackwood? She's of age, isn't she? She looks at least thirty-five.'

'She was keeping house for him. I guess he found that pretty useful. And he's a snob, a priggish sort of man who thinks Blackwood is not good enough.'

'Is he one of the important people of York, then?'

'He's a clerk to a lawyer or something of that sort. But he thinks rather well of himself.'

'I see.'

John gave her a sidelong glance. 'There's another thing. I guess Mr. Blackwood also didn't want Mrs. McPhail to know – I mean, he didn't want her to know beforehand. That was another reason for coming here.'

'Why not?'

He shrugged. '*I* dunno. Grown-ups are awfully silly sometimes. But look, you'll want to congratulate them. Come along to the hotel. I'll ask if you can have lunch with the rest of us – with the servants, I mean.'

The carriages had needed to do little more than cross the street, but clearly Mr. Blackwood had thought it beneath his dignity, on his wedding day, to walk those few steps. Besides, the ladies of the party were wearing thin and elegant shoes. So the carriages had crossed the street and were now standing in front of the Kingston Hotel. There had been a delay while duckboards were laid from the carriage doors to the hotel entrance for the wedding party to walk on. But now the bride and groom were in the lobby receiving the good wishes of the upper hotel staff, who had one eye firmly fixed on the tips which would be handed out when the party left. John made his way through the crowd, towing Emma behind him, until they reached the groom.

'Mr. Blackwood,' he said, 'here's Emma. She happened to be in town and saw you coming out of the church. Can she join in celebrating your wedding?'

'Of course, of course!' he said, as bluff and hearty as ever, but for a moment there was a worried look in his eyes. 'What brings you to Kingston, Emma?' It was clear that the question was not an idle one; he really wanted an answer.

John was watching her too; she realized that she had

not answered him when he had asked a similar question a few minutes ago.

'Business, Mr. Blackwood. Personal business.'

'Oh,' he said, trying to sound as though it didn't matter. 'I thought Mrs. McPhail might have sent you.'

She smiled to reassure him. 'Oh, no, Mr. Blackwood, nothing like that. And by the way, I'd like to congratulate you and Mrs. Blackwood. I hope you'll be very happy.'

She glanced towards the bride, who was some distance away talking to one of the wedding guests.

Mr. Blackwood's manner once again became that of a bridegroom. 'Thank you, Emma. We certainly intend to be. I hope you'll join the servants in the kitchen for the wedding breakfast.'

'Thank you, Mr. Blackwood.'

John led the way to the kitchen, off which was a room made ready for them. The other members of this party were three coachmen and a lady's maid who had dressed the bride that morning at the private house where she had been staying for several days. The four of them kept apart from Emma and John, talking about Kingston people and events. Emma and John said little; Emma, being hungry, made the most of the free meal. When they were finished, she and John went outdoors again.

'Do you have to attend Mr. Blackwood?' Emma asked, uncertain what John's duties were on this trip.

'Not until dinner-time,' he said. 'I have the afternoon to myself. Where do you want to go?'

'The harbour, maybe?'

So they walked down to the harbour and sat on one of the many piles of cordwood waiting to be loaded onto steamships.

Now that the mystery of John's affluence was solved, Emma's mind turned back to an unsolved puzzle. She told John about the midnight unloading of the cart behind Blackwood's stable which she had glimpsed a few weeks earlier.

'Is Mr. Blackwood involved in smuggling?' she asked bluntly.

John showed no surprise. Perhaps he was suppressing it, or perhaps he had his own suspicions. Whatever it was, he took his time about answering. 'I don't know. He could be. Or someone else might be using the shed.'

'Without Mr. Blackwood's knowledge?'

'It's possible. Those sheds face into the yard next door, which Mr. Blackwood bought last year after the house there burned down. He got it cheap. Anyone could get in through that entrance and not go near Blackwood's house and the main gate.'

'Could Ralph be doing it?'

John shrugged.

'Why was Ralph's brother beating you that day?' She could not have said why her mind leaped to that subject.

John grinned. 'He wanted me to do an errand and I said I wouldn't. I don't like Ralph and him.'

'You know he's in Kingston too, right now?'

'Who? Ralph?'

'No, the brother. I don't know his name.'

'Bick. No, I didn't know.' This time he was surprised. 'Where did you see him?'

'Outside the church. He was sort of skulking at the back of the crowd.'

John was silent for a few moments, absent-mindedly pulling bits of bark from the log on which he was sitting. They were both staring out over the busy scene in front of them. The ship on which Emma had arrived that morning was still being unloaded. A couple of smaller sailing vessels – batteaux or Durham boats, Emma thought – lay at another wharf and one was being loaded. A steamship was docked further away; Emma couldn't read her name because of a pile of crates and bales near the bow.

All of a sudden her eye caught two familiar figures. Farther down the wharf area, out of earshot but clearly recognizable, stood Mr. Michaels-Harbottle and Ralph's brother Bick. They were talking earnestly. Bick half-turned to gesture out over the water, then looked back at his companion and shoved his hand in his pocket.

Emma touched John's arm. 'There he is now,' she said quietly. 'And Mr. Michaels-Harbottle with him.'

John spotted them. 'I wonder what they're up to. What do you know about this Harbottle man?'

'Well, he's been staying in the hotel – I mean our hotel, Mrs. McPhail's – for three or four weeks. He's from Albany, or so his card said. He's sometimes away overnight or for a couple of days but he keeps his room on. Says it's easier not to have to pack, but he's only got one valise.'

'I've seen him in York. A businessman, he looks like, but he does a lot of his business in taverns, and in shops, and on the street. He and a red-haired fellow. I know about his travelling. Twice he's rented a saddle-horse from us, and I've seen him getting off the Niagara boat.'

'One of the men unloading the cart that night had red hair.'

'So do lots of people.'

Abruptly the two men began walking, still in conversation, heading straight for Emma and John.

'They'll see us,' Emma said in sudden anxiety. 'If they haven't already.'

'Come on.' John got up.

'Run away?'

'Come *on!*' He pulled at the cloak which hung over her arm – there had been no place to leave it and her bundle – and began walking purposefully towards the two men but closer to the water's edge. 'And that's a batteau,' he said, leading her along with one hand and pointing with the other. 'Used for going to the smaller ports that have no wharf. It hasn't any keel – or maybe only a little one, I'm not sure.'

'Hey, kid!'

'Oh, hullo, Bick,' said John.

'What're you doin' here?'

Since Bick had seen John coming out of the church with the wedding party, he obviously knew the answer to his own question. He was, Emma thought, trying to pull the wool over someone's eyes, perhaps Mr. Michaels-Harbottle's. It made Bick seem even more shifty and untrustworthy than he had appeared before.

'Came with the boss.'

Mr. Michaels-Harbottle nodded to Emma but his eyes were cold. For what seemed a very long moment, the four of them stood in an uneasy cluster. Bick was glaring at John, who cocked his head in a gesture of impudent unconcern and brushed a scrap of tree-bark off his handsome new coat. Courteously he moved aside to make way for a man with a heavy coffer on his shoulder.

The silence made Emma nervous. Once before she had seen Bick beating John, and the glowering look on the man's face now suggested that he was storing up more resentment for the future. Mr. Michaels-Harbottle did not look like a violent person but that did not mean that he was harmless. Clearly he was annoyed at having met Emma here in Kingston, or perhaps he was displeased at being seen with Bick. The fact that he *was* annoyed made this odd encounter more significant; if the man minded so much, it must matter somehow.

At last he said, 'Well, we must be on our way. Coming, Bick?' He glanced at Emma and John before turning to walk away.

Bick followed without a word.

When they were out of hearing, Emma said, 'Mrs. Jones says her husband used to get work loading and unloading boats when they lived here. She suggested – I don't think she actually said it – that sometimes he got paid more for working at night, and at those times he was unloading smuggled goods.'

'Lots of money in smuggling, they say.'

Emma almost told him that she had suspected him of earning money by distributing smuggled goods. But she was ashamed now of having jumped to conclusions in that impulsive way and of having been so ready to assume that John was involved in something illegal.

But he need not have had any choice in the matter. A boy could be forced to do things. And it could still happen; contraband might even now be stored in the shed behind Blackwood's livery stable.

***

Later that afternoon, they talked about more immediate problems. John asked Emma where she would sleep that night.

'I thought I'd sleep in a shed somewhere. I brought a little money but I can't afford to spend it on a hotel room.'

She hadn't yet told him that she had found his cache of money and borrowed from it.

'I'll talk to Mr. Blackwood,' he said. 'I have to wait on him anyway at five o'clock, when he goes to the house of some friends of his. He and Mrs. Blackwood are having dinner there and spending the night, and I'm to be on hand.'

'Where are you sleeping?'

'In those people's kitchen. We're going back to York tomorrow. Are you coming with us?' He gave her a slanting look. 'If your personal business here is finished.'

Since his abrupt question earlier about what she was doing here, he had not asked why she had come to Kingston. Perhaps he understood that she had been worried about him, or perhaps he was respecting her privacy just as she had respected his.

'Yes, I'll be going back tomorrow.'

That afternoon, John helped Mr. Blackwood move his luggage to his friend's house – the same house, Emma learned, where the new Mrs. Blackwood had stayed before her marriage. Emma tagged along, disliking the sense of being at loose ends. While John helped carry luggage into the house, she waited within view of the back door, sitting on a chopping block and, when one of the servants asked her business, explaining as well as she could why she was there.

Eventually John came. 'Mr. Blackwood talked to his hostess.' He jerked his head towards the handsome house behind him. 'You can sleep in the attic with the maids if you help with the dishwashing. With the wedding guests dining here, they can use extra hands.'

It was a tiring and unpleasant evening for Emma. More than once she wished that she had settled for sleeping in someone's shed. Among the servants of Mr. Blackwood's friends, and in the hurry of preparing and serving a formal dinner, she was either ignored or bossed. The dishwashing, beginning when the first pots were emptied into serving dishes, continued for several hours. Emma worked with an elderly woman who constantly nagged at her. Aware of her menial position, Emma tried to put up with the endless scolding for the way she dried the dishes, the way she stacked them, the rate at which she worked, the way she slouched.

There was a short break for the servants to eat their meal, and then *those* dishes were added to the pile to be washed.

When Emma was finally lying on a straw-filled pallet on the floor of the attic room occupied by two other maid-servants, she had a sore back and was so irritated that she was sure she wouldn't be able to sleep. She lay flat, willing herself to relax the taut muscles in her back and the feverish fidgeting in her mind. She ignored the whispering and giggling of the two women in the bed. All she wanted was to go to sleep.

Eventually she did. During the night she was awakened by one of the other women using the chamber pot, but except for that she slept until the other servants woke her up. For washing, she had to use the water that they had already used. But she was given a substantial breakfast, and she did not have to help with the dishwashing because it appeared that, along with the rest of the Blackwood party, she would have to leave directly after breakfast to catch the boat to York.

While walking to the docks, Emma compared her own life at her aunt's hotel with what she had seen of the lives of the servants in this house. At Mrs. McPhail's hotel, Emma's room was tiny but at least it was private, and she liked her fellow servants. She was never physically punished, unlike the maid-servant who, yesterday evening, had twice been slapped hard by the cook. All things considered, she was not badly off and she'd be glad to be back.

She and John were walking to the wharf together. On the way, they were overtaken by a cart loaded with garbage, pulled by a pathetic old horse. This reminded Emma of the two men she had seen yesterday loading refuse onto a cart. She mentioned it now.

'It's because of the cholera,' John said.

Everyone knew about the cholera epidemic which had swept across Europe the previous year, killing great numbers of people. It had come from Asia, so they said, and some people were afraid that it would reach North America. A week or ten days earlier, while serving breakfast at the hotel, Emma had overheard one of the guests saying that Sir John Colborne, the Lieutenant Governor, had declared next Wednesday to be a day of public fasting and prayer in the hope that the epidemic might be averted.

'What does garbage here have to do with the cholera in Europe?' she asked.

'They think that it's something to do with garbage being piled too close to the houses. Besides, it's not just in Europe – the cholera, I mean. I heard someone saying yesterday that it's reached Quebec now. It came on the ships.'

'So there's not much point in Sir John Colborne's day of prayer next week.'

'I don't suppose there's much point in shifting garbage either – or maybe there is.' He wrinkled his nose; the garbage cart, moving along just ahead of them, trailed a nauseating stink.

'York needs cleaning up too,' Emma said, thinking of the refuse dumped in the burned-down Parliament Buildings near the Freemans'. She remembered the pile of garbage, including dead horses and dogs, that had accumulated all winter on the ice of the harbour until, with the spring thaw, it had sunk out of sight in the water. And York must contain alleys that were just as bad as the one into which she had strayed yesterday.

* * *

The dock area was crowded, with the activity centred on the steamship *Great Britain.* It was an enormous ship, its hull high above the wharf, its two tall smokestacks and one mast soaring higher still. It was being loaded with cords and cords of firewood for its boilers and with some freight – though most freight was still carried by schooner. Besides the men doing the loading, there were what looked like hundreds of people milling around, some carrying bags and boxes. A number of them had the half-lost, half-hopeful look of immigrants newly arrived and travelling up-country. They had probably boarded the *Great Britain* at Prescott and had come ashore during this stopover in Kingston to stretch their legs.

The carriage bringing Mr. and Mrs. Blackwood had pushed part-way into the crowd but then stopped, impeded by the cordwood and freight waiting to be loaded. Mr. Blackwood, dismounting, shouted for John to help with the luggage. Under Mr. Blackwood's supervision, John and a porter began transferring a coffer and several valises from the carriage to the ship. Mrs. Blackwood also got out of the carriage and stood talking with a lady whom Emma had seen yesterday in the wedding party.

Emma was quite close and observed Mrs. Blackwood with interest. She was a plump woman, no longer young but with a pleasant, alert look. Her clothes were rather fussy for travelling, but after all she was just married and no doubt wanted to please and impress people. During a moment's lull in the noise of the crowd, Emma heard her laugh; and when her new husband returned from making inquiries of some official she gave him an affectionate look.

She was not a beauty, and Emma was surprised at Mr. Blackwood's having married her. Emma would have expected him to choose someone younger and more striking. But she looked good-natured and friendly.

In another lull, Emma heard a man behind her laugh scornfully and say, '... not rich enough to travel by steamship!'

Did a person have to be rich to travel by steamship? Emma wasn't rich and yet here she was....

The fare! She had been assuming that the fare to York on the *Great Britain* would be a dollar, the same amount as she had paid to come here on the schooner. But maybe it was higher.

How could she find out?

She looked around but saw no one who looked like an official; the man whom Mr. Blackwood had been talking to had disappeared. Close by, however, were a middle-aged lady and gentleman, decently dressed but not very rich or grand. The man carried two valises so probably they were travelling on the ship, not seeing someone else off.

Emma addressed the lady. 'Excuse me, please, ma'am, but do you know what the fare is?'

'On the *Great Britain*? I believe it's....' She turned to her husband. 'Herbert, here's someone who wants to know the fare.'

The man turned a calculating eye on Emma. 'You'd be travelling steerage, I suppose? The half-price cabin, they seem to call it on this ship. Where to?'

'York, sir.'

'You'll have to pay three dollars, then.'

Three dollars!

'Thank you, sir,' Emma said, curtseying and trying to hide her alarm. She didn't think she had three dollars. Making her way out of the crowd and turning her back on it, she got out her little knotted bundle of money. She counted carefully, translating the farthings and pence and half-crowns and American coins into cents and dollars as she went. She was used to the mental calculation; everyone in Upper Canada had to be able to deal with a variety of currencies because there was no standard one. But she did not usually have to do it in the palm of her hand and with the distraction of having to guard against the snatching fingers of a thief.

There were only two dollars and seven and a half cents.

She'd have to ask John or, even more embarrassing, Mr. Blackwood for a loan. The prospect made her lose all interest in the crowd, the trip, or the new Mrs. Blackwood. She had enjoyed travelling to Kingston on the schooner, but almost everything since then had been worrying or unpleasant. Travelling, she thought, was something she would try to avoid in future, unless she could go in comfort as the gentry did.

Abruptly John appeared. She explained the problem of the fare and also, to get it over with in one humiliating confession, admitted that she had already borrowed from his savings. It was not the borrowing that she felt so guilty about, because she would repay him, but the fact that she had invaded his privacy by having searched for and found his cache.

His brows drew together in annoyance, but after a moment he nodded. 'That's okay,' he said briefly. 'Thanks for telling me.' He reached into his pocket. 'Here, hold out your hand and we'll see what I've got. You can borrow it all if you need to, because Mr. Blackwood will pay my fare.'

He transferred his money, coin by coin, into her hand, counting aloud as he went. It still wasn't enough; she needed fourteen cents more to make up the amount of the fare.

Their eyes met. Emma was relieved to see that he was no longer annoyed. Now he shared her feelings: embarrassment at having to ask for money, a sense of insecurity at being so nearly penniless.

But, though nearly penniless, they were not friendless; they could ask Mr. Blackwood to lend them what Emma needed. Emma gave a thought to the immigrants around her. How many of them were nearly penniless after their long trip and, in addition, were far from friends and unsure of where to find help in a strange country?

'Come along,' John said. 'Let's go see Mr. Blackwood.'

Mr. Blackwood was standing talking to his wife and her friend. Of course Emma could not just go up and interrupt his conversation. She was only a servant, and someone else's servant at that. Even John could not interrupt, unless it was an emergency. But he could position himself so as to catch Mr. Blackwood's eye. This he did, and after a few minutes Mr. Blackwood noticed him. He looked irritated but did give John a moment's attention. Emma, who had been waiting nearby, joined him and helped explain their dilemma.

'How much do you need?' Blackwood asked. 'Fourteen cents?' He delved into his pocket. 'And don't forget to buy yourselves some food. You'll be travelling in the half-price cabin and you have to bring your own food. Better look after that right away – we'll be going on board in a few minutes.' He counted about fifty cents into John's hand.

'Thank you very much, sir,' John said. 'You can take it out of my wages.'

'We'll see about that later. Hurry, now.' He nodded in response to Emma's thanks and turned back to his wife.

Emma had overlooked the need to take food. 'Where can we buy something to eat – something to carry with us – just like that?' she wondered out loud.

John looked around with an intelligent eye, and again Emma realized how familiar he was with the ways of towns. 'A pub,' he said. 'Worth a try. There's always pubs near docks. Come along.'

He led the way towards a building with a swinging sign, went in, and walked straight up to the bar. He began talking before the barman even turned to face him.

'Excuse me, please. Do you sell food?'

The man turned. 'Food?'

'We're travelling on that ship out there. We need some food. Do you sell meat pies or anything?'

'Not meat pies, son,' the man said slowly.

'Do you sell *any* food? Otherwise we'll try somewhere else.'

The man still took his time, scraping his thumb against the bristle on his chin. Emma was in a fidget of impatience.

'Well, now, I don't sell no pies. But I got these.' From under the counter he produced a basket of big cookies. 'The wife bakes 'em. Handy for sticking in your pocket.'

They didn't look appetizing and would, Emma suspected, be very dry and hard to swallow without something to drink. On the schooner she'd been given beer by a friendly sailor, but there would probably be no free drink this time.

John's mind must have been following a similar course. 'Can we buy a small jug of beer from you as well?'

Again the man reached under the counter and brought out an earthenware jug that would hold about a quart, and a wooden plug.

From the ship at the wharf came a sudden bang. It was the firing of the small gun in the bow giving the signal that the *Great Britain* was beginning to take on passengers.

'How much?' John asked.

'Them cakes is a penny each. The jug'll cost you fifteen cents, and two cents for the beer.'

While John dug in his pocket, Emma did a quick calculation.

'We'll take the jug of beer,' she told the bartender, 'and six ... no, eight, of the cakes.'

She left it to John to count out the money while she opened one corner of her cloth bundle and put the cakes inside. John took the jug, now filled with beer, and they left.

Emma had been excited, the previous afternoon, to learn that they would be travelling back to York on the *Great Britain*, the largest and most luxurious steamship on Lake Ontario. She had overheard guests in her aunt's hotel saying that the ship had separate staterooms instead of just one cabin for all the ladies and another for all the gentlemen, both with tiered berths along the walls. Besides staterooms, the *Great Britain* provided unprecedented luxury and elegance; the cabin assigned to ladies for daytime use had sofas and mirrors and other splendid furnishings.

Of course she knew that she would see nothing of this when she was actually travelling on the ship. Along with the servants and most of the immigrants, she would occupy the half-price cabin or sleep on deck.

Still, she was excited as, along with the other passengers, she slowly moved up the gangplank.

Chapter Nine

This journey turned out to be very different from the one on the sailing ship. The steamship was noisy, its boilers roaring, its paddle-wheels splashing and creaking and clanking. The two funnels belched smoke, though the awning over the deck protected passengers from the shower of soot. The whole ship vibrated as it ploughed through the water.

In the crowd on board, Emma and John separated. Emma wandered around observing everything. Many of the steerage passengers, who had paid half-price, established themselves on deck, mothers with small children staking claims to a little patch or corner while the men stood in groups talking and the boys ran around chasing each other.

One woman sitting on the deck among her bundles was having trouble with two young children who were both crying fretfully.

'Can I help you soothe one of them?' she asked. The two little girls were very close in age but did not look like twins.

The woman, with a grateful look, handed over one child. 'Oh, you *are* kind.'

'Have you just arrived from England?'

'Lord, yes, and nobody told us it'd be such a long trip! All that water – ocean, and river, and now this huge lake! We're from inland – I never dreamed there was so much water in the world!' On her face was an expression of uncomfortable surprise, perhaps even fear. But then she gave a little laugh. 'Live 'n' learn, that's what they say.'

Emma, now sitting on the floor beside the woman, rocked the child in her arms. 'I'm from inland too. I keep thinking that the ocean can't possibly be bigger than Lake Ontario, though I know it is.'

'Is that what this is called? Lake Ontario?'

'Yes.'

'The place we're going to is York. Funny – there's a York in England too.'

Emma had a mental image of the English York. In one of the books her father had owned there had been an engraving showing a walled city with the massive, square-topped towers of the Minster rising above the walls, not a bit like the York in Upper Canada.

'Did you arrive in Canada this spring?'

'Oh, yes – the first ship, they said. We saw icebergs out at sea – huge things, bigger'n the church at home.'

'Did you see any cases of cholera in England before you left?'

'Dearie me, yes.' She turned to look directly at Emma, her face grave and her eyes wide. 'So awful, you wouldn't believe. A person'd be well in the morning and dead before tea. We had several cases on the ship coming from England but, God be praised, we're alive.'

'On the ship! So you've....'

The woman stared uncomprehendingly.

'We haven't had it yet,' Emma explained. 'I heard just today that it's arrived in Quebec.'

'Quebec. That's where we landed,' the woman said, apparently having missed Emma's main point.

'So you had cases of cholera on your ship?' Emma looked at the woman, then with a sudden revulsion nearly pushed away the child in her own arms. The little girl, the woman beside her, any of the people crowding the deck might be infected! It was people like this who brought it.

She realized that she didn't know the signs of the disease. 'What is it like?' she asked. 'I mean, what happens when a person has it?'

The woman's face, though still turned towards Emma, took on a look of seeing past or through her.

'They have the runs real bad, and they vomit. They're all twisted up with cramps. They pass out. And then they die. All in a few hours. It's horrible ... I can't tell you. Little children....'

The hesitant, reluctant, awed speech, and the staring eyes, did more than the sparse words to convey to Emma the horror of cholera. At the mention of little children, Emma's arms again twitched around the child she was holding.

After a moment, the woman's eyes focussed on Emma again. 'There's none at York, then?'

'Not yet. Do people who catch it ever get better instead of dying?'

'Some do, they say, but I haven't seen it. I've only seen people die.'

Emma shivered at the woman's bleak tone. As though in sympathy, the child in her arms whimpered and shifted but settled again.

The woman sighed deeply. 'Well, no use worrying. Tell me some more about York. And what's your name, lass?'

'Emma Anderson. What's yours?'

'Staples. Mrs. Staples. My husband's a carpenter. That's him over there, smoking the pipe.' She pointed at a group of men standing talking by the rail of the vessel. The man with the pipe was short and sturdy, with an agreeable face.

'Do you have any more children besides these two?'

'We got a boy, Jimmy. He's nine. He's about somewheres. We had two more but they died as babies. Amy, there ...' she nodded towards the little girl in Emma's arms, '... she's my sister's child. My sister died and her husband married again and didn't want her.'

'Have you got a place to go to in York?'

'My husband's planning to take up land and start farming,' Mrs. Staples said. There was pride in her voice, but her eyes took on a look of bewilderment as she stared at the endless wooded shore, with only here and there a tiny settlement of a few houses in a stump-filled clearing.

'Well, there's lots of land,' Emma remarked.

'There seems to be, sure enough. All them trees....'

'But when you get to York, what will you do? I mean tomorrow morning, when we land.'

'Tomorrow morning!' Mrs. Staples gave a gasp that was more alarm than pleasure. She turned wide-eyed to Emma. 'I can't hardly believe it, after all this time.'

Emma's sensible question received no answer. The Staples family, like many immigrants, trusted in luck or Providence to supply them with food and shelter when they arrived. Emma had seen it over and over again. It was for this reason that a committee of substantial people in York had been set up. Its purpose was to help immigrants when they landed and find employment for them in York or speed them on their way to the backwoods where their newly acquired land lay. The committee's motives were benevolent but also very practical; many of the immigrants had exhausted their forward drive by the time they reached York and, short of money, unsure of what to do next, daunted by the unexpected size and emptiness of the land, simply lingered in York. A few found work for themselves but others turned to crime or begging to support them from day to aimless day. The committee wanted to prevent that if possible; York already had slums and a red-light district, beggars and criminals.

Now, with the threat of cholera, the committee might have to look after immigrants who were sick as well as friendless, penniless, and exhausted.

As Emma was brooding on this, John came towards her. She freed one arm to wave to him.

'There you are,' he said. 'Can you come here a minute?'

Emma transferred the sleeping child to Mrs. Staples, said a few encouraging words, and went to John.

'What is it?'

'Mrs. Blackwood wants to meet you.'

'Meet me? Why?'

'I mentioned you.'

He led the way to the part of the deck reserved for the first-class passengers – an area where he, as personal servant to such passengers, was allowed to go.

Mrs. Blackwood was standing by the rail on the sunny side of the ship, looking out over the wide expanse of the lake, shading herself with an elegant parasol. Near her stood the lady whom Emma had seen on the wharf and who had also been at the wedding. Since she was travelling back to York, she was probably a friend of Mrs. Blackwood's who had accompanied her to Kingston as companion and supporter.

John made introductions briefly but efficiently.

Emma bobbed a curtsey and Mrs. Blackwood gave a friendly nod.

'I'm glad to meet you, Emma. I've heard about your

misfortune of a few years ago and about the way you've adapted to your new life. I admire you for it.'

Two strangers standing nearby, overhearing this, gave Emma curious looks. That, on top of Mrs. Blackwood's kindness, made her blush.

'Oh, thank you,' she mumbled. 'But I don't think....' Then she gathered her wits; this was no time to seem childish. 'It's kind of you to say so, Mrs. Blackwood, but it was not too difficult. And may I offer you my congratulations. I'm sure this is a happy occasion for you.'

'Thank you. I mean to be happy and useful. Jeremiah is going to show me how to do the bookkeeping for the business.'

'Will you enjoy that?'

She gave a slightly self-conscious little laugh. 'I won't know until I've tried, I'm afraid. I know that Jeremiah doesn't like the work but I'll be glad to attempt it.'

She was no doubt right about her husband's not enjoying bookkeeping. Blackwood was an outgoing, sociable man. Emma could see him now, further along the deck, talking to three men and laughing boisterously.

All the same, the mention of the livery stable reminded Emma of the scene she had witnessed on the night she had gone to fetch Dr. Ross. If Blackwood were involved in dishonest dealings, would he let his wife do the bookkeeping? Wouldn't there be a risk of her noticing suspicious items in the accounts or being approached by people who had illegal business with the livery stable?

Mrs. Blackwood began to say something about the fine weather when her voice was drowned out by the clanging of a bell.

'That's the signal for our dinner,' she said when she

could make herself heard again. 'I'm sure we'll meet again, Emma.'

'I hope so.'

As Mrs. Blackwood joined the first-class passengers filing into the cabin, Emma looked after her. A nice woman, she thought.

Then, staring thoughtfully past the heads of the passengers and wondering what *their* dinner would consist of, she caught sight of Mr. Michaels-Harbottle, already in the cabin. So he was travelling back to York too! She wondered if Bick was somewhere on the half-price deck, where he and John would come across each other. Uneasy again, she turned away and went to look for John. He was not far away; together they found a place where they could sit and eat some of their cakes and drink from the jug of beer. She mentioned Mr. Michaels-Harbottle's presence and asked John if he had seen Bick.

'No. He may not be on board.'

'You'll be careful, won't you? He's beaten you up once already.'

'I won't pick a fight, if that's what you mean. Don't *worry* so much about me!'

He was obviously irritated, and Emma was sorry for having been tactless. Perhaps she did fuss too much. Probably he realized that she had travelled to Kingston to look after him, and maybe he resented it.

As it turned out, he had not been in trouble. Furthermore, he had shown himself perfectly capable of looking after himself and, she admitted, had made most of the arrangements for her as well.

She would not stop keeping an eye on him, but she should do it more tactfully and trust more in his competence and good sense.

That night Emma and John, like most of the other half-price passengers, slept on deck. In the morning the ship arrived in York.

***

When they had disembarked, Emma and John separated. He had to go with the Blackwoods, and Emma had to report to Mrs. McPhail.

As she walked up from the docks, she worked out what she could say. She had talked to the Blackwoods that morning; it had been agreed among the three of them that she would not mention the runaway marriage. Mr. Blackwood had said with a laugh of slightly nervous bravado that he would 'break the news' himself later in the day. Emma would have to try to make her explanation and apology without that.

She was not looking forward to it. She and Mrs. McPhail had had several confrontations in the past; although Emma had won a few points here and there, she dreaded facing her aunt's controlled, icy disapproval.

When she walked in by the back door, the first person she saw was Mrs. Jones rolling dough for pies.

'Well! So you're back! You did give us all a surprise, taking off like that.' Despite the sharp edge on her words, her manner was more amused than angry.

'I suppose so. Is Mrs. McPhail in?'

'In her room, so far's I know.'

'What's her mood like?' Emma asked, hanging up her cloak on a peg behind the back door and setting down her bundle.

'Dunno – I haven't seen her this morning, and Ruth hasn't said. But don't expect her to praise you. She don't like servants taking leave without asking first, and you can't blame her.'

'I don't.'

Emma knocked at the door of her aunt's private room and was bidden to come in.

'Oh, it's you!' Mrs. McPhail said, looking up from a letter she was writing. 'Sit down.'

Emma took the chair beside the desk. 'I'm very sorry for leaving like that, Mrs. McPhail,' she said. 'I had reason to believe that John was in trouble. But it turned out that he went to Kingston on business for Mr. Blackwood. So I came back as quickly as possible.'

'Didn't you think of the nuisance you were causing to the Freemans and to us here at the hotel?'

'Yes, I did think of it. But there was no time for me to talk to you and arrange for someone to do my work. I had to leave at once. The sooner I went, the better my chance of helping John if he needed it. He's only thirteen and I'm responsible for him.'

'We were very inconvenienced. Mr. Freeman sent Charlie with a message asking when you'd be back.'

'I left a note on his front step.'

'So he said. Not a very informative note, I understand.'

'I had no information to give. I didn't know what I'd find in Kingston, or when I'd be back. All I could do was say that I'd return as soon as possible. Really,' she urged, 'I did try to be as reasonable as I could and not give you all cause to worry about me.'

Mrs. McPhail gave her a cold, considering look. 'You take a great deal upon yourself. You constantly ignore the fact that I am John's guardian, as well as yours.'

'You are our legal guardian,' Emma said, choosing

her words carefully, 'but Father told me to look after him. I mend his clothes and make sure that he gets enough food and sleep.' Sometimes, she wanted to say, you don't see him for days!

'And that includes rushing off to Kingston after him?'

'Yes, it does,' Emma said firmly, meeting her aunt's eyes. 'It *certainly* includes that.'

'Well, the episode is over. You will lose three and a half days' wages, of course, and will have to apologize to Mr. Freeman. Instead of doing your own sewing during quiet periods at the store, you will take sewing for the hotel. Mrs. Jones has a supply of linen to be made into pillow-cases. You had better go to Freeman's now and do your usual afternoon's work.'

As she walked to Freeman's, Emma reflected that the punishment was not severe. The withholding of her wages was fair, and she would probably have had to make the pillow-cases anyway. Perhaps Mrs. McPhail had not been able to think of any other penalty; she seemed not to favour corporal punishment, and she could hardly add any more work to Emma's already full schedule.

But it had been an unpleasant encounter. Mrs. McPhail had been so cold, so much more an offended employer than an aunt. Maybe that was natural, but as she trudged along Emma sighed and wondered whether and how she would ever be able to free herself of Mrs. McPhail.

Chapter Ten

Emma found Mr. Freeman in the shop, sitting in the armchair by the cold fireplace, with the whiskey jug on the floor beside him. When he saw her, he surged to his feet and looked so threatening that she retreated a step.

'Oh, so you decided to come back!'

'I said in my note that I'd be back.'

'Note! Huh!' He slouched across the floor. At the far end of the room he turned and glowered at her. 'I've heard about your proud ways. Think yourself a lady, don't ya, with a right to make up your own mind, do what you want. Well, not here, girl. Not here. You're just hired help, see?'

'Mrs. McPhail pays my wages, sir. So I'm not really *your* hired help.'

'Oh, so you're here out o' the goodness of your heart – come here as a favour, like.'

'Out of the goodness of *her* heart,' Emma corrected, but he was concentrating so hard on his grievance that he did not hear her. No doubt her absence had forced him to stay home in the afternoons, just when he had developed the agreeable habit of leaving her in charge of the shop and going off on his own business.

'Lookee here, girl, either you work here or you don't. You don't just take it or leave it. It's no use unless we kin depend on you. Got it?'

'Yes, Mr. Freeman,' she said, trying to soothe him a bit without being too submissive.

'You here for the afternoon now, or just ... droppin' in?'

The sarcasm was more unpleasant than his raging

had been. 'I'm here for the afternoon,' she said curtly.

'I'll be off, then. Stay here till I get back, you hear?'

'Yes, Mr. Freeman.'

He took a long swig of whiskey – she could see his Adam's apple bobbing several times – then corked the jug and, with a surly look at her, carried it away with him. She heard him open the hallway door, tramp up the narrow stairs, move around overhead, then come down and leave by the back door.

When he was gone, she went to the kitchen. Dinner was long over and Mrs. Molloy had left. Mrs. Freeman's door was ajar but the only sound was a soft snore. She must be used to sleeping through her husband's fits of noisy bad temper.

Because of all the upheaval, Emma had missed her midday meal. Now she found a piece of stale bread in the cupboard and put it on a plate. The usual pot of soup or stew was hanging from the crane in the fireplace; it was only lukewarm but she spooned some over the bread and ate it.

This was the first quiet moment she had had since that wonderfully tranquil voyage to Kingston in the schooner three days ago. She let the quiet settle around her. But she was not inwardly at peace. She felt dislocated and disoriented after her trip; she felt as though the floor under her feet were rolling and trembling like the deck of the steamship. The transition had been very abrupt; surely it could not be more than two hours since she had disembarked.

The door tinkled; it was one of the neighbour women wanting to buy four ounces of tea. Emma weighed it out and wrote down the transaction in the book. When the woman was gone, she sat down in one of the chairs.

She thought about Mrs. McPhail's fairly reasonable reaction to her absence and about Mr. Freeman's anger. It should have been the other way round. Mr. Freeman had no right to be so demanding, while Mrs. McPhail might have been expected to punish her more severely.

But neither of them had scolded her for what she felt had been her real mistake. She had been much too ready to suspect John of being involved in smuggling, and she had treated him tactlessly, revealing that she worried about him and considered him unable to look after himself. She herself hated to be treated like a child; that made it doubly wrong of her to treat him so. Naturally he would dislike it as much as she did.

Her eye lit on the scales, which she had just used to weigh the customer's tea. There were different kinds of weighing. Now she weighed herself, her decisions and actions of the past few days. She had been wrong, hasty, tactless, thoughtless. Had she considered more carefully she would probably not have hurried off to Kingston to fuss over John. She'd have to learn from this experience, that was all, learn to think things over more carefully *before* acting rather than afterwards.

And on top of it all she had spent more than four dollars, which was two months' wages for her. She would repay John and Mr. Blackwood what she had borrowed, but it was a great deal of money to spend on an impulse, especially when it bought nothing except a bitter new knowledge of herself.

She could do nothing further at this moment to reform her behaviour for the future, only resolve to remember. Abruptly she yawned. These last few days had been tiring and unsettling, and last night's sleep on the deck of the *Great Britain* had been disturbed by the cold, the noise of the engines and paddle-wheels, and the stops to take on more cordwood.

In the afternoon quiet of the house and shop, she leaned her head back and slept.

***

In the hotel that evening, when she was on her way to bed, Emma was stopped in the lobby by Mrs. McPhail.

'There you are, Emma. Will you come into my room for a moment?'

Emma put down her hot-water jug and candle and followed Mrs. McPhail.

'I gather that you had the advantage of me in learning about Mr. Blackwood's marriage.'

Emma, who had been sagging with weariness, jerked to attention.

She had forgotten about this. Mrs. McPhail did not sound particularly angry, but it was not wise to relax.

She looked at Mrs. McPhail's face and hands, watching for further reactions.

'I was bidden not to speak of it,' Emma said. 'What ... what do you think about the marriage?' It might be a risky question to ask, but Emma had to know. Mrs. McPhail and Mr. Blackwood were friends; now Mrs. McPhail would have to exclude Mr. Blackwood from her circle or admit the new Mrs. Blackwood.

Mrs. McPhail smiled, but there was a tightness at the corners of her lips. 'I'm very impressed. I had not given him credit for so much sense.'

'Do you know her?'

'I had not met her until this afternoon, when they called here. She seems a pleasant, sensible person – though not very elegant in her appearance.'

'You're not displeased?'

'Not at all, though I gather from their manner that they thought I might be.' She smiled, but to Emma's eyes there was something tigerish in the expression. 'They seemed to consider their marrying more important than it actually is.'

'It's important to them, of course.'

'Naturally. And to her brother. But hardly to me.'

The last words somehow rang false. Mrs. McPhail was trying too hard to show that she didn't care. Her left hand, almost buried in the folds of her skirt, clenched.

Emma took careful note of these signs. Mrs. McPhail's mood was of concern to everyone around her; if she were angry about this marriage, everyone would be affected, not only the newly married couple. For some reason, Mrs. McPhail had decided to act out a little drama designed to show that she did not object to the marriage – that, if anything, she found it amusing and perhaps slightly ridiculous.

If her real reaction was anger and resentment, then Mr. Blackwood had been right to elope. In that case, his judgement of Mrs. McPhail's character and temperament deserved respect.

All this passed through Emma's mind as she watched her aunt's hand clench. It was all the more reason why she should join in the pretence.

'I'm glad you welcome the marriage,' she said, 'and that you're not annoyed at my keeping quiet about it this morning. May I go to bed now?'

'Certainly, Emma. Good night.'

***

The next morning Emma was back to her usual routine. She was up early and worked in the hotel until breakfast was over and the guests' rooms were clean, then set off for the store. In her cloth bundle she carried the material for the first pillow-case that she had to sew.

The weather had turned rainy; she picked her way along such solid spots as there were in the muddy street but could not help getting her feet wet. She drew her hood over her head and kept her arms and bundle under her cloak.

It was market day. In spite of the rain, the streets were busier than usual with the farmers and their customers, and the market place on King Street was thronged. At this time of the year the farmers had no fresh vegetables to sell but they did have dairy produce, live and dead poultry, home-spun yarn, weaving, needlework – and there were always people selling horses, cattle, sheep, tools and implements. Around the fringes of the crowd were the Indians selling fish, venison, moccasins, and baskets.

Emma was approaching the store but was still on the Kingston Road when the door of Freeman's burst open and Mrs. Molloy came rushing out in a flurry of skirts. When she saw Emma she threw up her hands.

'Oh, thank the Lord you're here! Hurry, hurry!'

'What's the matter?'

'It's Mr. Freeman. He's had some sort of attack. He just fell down! I'm going to the neighbours to get someone to fetch the doctor. You go and stay with them.'

Emma found Mr. Freeman on the floor in the shop. He lay on his back, arms and legs sprawled. His face was twisted, and his breath came in snorts. She hovered over him for a few moments but had no idea what she could do.

As she stood there, a thump sounded from the back of the house. Mrs. Freeman called out, 'Mrs. Molloy! What's going on?'

Emma went to her. Mrs. Freeman was sitting on the edge of the bed, painfully trying to get to her feet.

'Oh, Emma!' she exclaimed. 'Something's wrong! There was an awful crash, and then Mrs. Molloy cried out, and now she seems to be gone. I don't know what's happening.'

'It's Mr. Freeman. He fell down and appears to be ill. Mrs. Molloy has gone to send someone for the doctor.'

'Abner? Ill? I've got to go to him. Maybe I can get up if you help me.'

'I don't think there's anything we can do.' Rose Freeman was struggling to get to her feet, though her face contorted with the pain and effort. 'No, please, Mrs. Freeman, please stay in bed. Otherwise you'll fall too....'

'Abner needs me!'

'Mrs. Freeman, please, he's lying very quietly on the floor, not uncomfortable or anything. As soon as you're back in bed, I'll go and stay with him until the doctor comes. Won't you please get back into bed?'

Rose had been making one last effort, but apparently her legs lacked the strength to hold her up. The feet visible below the edge of her nightgown were swollen, with reddish blotches, and were turned a little inwards, and the part of the leg showing above the ankles was pitifully wasted away.

Now she gave up and sank back. Emma helped her swing her legs into the bed and spread the covers over them. For a moment she took the woman's swollen hands in her own and, when Rose lifted her eyes in silent but anguished appeal, gave what she hoped was an encouraging smile.

'I'll do what I can for him, Mrs. Freeman, and come back in a minute to tell you how he is.'

'And Charlie! Someone ought to go and tell Charlie.'

'First the doctor, I think, Mrs. Freeman. But we'll certainly send a message to Charlie as soon as possible.'

'Yes, of course.'

Afraid of what she might find, Emma went back to the shop. Mr. Freeman was still breathing, but the breaths seemed to be more laboured. Driven by the need to do something, she fetched a shawl from one of the pegs in the passage and folded it to make a pillow. For the rest, she was unwilling to touch him. She went to the front door, reaching it just as Mrs. Molloy returned, red-faced and breathless.

'They've sent a boy,' she gasped. 'I gotta sit down before I drop too.'

She plunked down on the doorstep, ignoring the rain, and used her apron to wipe her perspiring face. 'Any change?'

'He's just lying there, breathing in that awful way. Mrs. Freeman was trying to get up but I persuaded her not to. She wanted Charlie fetched. I said we'd do that when we had sent for the doctor.'

'I told the boy to go to Doel's brewery after he's been to the doctor. Poor things – an unlucky family.'

'I'll go back to her,' Emma said.

The doctor, when he had examined Abner Freeman, said that it was an apoplexy. He bled the stricken man but without perceptible results.

Emma, having been on hand during the bleeding procedure in case the doctor needed someone to help or run errands, went back to the kitchen. She found Mrs. Molloy standing in the doorway of Rose Freeman's bedroom.

'We'll have to get him to bed,' Emma said to them.

Mrs. Molloy gave a pessimistic grunt. 'We was just talkin' about that. I don't know how we'll ever get him up them little twisty stairs to his own bed, and he just a dead weight.' She tipped her head towards the hallway; from behind one of the doors there, the stairs curved up steeply and in a tight coil to the floor above.

Emma winced at the choice of words.

Mrs. Freeman again made a motion to get up. 'Why not bring him in here? If you'll help me....'

'No, no, Mrs. Freeman, please don't,' Emma said hastily, going into the room to prevent her. 'Why can't Mr. Freeman lie in the parlour?' Although she had never been in it, she knew that the room across the passage from the shop was the parlour, almost never used now that Mrs. Freeman no longer entertained visitors. 'We can bring his own bed down from his room. I suppose it can be taken apart to get it down the stairs?'

'That's a good idea,' Mrs. Molloy said. 'You just stay there, Mrs. Freeman, and let us make him comfy in the parlour.'

'Well, if you think....'

Emma went to the shop to confer with the doctor. She found him kneeling beside the sick man, feeling his pulse and watching his face closely.

'We've been trying to decide about a bed for him,' Emma said softly. 'His own room is upstairs, up a narrow little staircase....'

The doctor gave her a quick look, then turned back to Mr. Freeman. 'You may not have to worry,' he said. 'I'm afraid he's going.'

Emma also looked at the man lying on the floor, then knelt down beside the doctor. The harsh breathing filled the shop and seemed to vibrate through the floor. While she watched, he gave a desperate gasp and was silent.

After a moment the doctor laid the hands on the chest and pulled down the eyelids. Then, with a sigh, he got heavily to his feet.

'I'll tell Mrs. Freeman,' he said.

Emma stayed where she was. Another death, she said to herself. First her parents and baby sisters, then Granny Wilbur, now this. She had a vision of the long corridor of the years to come, marked by the deaths of people near her.

As a small tribute to the dead man, she touched his hand with her finger. But there was nothing there. The spirit was completely gone.

At once, in a blaze of vision, she saw how beautiful it was. His spirit was free! She had heard religious people talk about the soul and the body but had never understood it until now. What was left lying on the floor had to be treated respectfully, but Abner himself was free.

She got up and went outdoors. The rain had stopped and the clouds in front of the sun were breaking. Some quality in the breeze reminded her of the wind over the lake that had taken her schooner to Kingston – and of that other wind over the lake which, on that Sunday-afternoon walk with John last fall, had given her a glimpse into her own boundless potential. Now she lifted her face to the stroking of this breeze and closed her eyes. The potential was still there; perhaps the spirit could be free even while she was still alive, not have to wait until she died.

Behind her the door opened. The tinkling bell,

together with her recollection of the Kingston trip, reminded her of her return yesterday and of having to apologize to Abner for her absence.

She turned and, as she had expected, found the doctor just putting on his hat and closing the door behind him.

'Could I ask you one question, doctor?' He said nothing but stood listening, waiting for her to continue. 'Could it ... Mr. Freeman's apoplexy, I mean ... could it have been caused by....' She stumbled and tried again. 'He was very angry at me yesterday. I had done something wrong and he was furious. Could that...?'

He understood. 'Anything could have caused it, but it's much more likely to have been something that happened shortly before the attack. This morning, say. But it could have been anything. He'd been drinking too much for years, and he was a bad-tempered man.' His eyes grew abstracted, as though in his mind he was again seeing the dead man lying on the floor of the shop.

'So you don't think....'

He turned his attention fully on her. 'My dear girl, don't agitate yourself. Most of us have enough to worry about without assuming more burdens than we need to. I can't tell you for certain that his getting angry at you yesterday did *not* bring on this apoplexy. But I don't think it's the most likely cause. That is the plain truth. You really would be foolish to blame yourself.'

Their eyes met and Emma could see that he was being as clear and honest as he could be. It was a kind of compliment; had he given her a bland reply intended to soothe her rather than answer her worry, she might have remained unsatisfied for ever.

Something in her reached out to the doctor as a

man. He was no taller than she, a thin man with grey hair, a grey face and respectable but somewhat untidy clothes. His eyes held a tenderness that was almost sadness, not for her but perhaps for people like Abner Freeman.

'You're very kind, doctor,' she said. 'Can I offer you a cup of tea?' It was the only comfort she could think of.

'Thank you, but no. I have other calls to make.' He touched the brim of his hat.

She watched him walk to his horse, mount, and ride away towards town. How good of him to answer her so honestly! And how strange that out of the sadness of Abner Freeman's death should have come that feeling of exaltation, of hope.

***

After that, Mrs. Molloy took over. By some means which Emma never discovered, she sent for several old women who were friends of hers and were used to laying out the dead. They set up a trestle table in the parlour and moved Mr. Freeman to it; Emma was astounded at the handy way in which five elderly women lifted and carried his huge bulk. Rose Freeman let them do it; someone had to, and she couldn't do it herself. Emma sat with Rose for part of the time, holding her rheumatic hands and trying to be a comfort. Several times the doorbell rang; Emma served the customers, thinking that it would not be fair to turn them away.

Charlie arrived home in the middle of the afternoon. Emma was in the shop, having just served a customer, when she saw him come running along the Kingston Road.

She went out to meet him. All he knew so far from this morning's message was that his father had been taken ill. She wanted to prepare him for the chattering women moving back and forth between the parlour and the kitchen, getting hot water to wash and shave the corpse, making tea for themselves, enjoying the occasion in a ghoulish way yet treating it all as a commonplace event.

'Your father, Charlie....'

'How is he? What's...?' Then he saw the answer in her face. 'He's dead, ain't he?'

'I'm afraid so. The women are here, laying him out.'

'I gotta go to my mother.'

Emma returned to the shop, the only place where she would not be in the way. She looked at her bundle of sewing but decided that it would not be suitable to stitch pillow-cases at a time like this. So she pottered about straightening the rows of bottles on shelves, dusting the scales, tidying the merchandise in the drawers. She sold tobacco to an old man and tea to a girl of about ten. A young man identifying himself as an assistant to the Reverend Dr. Strachan, rector of St. James' Church, called to discuss the funeral; she ushered him to the little room off the kitchen where Rose and Charlie were.

Towards the end of the afternoon, Charlie came to the shop.

'Mother'd like a word with you,' he said. 'Kin you come?'

She went with him and, at Mrs. Freeman's gesture, sat down on the stool while Charlie leaned in the doorway. As usual, with three people in it the stuffy little room felt almost intolerably full.

'Poor Emma,' said Mrs. Freeman. 'We haven't paid

much attention to you. But actually we've been thinking about you – about the shop, you know. Of course tomorrow's Sunday so we're closed anyways. The funeral will be on Monday so we'll stay closed then. But Tuesday.... Well, Charlie wants to try if he can keep it going.'

'You mean he'll stop driving for Mr. Doel?'

Charlie answered. 'If I have work that I kin do at home, I kin look after Mother. Simpler.' But he looked very dejected, and Emma thought there was more to this than grief at the death of his father. He had never wanted to work in the shop. Now it looked as though he might have to.

'However,' Mrs. Freeman went on, 'he doesn't know very much about the business. We'd both like you to stay on for a little while until he learns. I can help by lying here and giving advice.' She tried to smile but her eyes were dark with sorrow and she looked much older and more drawn than usual. 'The three of us can work together – if you don't mind staying. Of course you'll have to ask Mrs. McPhail....'

'I don't think she'd object,' Emma said, recalling why she had originally been sent to the Freemans. 'In any case, I'll be here on Tuesday.'

'That's good of you. And, Emma, thank you for your help today.' Her voice trembled on the last words.

Charlie walked to the front door with her. 'On Tuesday ...' he began, mumbling almost inaudibly, '... on Tuesday, kin you be here early? To open up? I don't....'

'Sure I can,' she said reassuringly. 'I'll see you then.'

Chapter Eleven

On Tuesday, therefore, she left the hotel earlier than usual so as to be at Freeman's at nine o'clock. The house, when she approached it, looked dead. There was no smoke coming from the chimney. A cock crowed, but there was no sign of human life.

There was no tinkle as she opened the door; probably someone had temporarily removed the bell because its tinkle was unsuitable to a house of mourning. The absence of that familiar sound emphasized how silent the whole house was. It clutched at Emma and almost frightened her. In one panic-stricken moment she had the horrid thought that she might find Rose and Charlie dead too.

She closed the door gently and tiptoed down the corridor. As she passed the door to the shop she glanced in. It was, of course, empty.

She stopped just before entering the kitchen. That room, usually so warm and alive, was dark and chilly.

Emma was becoming really worried. She didn't realize how tense she was until a noise made her jump. It was the sound of a boot scraping along the floor.

The noise came from Rose Freeman's room. Emma went through the kitchen to the small bedroom.

Rose lay in bed as usual, her eyes in a blank stare. Charlie sat on the stool, his hands dangling between his knees, his eyes also fixed. Across Rose's bed, probably weighing uncomfortably on her legs, lay what appeared to be a bundle of Abner's clothes. They added a further musty and unaired smell to the room's already oppressive atmosphere.

'Hello,' Emma said softly.

'Goodness!' Rose exclaimed, shaking herself and focussing on Emma. 'It's you! What's the time, then?'

Charlie looked up at Emma, his mind coming back from some far place. 'We were lookin' for something black of Dad's for me to wear. Yesterday for the funeral I wore his best suit. But it's all too....' He turned to his mother. 'I can't wear this stuff,' he said with a tightness in his voice. 'And I can't wear his best suit for everyday. So it'll have to be just a black armband. That okay?'

'Of course, my boy.' She looked up at Emma. 'We're all at sixes and sevens this morning 'cause Mrs. Molloy isn't coming. It's her legs again.'

'It's not her legs, it's drink,' Charlie said, getting wearily to his feet and gathering up the dead man's clothes. 'I'll take these away.'

'Why don't you hang them on the clothesline?' Emma suggested. 'They smell sort of musty.'

'Yes, do that, Charlie,' said his mother. When he was gone, she turned to Emma, while at the same time lifting her swollen hands to pat her hair into place. 'I'm afraid, with Mrs. Molloy not here, that no one's got the fire going.'

'Have you had any breakfast?'

'Oh, yes, Charlie made me some bread and jam. But I'd be real grateful for a cup o' tea. And there's some soup left from yesterday, that Mrs. Wilkins brought. Some cold chicken, too, I think. You could hang the soup over the fire to heat up for dinner.'

So Emma stirred the fire and boiled water for tea. While the water was heating, she helped Mrs. Freeman tidy herself and the bed.

When Mrs. Freeman was supplied with tea, she decided that the next thing to do was to show Charlie how the shop worked. She used the same procedure that Abner had used with her, explaining the book, showing the pile of old newspapers available for wrapping, opening drawers and cupboards to indicate where everything was. She mentioned some prices but found that he couldn't remember them – or didn't want to.

'I'll write them down,' she said, trying to be helpful but finding it very hard to cope with Charlie's refusal to be interested.

Towards midday she went to the back of the house to do the work that Mrs. Molloy should have done, sweeping Mrs. Freeman's bedroom and the kitchen, collecting dirty dishes, and generally tidying up.

Charlie lounged around watching her until she sent him to feed the livestock and fetch firewood and water. When he had finished that he came back and sat down at the kitchen table, following her with his eyes.

A little later, the front door opened. Emma was busy at the fire, moving the kettle of hot water off the crane and replacing it with a pan of soup. She was handling the heavy vessels carefully to avoid accidents and at the same time partly averting her face from the heat of the fire.

Charlie was still lolling at the table. Not only had he not offered to help her move the heavy iron pots, but when the front door opened he didn't move.

Keeping her eyes on the hot water, she said, 'Maybe you can look after that customer, Charlie. I'll come in a minute if you need me.'

'Me?'

In her annoyance, Emma wondered whether after all he *was* feeble-minded.

But he got up and went. Emma could hear voices. In a moment he came back to the kitchen. 'She wants boot-laces and tobacco and tea and something for her husband's lumbago.'

Emma wiped her hands and went to the shop. The customer was a stranger, a small woman who moved briskly in spite of a noticeable limp. Emma helped her while Charlie leaned in the doorway watching. When she was gone, Emma looked straight at him.

'Are you really going to keep up this business?' she asked. 'If you are....' She deliberately let her sentence hang uncompleted in the air.

He shrugged the shoulder that was not leaning against the wall. 'It's all I kin do. If I keep on driving for Doel's, I gotta hire someone to look after Mother in the afternoons. If I run the store, I look after her myself. Maybe increase the business. Town's growing, they say.'

Emma wanted to remark that he wouldn't increase the business if he didn't bestir himself. At the very least he had to familiarize himself with the merchandise, the prices, the procedures. He had to improve his manner and appearance. But she kept silent. His father was only just dead, and Charlie ought to be allowed a few days to adjust to that and to the idea of being a shopkeeper.

On the other hand, if the customers once stopped coming....

'Well, I'll help you all I can,' she said, trying to sound sympathetic and briskly encouraging at the same time. 'You'll have to learn the prices of things, find out how your father's bookkeeping works.... I don't know much about the bookkeeping, only about the way he recorded what credit the customers got and when they paid it off. But I think I know all the prices now.' She smiled, trying to evoke some of the friendliness that they had shared before, when he showed her his carvings. But he was staring at the floor.

Dinner was a gloomy affair. Rose ate two mouthfuls of soup and then burst into tears. When Emma tried to comfort her she asked to be left alone and gestured to Emma to close the bedroom door. So Emma returned to the kitchen table and went on eating her soup, face to face with a completely silent Charlie. After dinner he laid down his spoon and went out; through the window Emma saw him walking towards the marshes, carrying a gun. She knew he was fond of shooting birds and had not yet begun to understand how he could shoot birds and also carve those delightful little portraits of them.

She washed the dishes and dusted the shop. Two customers came in and kept her talking for half an hour about the sadness of Abner Freeman's sudden death. She welcomed their inquisitive but friendly chatter; it was a relief from Rose's tears and Charlie's silence.

'They're lucky to have you here,' one of the women said. 'Staying on, are you?'

'I don't know yet.'

When they were gone, she thought about it. As long as she was there, Charlie might well feel that he had no need to learn the business. She had come as a temporary help but was becoming a fixture – an unpaid shop assistant, ready to turn her hand to housekeeping and nursing, convenient for the bereaved Freemans. It was not Rose's fault except that she could do more to encourage Charlie to take on the work.

What rankled, of course, was Charlie's behaviour that morning. She remembered having taken a liking to him when she first met him, but since then....

If she kept coming to the store as she was doing now, Charlie would never take over. She'd have a word with

Mrs. McPhail. The best plan might be for Mrs. McPhail to limit Emma's hours of work at the shop.

At the usual time, she made tea and knocked at Mrs. Freeman's door. When she was invited in, she was pleased to see that the invalid had overcome her tears. She was pale and looked old and tired, but she was composed.

She asked where Charlie was. Emma reported that he had gone to hunt in the marshes and was not back yet.

'Poor boy,' Rose said. 'This changes everything for him. He didn't like his father, but now....' She put her deformed hands to her face. 'I can't ... I can't....'

Emma was overcome by sympathy, and by remorse for her earlier uncharitable thoughts. Of course it was too soon to expect Rose and Charlie to carry on as though nothing had happened. They were entitled to forbearance and support from their friends. She went to sit on Rose Freeman's bed, balancing awkwardly on the upright board that kept the straw mattress in place, and put her arm around the woman's shoulders. 'I know, Mrs. Freeman. I ... I've lost people too. It's hard. It's very hard.'

'He was ... he was sometimes not very easy to live with. But mostly we were comfortable together. And now, for me, handicapped like this.... There's no point in my living. I'm completely useless. Abner needed me, in his way, but Charlie....'

'Charlie is going to have *great* need of you in this difficult time.'

'If I weren't here he ... he could do whatever he liked.'

'I think he'd be lost without your support and encouragement.' She searched for something positive to suggest and then thought of Mrs. Blackwood. 'If Charlie is going to run the store, you might be able to help with the bookkeeping. And with planning and making decisions. There's lots that you could do lying here. Today already there's some money in the drawer that should be recorded and put away. Mrs. White paid something on her account, and Mrs. Thorpe asked if we'd take eggs as part payment – she'll bring them in later this week and hopes you say yes. Someone has to decide those things and keep track of everything. With your experience of how the store works, you could really help Charlie. And everyone tells me how pleasant the atmosphere of the store was when you were able to work and talk to the customers.'

Mrs. Freeman wiped her eyes. 'I could discuss things with him all right. But I don't know about keeping the books. There's days when I wouldn't hardly be able to hold the pen 'cause my hands are too bad for me to grip one of those narrow quills.'

'Then you can do the bookkeeping on your good days, and at other times talk with Charlie, help him make decisions. But I'll bet we could make a fat quill for you, wrap something around the stem so that it's thicker and easier to hold. We could fix up some sort of board or low table across your bed to put the book on, and the inkwell can stand on the stool where you can reach it but not knock it over. Or you could use a pencil.' She had been carried away by her own enthusiasm, but now she paused. 'Not if it's going to be too much for you, of course. And anyway, it's for you and Charlie to arrange. I'm just....'

'No, no, it's a good idea.' Rose did not sound enthusiastic, but Emma hoped that she might still become so.

'Didn't you do the bookkeeping before you became ill?'

'No, Abner always did. He'd go into the shop in the evenings and spread the book out on the counter. I'd hear him muttering and swearing....' She swallowed hard and Emma was afraid of more tears, but Rose didn't give in this time. 'I can read and write and do figures, sort of. Your granddad paid for me to go to some classes. I may have forgotten some things, of course....'

'It will come back to you,' Emma said encouragingly.

Meanwhile Charlie was still not home. Emma decided that she might as well heat the soup for supper. At the same time she checked supplies in the kitchen and discussed them with Rose, decided what was needed, what their own shop could supply and what would have to be bought at one of the bigger stores in town.

About dusk, Charlie came home. He was still quiet but seemed less sullen, and his 'See you tomorrow' to Emma was not unfriendly.

Emma went home feeling that she had had an exhausting day. And she felt in her tired bones that there were more troubles to come before Rose and Charlie Freeman would be able to manage their lives by themselves.

Chapter Twelve

That night Emma was awakened by noise from next door and red light coming in at the quarter-pie window and flickering against the ceiling.

'Fire!' someone outside shouted. 'You, there, in the hotel! Fire!'

She shoved her feet into her boots. She and John and Mrs. Jones met in the open area of the attic and clattered down the stairs – there was no point in keeping quiet for the guests' sake when there was a risk of fire.

The blaze was burning in a shed where the neighbour kept his horse, hay, a few hens, and firewood. Less than four feet away, on the hotel side of the fence, was the hotel's wood-shed. If it caught, the resulting fire would be big enough to threaten other buildings, including the hotel itself.

Emma, John, and people from the neighbour's household began the work of putting it out. The livestock had already been taken out of the shed – Emma saw one little boy with a hen in his arms, and well out of the way was a small portable coop holding a mother hen and a number of very young chicks. Now the able-bodied people present began drawing water from both wells and flinging it in bucketfuls at the fire. It was slow work; someone ran across the road to use the well of the people who lived there. Those who couldn't be kept busy with buckets watched carefully for burning bits of debris and stamped them out at once. Mrs. McPhail sent John to ask that the bell of St. James' Church be rung to summon the town's firefighters.

By then other people were assembling, some to watch – Emma had a brief glimpse of Mr. Michaels-Harbottle in a handsome dressing gown – and others to help. Mrs. McPhail asked Mrs. Jones to stir up the fire in the kitchen and begin heating water so that the firefighters would be able to wash later.

Emma carried buckets and flung water at the burning shed. She was feverishly impatient at the slow supply of water, every bucket of which had to be drawn up out of one of the available wells. At one moment, when she saw burning debris fall on the woodshed roof, she climbed on a chopping block and reached out with a rake to beat it until it was extinguished.

After what seemed a long time, the bell of St. James' Church rang the tocsin to give the general alarm, and later again one of the fire engines arrived. It was a horse-drawn cart with a barrel and pump on it, and it came careering up Yonge Street, some of the volunteer firefighters clinging to the cart and others running behind. Emma drew back and watched the men go into action, pumping vigorously by raising and lowering a long handle.

From the first cry of 'Fire!', Emma had been reminded with terrible vividness of the fire which, two years ago, had killed her parents and baby sisters. While she was actively fighting the blaze, the memory gave her a frantic energy, but when she was merely watching, it became so strong and fearful that she could not bear to look at the flames. She went indoors.

'You'll have to have a good wash,' Mrs. Jones said, handing her a cup of tea. 'Look at you.'

Emma glanced down. She had been working in her nightgown, a roomy garment made of thick white linen. Now it was covered with soot and mud. Her hands were filthy and she had torn two fingernails. Her boots were muddy. It would take her a while to clean up sufficiently to meet Mrs. McPhail's exacting standards.

'What time is it?' she asked Mrs. Jones.

'Getting on for five.'

'And I've got to wash and get ready for the day! I'll be late!'

'Well, at least I've plenty of hot water for you. Take some upstairs with you. And bring that nightgown along when you come down. Mrs. Tubb has to do a laundry today and can do that as well.'

Cleaning up took even longer than Emma had expected and she was more than half an hour late going downstairs to start the day's work. Some of the guests, wakened because of the fire, were up early and idled about waiting for breakfast and getting in Emma's way as she cleaned the lobby and dining parlour and set the table.

Later, in the course of serving breakfast, Emma put down the refilled teapot in front of Mrs. McPhail. As she did so, Mrs. McPhail reached forward and pointed to dirt under one of Emma's fingernails. Their eyes met and Mrs. McPhail gave a small but significant frown: it was the rule that Emma's hands should be clean when she waited at table. The dirt had escaped her notice because she had been washing by the light of one candle. Probably none of the guests had observed the silent reprimand; Emma, however, obeyed the unspoken order and went to the kitchen where, with a splinter of firewood, she dug under her nail until the dirt came out. But inside she was fuming; Mrs. McPhail might have been a bit more lenient, knowing that the dirt was soot from the fire which Emma had helped put out.

After all this delay and upheaval, Emma was later than usual in leaving to go to Freeman's. She was still in the hotel kitchen bundling up the pillow-case she was sewing and looking for her shawl when Mrs. McPhail and Mrs. Jones began planning the day's dinner. At the same moment John came in. He had left for work earlier; now, clearly, he was on the job, delivering a folded note to Mrs. McPhail.

'From Mrs. Blackwood, ma'am.'

'Mrs. ...?'

The rasping edge in Mrs. McPhail's voice caught Emma's attention. She glanced at her aunt who, having been caught by surprise, was holding the note as if it were poisonous.

'Mrs. Blackwood, ma'am,' John repeated, thinking that she hadn't heard him.

Mrs. McPhail read the note. 'It requires no written answer. You can tell Mrs. Blackwood that we have no rooms free for tonight.'

'But we have!' Emma exclaimed. 'Mr. and Mrs. Peterson are leaving today.'

It was only when Mrs. McPhail looked at her that she remembered how foolish it was to blurt things out.

'I beg your pardon, Emma?' Mrs. McPhail's hand was clenching and flexing among the folds of her skirt.

Emma would have retracted the words if she could. But she couldn't, and besides, they were true. 'We do have a room free for tonight,' she said.

Mrs. Jones, trying to ease matters, asked, 'Why does Mrs. Blackwood need a room here?'

'An unexpected visitor, apparently,' Mrs. McPhail explained briefly. 'Her own guest room is being repainted.' But her eyes were still on Emma. '*I* decide whether we have rooms empty, Emma.'

'Yes, Mrs. McPhail.'

As she walked to Freeman's, Emma's mind was in turmoil. The fire in the neighbours' shed had revived all her worst memories. And then the rush and disorder of the next couple of hours – and the business about her dirty fingernail – and now this about whether there was a room free.

Mrs. McPhail's reaction had nothing to do, of course, with whether there was an empty room in the hotel. It had to do with Mrs. Blackwood. Mrs. McPhail resented Mr. Blackwood's marriage. Perhaps she, being an attractive woman still, had hoped to marry him herself. Perhaps it was just that she resented his doing such a thing and doing it secretly.

But Emma had not expected her aunt to be so petty as to lie about having a room empty, just to spite Mrs. Blackwood. It *was* a lie. The Petersons were definitely leaving – Emma had heard them talking about it at breakfast – and if other guests were known to be coming Mrs. McPhail would have put a note beside the hotel register so that whoever received them would be able to welcome them by name. So it was quite certain that no one was expected to occupy that room tonight. Emma had been right in her facts, even though she had been wrong to contradict her aunt.

There was something further in this matter, however, that worried and frightened Emma. It gave a new insight into Mrs. McPhail's character. It showed a jealous, possessive streak in her. If she resented Mr. Blackwood doing a perfectly sensible thing like taking a wife, might she not be equally resentful if Emma wanted to become independent?

Brooding over all that, Emma reached the store in an agitated state of mind. She went in by the front door as usual. The door tinkled and she was just observing that someone had put the bell in place again when she heard voices in the shop.

Charlie was behind the counter, and a male customer stood facing him. 'Cloves,' Charlie said. 'And what else?' It was not cloves, however, but cinnamon sticks that he laid down beside the things which the customer was buying.

For the second time that morning Emma spoke without thinking. 'That's cinnamon, Charlie, not cloves!' she said, striding into the shop.

Both men looked at her, the customer surprised and Charlie scowling.

She realized that again she should not have spoken so abruptly, that she should have found a more tactful way to correct Charlie's mistake. And her tactlessness couldn't have come at a worse moment, just when Charlie was, for the first time, taking his place in the shop. But, again, the damage was done. All she could do was try to smooth things over a bit. She turned to the customer, who was a stranger to her.

'Were you looking for cloves, sir?'

'Yeah. The wife sent me. She just said cloves. I dunno what they looks like, 'n' neither does this young fella, I guess.'

Charlie, still glaring, now blushed with embarrassment. He shook his hair forward so that it nearly hid his eyes. Emma could think of nothing to say to placate him, at least not while the customer was there. She gave him a smile and went behind the counter.

'There's the cloves, Charlie,' she said. 'The jar at the end of the row.'

He turned away resentfully. 'You do it, then, if you're so smart.'

As he spoke, Emma realized how the confusion had happened. The spices were kept in round glass jars with the names printed on them. But some of the jars had got partly turned around so that a portion of the name was out of sight. The cinnamon and cloves jars had only the first bit of the names visible. It was obvious why Charlie had confused them.

'How much cloves, sir?' She held the jar towards the customer so that he could see what he was buying. 'You see, they're quite small.'

He looked puzzled. 'She said a few. But they're awful small. Measure us out a couple dozen, lass.'

She scooped about twenty into the pan of the scales. 'That'll go quite a long way, sir. They're just used for seasoning, for the flavour.'

He stared at the cloves in the pan of the scales. 'Maybe three or four more.'

She counted them out, and he nodded. 'Yeah, that should be okay.'

While wrapping the cloves in a bit of old newspaper, she glanced at Charlie to see whether he wanted to finish serving the customer. But he was standing with his hands in his pockets staring out of the window.

'Anything else, sir?' she asked the customer.

'Just some boot-black, please, lass.'

'Are you paying cash, sir, or do you have an account?'

'Er ... cash.'

She added up the cost and told him the total. When he had paid, he put the purchases into his various pockets.

'G'day, lass.'

'Good day, sir. Hope to see you again.'

'Sure. G'day, young sir.'

'Good day,' said Charlie, not turning around.

The customer's departure left Emma alone with Charlie. Now she would have to apologize. She had been tactless, there was no denying it, and she deserved his resentment. Had they known each other better he might have forgiven her, but as it was she had hurt his feelings and humiliated him before a customer. It wasn't something that he would forgive easily.

She had drawn breath to speak her apology when he turned around to face her. 'You were late!' he accused. 'It wouldn't have happened if you'd been on time. You said you'd come early.'

That squashed her apology before it was spoken.

'I couldn't come any earlier because we had a fire this morning. I had to help fight it. It's no joke having two jobs at the same time. And remember that you're getting my help free. You're not paying me a penny!'

For a moment they confronted each other like fighting cocks, both blazing with anger. Then he turned and went out. She heard him storm through the kitchen and out by the back door.

'Emma?' came Mrs. Freeman's voice.

'Coming, Mrs. Freeman.' She tried to speak cheerfully, but as she went down the passage she gave a despairing sigh.

'Good morning, Mrs. Freeman. Have you had breakfast?'

'Yes, thanks, Emma. Mrs. Molloy's here today. She just stepped across to the neighbours to borrow something. But what was going on between you and Charlie?' When Emma was silent for a moment, wondering where to begin, she said gently, 'Tell me about it, dear. Maybe I can help.'

So Emma did, starting with the fire in the

neighbour's shed and digressing to talk about her parents' death. Remembering in time that Rose was a friend of Mrs. McPhail's, she said nothing about the two little encounters she had had with her aunt that morning, only describing the upset in the hotel's routine and the irritation that had caused.

When Emma came to the confusion about the spices, Mrs. Freeman looked concerned. 'How did that happen?'

Emma explained about the jars having got turned around. 'I didn't notice yesterday that they were not facing forward. But I know what the spices look like, so I don't need to read the labels.'

'Oh, dear,' Rose sighed. 'This is going to make it hard. I had a long talk with Charlie last night. He doesn't much like the idea of being a shopkeeper – but I guess you know that. He thinks it isn't a real man's job, though lots of men do it.'

'It's not like working with horses and kegs of beer,' Emma said with just a touch of irony.

'Well, I got him to say that he'd try it and do his best.'

Rose Freeman looked up and met Emma's eyes. Neither of them needed to express the thought that Emma's tactlessness might have undone all Rose's constructive efforts.

'I'm so sorry,' Emma said, feeling very remorseful. 'I seem to have made an awful mess of things.' She felt the tears coming to her eyes but tried to keep them back.

'Where has Charlie gone?' Rose asked. 'I heard him run out.'

'He didn't say.'

'Well, we can't do anything until he comes back. I'll

talk to him again, explain that you had a bad morning at the hotel. Is it okay if I mention that?'

'Whatever you think best. I'll apologize when I see him, but you can tell him that I'm sorry for what I said and that I'd ... I'd like to be friends.'

But Charlie did not come back. At the end of the afternoon Emma gave Mrs. Freeman a supper of bread and cheese, and then Rose sent her home. 'You've had a very long day, dear.'

'Will you be all right alone?'

'Of course, for a little while. Charlie won't stay out all night. He's probably lurking somewhere waiting to see you leave before he comes in. Just make sure the fire is safe. And ... Emma ... don't brood about all this. It'll work out. Everything works out somehow.'

Impulsively, Emma hugged her. As she left the house she reflected that Rose at least was taking hold of things again in the wake of her husband's death.

***

But she could not obey the advice against brooding. In fact, it seemed to her as though only by thinking about things could she understand them. So, as she walked along the Kingston Road and King Street, she went over the events of the day again and particularly wondered how she could, in the future, stop herself from blurting things out. Maybe she could think everything over before she spoke – but that would make conversation impossible, and would certainly make everyone think that she was slow-witted.

What other cure was there?

She was still fretting over this when, in the centre of town, she saw ahead of her two familiar figures, the tallish military one of Major Heatherington and the shorter but equally trim one of his wife. They were walking away from her; Emma hurried into a run to catch up.

'Mrs. Heatherington!' she called when she was within range.

The Heatheringtons stopped and turned. When Emma reached them they all clasped hands and broke into a confusion of greetings.

'When did you get here?' Emma demanded.

'This afternoon,' Major Heatherington said, with that expression on his face which was not quite a smile but was just as friendly as if it were.

'We went to the hotel to look for you,' Mrs. Heatherington added, 'but you were out.'

'I was at the Freemans' store. I wrote you about that. And since I wrote that letter Mr. Freeman died and.... Oh! it's all very complicated.' She resisted the temptation to pour out all the miseries of the day.

Then she realized the significance of what Mrs. Heatherington had said. 'Aren't you staying at the hotel?'

'No, with Caroline,' said Mrs. Heatherington. Caroline was their daughter, a year or two older than Emma, who had married a military officer serving in the Lieutenant Governor's guard of honour. Emma knew Caroline but, moving in such a different social circle, had little contact with her.

'Oh, yes, you wrote to me that she was expecting a baby.'

Mrs. Heatherington nodded. 'We're rather anxious about her. Last time she had a miscarriage, you remember. So I decided to come and be with her for this confinement. It was rather a sudden decision; otherwise I'd have written to tell you that we were coming.'

'I wish you were staying at the hotel. Then I'd see you sometimes. Now....'

'Do you have Sunday afternoons free still?'

'Yes. I usually wash my hair then.' She smiled to suggest that she was not complaining, but in fact today's problems had made her feel overburdened with work and difficulties.

'Well, we'd like you to come and have tea with us at Caroline's house on Sunday afternoon.'

'Oh, but...!' The thought of visiting at one of the houses of the gentry dazzled and alarmed Emma. What would she wear? The only dresses she owned were the black ones she wore for work and for going to church. The blue-flowered one was not nearly ready.

She would just have to finish it in time. Today was Wednesday; could she possibly finish it by Sunday?

Mrs. Heatherington must have guessed what was going through Emma's mind. 'It won't be a party with a lot of people,' she said reassuringly. 'We'll just be the three of us in the little back parlour with a cup of tea, catching up on the news.'

'We're going to be late for dinner, Jane,' Major Heatherington said to his wife.

'Goodness, yes, we must hurry. We count on seeing you on Sunday afternoon, then, Emma. About three o'clock.' That, too, was considerate of Mrs. Heatherington. Three o'clock was early for tea, but she knew that Emma had to return to the hotel in time to help prepare dinner for the guests.

The encounter with the Heatheringtons cheered Emma but did not make her forget that in a few minutes she might have to face Mrs. McPhail. The events of that morning came to mind as vividly as though nothing had happened in between. Would Mrs. McPhail still be angry at her? What would have been done about Mrs. Blackwood's request for a hotel room for her visitor?

As usual, Emma went in at the back door. She found Mrs. Jones just finishing the setting out of the various dishes of the guests' dinner. Ruth was carrying them into the dining room.

'Not many people dining tonight?' Emma asked, assessing the amounts of food with an expert eye.

'Only six,' Mrs. Jones said, pouring sauce from a pan into the sauce-boat. When she finished, she straightened up and poked some straying hairs back under her cap. 'What sort of day have you had?'

'Awful. What did Mrs. McPhail decide about the Blackwoods' guest?'

The cook gave Emma a meaningful look. 'I believe the guest is staying at another hotel.'

'So Mrs. McPhail won! Then she ought to be in a good mood.'

'Tolerable. She's also pleased that the woodshed was saved this morning. Why? Do you have to speak to her about something?'

'Not unless she wants to speak to me,' Emma said, tiredness sweeping over her. 'Does Ruth need my help with the serving?'

'No, just you take it easy till dinner,' she said, referring to the servants' dinner, eaten after the guests had finished theirs. 'Oh, by the way, the Heatheringtons were here looking for you. Remember, those people who....'

'I met them just now on the street. I'm going to have tea with them on Sunday.'

When she reached her bedroom, Emma got out the

bundle of blue-flowered material that was so slowly becoming a dress. She had been working on it since last fall, when an unexpectedly large tip from a departing guest had increased her savings to the point where she could afford to buy the material. Now she laid it out on the bed to remind herself of what still needed to be done.

The main part of the dress was finished but the sleeves still had to be sewn up and attached to the bodice. Then the final things had to be done, like buttons and buttonholes, lace trimming.... Emma's heart sank. She had so little time. But at least for the rest of the week she'd defy Mrs. McPhail's instructions and take this sewing to the shop with her instead of the pillowcases. In a pinch she could leave off the lace trim, or perhaps invent some short cut with the buttons. She might have to work late in the evenings, though it was not easy to sew neatly by the light of a single candle.

One thing she was sure of: she would *not* go to tea with the Heatheringtons wearing the black uniform of a servant.

Chapter Thirteen

The next morning Emma did take the unfinished dress with her, but as she walked along her mind was on what she would find at the store, especially what mood Charlie would be in. Mrs. Freeman had promised to talk to him, to act as a mediator, but could she really achieve anything when at heart she must be on Charlie's side?

Charlie was alone in the shop when she arrived. He looked up and stared unsmilingly at her.

'I'm ... I'm sorry about yesterday, Charlie,' she said.

His eyes fell. 'Oh ... uh ... sure,' he mumbled. It was not clear whether he accepted the apology or forgave her. He came from behind the counter, pushed past her, and left the house. Emma, taken aback, stared after him.

Mrs. Molloy shouted from the kitchen. 'Emma? Rose wants to see you.'

Emma hung up her shawl. She was dismayed by Charlie's abrupt departure, which seemed to signify that he was not going to stay and learn the business, that he did not want to be there at the same time as she was. But if he intended to run the shop he would have to spend time here with her, learning more about the prices and qualities of things, the procedures of doing business, the ways of dealing with customers.

Rose Freeman looked more ill than usual, her face pinched and her eyes underscored with blue smudges. When Emma came in, she began without greeting to talk in a rather hectic, forced way.

'I heard Charlie go out,' she said, 'but he's coming back. I talked to him last night. I ... I explained about your ... your problems at the hotel yesterday. He's gone now to do a few errands of his own but he'll be home for lunch and start ... start learning about the shop. If you'll still teach him?' She looked pleadingly at Emma.

Emma was not sure whether Rose was pleading on her own behalf or passing on Charlie's appeal. Either way it embarrassed her. Did they regard her as some sort of monster who had to be appeased? Couldn't they behave in an ordinary way?

But she remembered again that Abner's death and Rose's illness distorted things. These were not ordinary circumstances; allowances had to be made.

'Of course, Mrs. Freeman. It isn't hard. He'll learn it in a couple of days.' If he really wants to, she added silently to herself.

'And I'm going to look over the books,' Rose said with an attempt at cheerfulness. 'Charlie will make a list of what's in the shop now, an inventory. Then we can decide what has to be ordered. We'd like your advice about that.'

'That's a good plan,' Emma said encouragingly. 'When you go over the books, wouldn't it be a good idea to make a list of the customers who still owe you money? It would be useful to know.'

'Yes, yes, I'll do that. I'll get Charlie to bring me a separate sheet of paper.'

Charlie was home for lunch but, with mumbled and incomprehensible explanations, went out again immediately after. However, he did return about half past three and spent an hour in the shop with Emma. They were embarrassed and awkward, not meeting each other's eyes, talking about nothing but the job at hand, but they did cover some more details of the shop's operation.

During that hour, a customer came in. Emma stepped aside and let Charlie serve her, keeping an eye on him without seeming to. He was slow and clumsy and appeared to be distracted by the woman's constant chatter. Worse, he made a mistake when adding up the woman's bill.

'Eighty-eight cents, please,' he said.

Emma, doing the sum in her head, had arrived at a total of seventy-eight cents.

What could she do? She was determined not to be tactless again, but she couldn't let him overcharge a customer. Quickly she did the addition again; the total definitely was seventy-eight cents.

She tried to catch Charlie's eye, hoping in some silent way to suggest that he check his arithmetic. But he ignored her.

As it turned out, the customer asked to have it put on her account. That postponed Emma's problem but did not solve it by any means; she would still have to find a tactful way to draw the mistake to Charlie's attention.

***

By the afternoon of the next day they had gone over all the merchandise so that Charlie was at least aware of what was in the store and where it was kept. While they did this review, Emma had discovered that Charlie did not know some things that she had known even before coming to work here. For instance, customers might ask for a remedy for a certain illness; she pointed out to Charlie that the labels on the medicine bottles stated what each medication was for and that he could offer the customers something appropriate. 'Of course you never promise that it will work. You let them decide whether to try it.'

Another thing he had apparently not realized was that if he could not supply the customer with exactly the requested merchandise he could suggest something similar. 'You can ask what it's wanted for and then discuss whether something else would do. Shopkeepers do that all the time.'

They were discussing how to organize the inventory for Rose when a horseman arrived and tethered his horse to the fence. A moment later he came into the shop, a tall man who strode in and set a pair of saddle-bags on the counter. He took off his hat and wiped his face with a red handkerchief.

'Yes, sir?' Charlie asked, stepping forward. Emma, pleased, withdrew to the side. 'Can I help you?'

'Like to speak to Abner, please,' the man said in a voice with an American twang, reminding Emma of Mr. Blackwood's.

Emma and Charlie exchanged glances. 'I'm ... I'm afraid you can't,' Charlie said. 'My dad's dead. I'm carryin' on the business.'

The man stopped in the middle of putting his handkerchief in his pocket. He looked hard at Charlie, his face startled and almost alarmed. 'Dead? Is that what you said, son?'

Charlie nodded. 'Last week.'

The man frowned, glancing swiftly back and forth between Emma and Charlie. Then he swung the saddle-bags onto his shoulder again and picked up his hat. He gave a brief nod to them both.

'G'day to you, then,' he said, as though finishing a perfectly normal and satisfactory piece of business, and strode out, putting on his hat as he went. Through the window they watched him mount his horse and set off at a canter.

Emma and Charlie stared at each other.

'That's odd,' Emma said. 'Could he be a personal friend of your father's and not a customer?'

'I've never seen him before. If he was a friend, wouldn't he introduce himself, or ask more about Dad's death?'

'He must have had business with your father. Perhaps bringing in merchandise to pay a bill. Then why not pay it? And he's not a regular customer because I've never seen him either. His business must have had something to do with those saddle-bags or else he'd have left them on the horse. Why bring them in?'

She looked at the counter as though trying to reconstruct the image of them and deduce something from it. Then she reached forward, picked up a tiny black thing, and laid it on the palm of her hand. There were a few others but she took just one and examined it closely.

'A tea-leaf,' she said. 'It fell from his saddle-bags. I wiped the counter after the previous customer left.'

They bent their heads over it.

'It's tea, sure enough,' Charlie agreed. 'A tea salesman.'

'A smuggler, more likely,' Emma said, speaking before thinking.

They looked at each other.

'A smuggler?' Charlie asked doubtfully. 'You think so?'

Emma thought of what she had seen and learned in the last few weeks. 'It could be. I'm not saying it is.'

Charlie was now staring at the place where the tall man had stood. 'He figured that Dad'd take the tea in his bags, otherwise he'd have left them outside, on his horse. That means he's had dealings with Dad before.'

A further logical conclusion hung unspoken in the air between them.

'Smuggling's illegal,' Emma observed tentatively. 'Your father could have got into trouble....' She eyed Charlie anxiously, wondering whether he could be punished for a crime his father had committed. But of course they might be wrong and Abner might not have been handling smuggled goods. Perhaps these little signs led to a completely different conclusion – or meant nothing at all. At this moment, though, Emma could not see where else they might lead.

'Let's go and talk to your mother,' she said.

'No!' Charlie burst out. 'She don't need to know.'

'She may know already, from working in the shop with your father. And besides, she may notice something in the books.'

Charlie, wearing a mutinous look, stuck his hands in his pockets and idly kicked at the base of the counter.

'I really do think we have to talk to her,' Emma insisted gently, understanding very well that he wanted to protect his mother, and perhaps his father's memory, but feeling that it was more important to discuss what they had stumbled on.

'She's sick.'

'She's not too sick to take an interest in things. And if you report this to ... to the authorities, she'll learn about it anyway.'

'*Report* it?'

'I think you have to, don't you? Otherwise you're guilty too, guilty of hiding it.'

'It's only guessing. We're not sure.'

She said nothing, watching him as he flung away

around the end of the counter and went to stand at the window. After a few moments he turned back to her.

'I guess you're right. We'll tell Mother and report it to whoever it is. The customs inspector, mebbe?'

'Probably.'

'We ought to tell Mrs. McPhail too.' He said it as though it were some sort of challenge, as though Emma would be as reluctant to tell her aunt as he was to tell his mother. He seemed to be daring her to tell Mrs. McPhail.

But Emma had already been thinking about Mrs. McPhail, who had a financial interest in the store and had sent Emma there to 'keep her eyes open.'

So she responded calmly to Charlie's challenge. 'Yes, of course. She could help us. She'll know who to speak to.'

'*If* it's smuggling. How do we find out for sure?'

'Let's go and talk to your mother.'

Mrs. Freeman was resting but not asleep; her eyes opened the moment Emma and Charlie appeared in the doorway and she smiled when she saw them together, apparently on good terms. But the smile faded when she saw their sober faces.

Charlie was silent, but Emma felt that he should be the one to recount what had happened. 'There was a man in the store just now,' she said. 'Charlie will tell you. I'll put the kettle on for tea.'

As she stirred and fed the fire and filled the kettle she could hear their conversation, and when Charlie mentioned the leaf of tea that had fallen out of the saddle-bags she picked the tiny thing up from the corner of the kitchen table and took it to show Rose Freeman.

Rose inspected the black twist. 'That's tea all right.

But he could just be carrying some provisions in his bag....' Her voice tailed off as she realized how unlikely that was.

'Have you noticed anything strange in the books?' Emma asked her. Yesterday, when the shop closed, Charlie had taken the ledger to her; he had also found a pencil among his father's belongings, and Rose had decided that it would be easier to handle than a quill. So Emma assumed that Rose must at least have looked at the ledger yesterday evening.

'No ... I ....' She looked up at Emma and Charlie, then down at the rheumatic hands lying in her lap. 'I don't seem to be able to manage very well. The book is so big and heavy, and lying across my legs it's too far away for me to read easily....'

That was very likely true. Or perhaps Rose was unwilling to admit that she couldn't read or do arithmetic well enough. Emma was sorry now that she had suggested it; she had done so only because she had the mistaken impression that Rose had formerly done the bookkeeping.

'I need someone to look at the books and sort of tell me....' Charlie gave an embarrassed glance at Emma. 'Myself, I can't.... Someone who's familiar with business. I'll get the person to explain so that I kin carry on after that.'

'Could you ask Mrs. McPhail?' Rose suggested. 'She's very clever, and she's already got connections with the shop. Oh, but if Abner was selling smuggled goods....' Her face grew anxious. 'She'll be very angry and take her money out of the business.'

'We thought that she should be told anyway,' Emma said. 'She'd be even angrier to be kept in the dark. Besides, she would know whom to notify.'

When she had made the tea and brought cups to Rose and Charlie, Emma went into the shop and carefully gathered the other tea-leaves that had spilled from the saddle-bag. There were about twenty of the little black specks and, thinking back, she thought that they had probably come from between the stitching of the bag or from some corner that had worn into a tiny hole. After pondering for a moment, she laid them on one of the pieces of newspaper used to wrap spices and made it into the usual little package, rolling it up and twisting the ends firmly. As she did so, she remembered the first time she had made a package like this. It was for Mrs. Ferguson. That brought Abner Freeman vividly to mind, stamping around the shop saying, 'We can't offend Mrs. Ferguson.' At that time Emma, occupied with her own worries and resentments, had only seen him as the boss whom she had to obey, who was making her do something hateful and humiliating. Now, looking back, she felt again that curious impulse of sympathy for him, the same sympathy and understanding she had had on the day she first came to the shop.

Now it looked as though he might have been involved in smuggling, or at least in selling smuggled goods. If this had come to light while he was still alive, it would have been her duty to turn him in. Could she have done it, knowing that if he were found guilty he would be severely punished?

Standing behind the counter thinking about this, she held the little package of tea on the palm of her hand, absent-mindedly weighing it as though her hand were one pan of the scales.

The question of whether to report smuggling was not as straightforward as she had thought. Abner was dead now and could not suffer, but if Charlie reported that his father had been engaged in this illegal activity....

What would come of it?

***

Emma had no chance to talk to Mrs. McPhail before dinner that day. But later in the evening she asked if she might have a private word with her. 'About the Freemans,' she said.

Mrs. McPhail led the way to her own room off the lobby. She sat down at her desk and gestured to Emma to take the visitor's chair.

Emma began bluntly. 'Something happened today – Abner Freeman may have been selling smuggled goods.'

Mrs. McPhail was always a good listener, but now her attention sharpened. She listened closely to Emma's story and looked at the tea-leaves in the newspaper package.

'Mrs. Freeman and Charlie need your advice about the bookkeeping and about reporting the smuggling,' Emma said in conclusion. It was a relief to turn it over to Mrs. McPhail; Emma had the sense that the Freemans depended heavily on her to solve their problems but knew that she couldn't do so.

'I'd better have a look at the books before anything further is done,' Mrs. McPhail said. 'Have you seen any other signs of suspicious activity at the Freemans?'

'Nothing definite. Several times people came and talked to Abner privately, and Miss Morgan told me that his tea was cheaper than other merchants'. I suppose cheap tea would be a sign – I mean, if duty had not been paid on it, it would be cheap, wouldn't it? But that may not be very much to go on.' She paused and then, before Mrs. McPhail could speak, she asked the question that had been on her mind since the word 'smuggling' had first arisen between her and Charlie that afternoon. 'Did you expect me to find something like this when you sent me to work there?'

Mrs. McPhail's face was expressionless for a moment. Then she smiled slightly. 'Let's say that it doesn't completely surprise me.' Her expression darkened. 'It's a serious business. There's been more talk than usual about smuggling. It used to be considered normal and acceptable, even admirable. Everyone knew it happened, and almost everyone benefited. Smugglers made a good living if they weren't caught, shopkeepers could earn more profit on smuggled goods than on things for which duty had been paid, and customers paid lower prices. Now some respectable people are beginning to disapprove of it – at least they *say* they disapprove.'

'But really they don't?'

'Well, they'll drink smuggled brandy if no one knows that it's smuggled.' She paused for a moment. 'I myself wouldn't like it to be said that I served smuggled liquor and tea here in the hotel. But it's not just a matter of reputation. If this hotel were suspected of using smuggled goods, we could ... I suppose we could be raided, or I could be fined or imprisoned. These things don't happen often because there are not enough customs officers to catch everyone, but they do occur.' She gave Emma a dismissive nod. 'Thank you for telling me.'

Emma slid forward on her chair but did not get up. 'What are you going to do, Mrs. McPhail? I mean about the Freemans?'

'I must look into this more fully.'

That was Mrs. McPhail being evasive and secretive again. But this time Emma felt entitled to know more precisely what her aunt was planning.

'You'll tell me what you intend to do?' And, when Mrs. McPhail looked uncommunicative, she added, 'If I'm to keep working for the Freemans, and carry messages between you, and be tactful when I'm there, I ought to know what you intend to do.'

After a moment's further reflection, Mrs. McPhail nodded. 'Yes, I can see that. Tomorrow evening I'll call on Rose and Charlie and talk with them, maybe glance at the books. What I do after that depends on what I discover.'

Something in her manner suggested that Mrs. McPhail was still not revealing all her plans, but Emma felt that she had pressed as hard as she could. Besides, she wanted to go upstairs to her room. Though tired, she hoped to spend an hour working on the blue-flowered dress.

She was aware that John did not come home until a little after eleven o'clock but, remembering her resolve to stop fussing over him, she stayed in her room and did not make an excuse to go out and talk to him.

Chapter Fourteen

The next day, Saturday, was a quiet one at the store. Charlie was away part of the time, and Rose told Emma that she was afraid that all the talk of smuggling had revived his dislike of shopkeeping. But she was pleased to learn that Mrs. McPhail would be coming that evening to talk over the problem.

Because the day was so quiet, Emma made good progress on the dress. By that evening it was ready. She had even been able to put the lace trim on the collar and cuffs.

On Sunday, as usual, she was allowed to get up half an hour later than on weekdays. She spent the morning doing her usual chores in the hotel and found time to iron her new dress. For once there were no guests lunching in the hotel; the servants had an early and quick lunch and after that Emma washed her hair, drying it in the yard in the May sunshine. Then she went up to her room to prepare for going to tea with the Heatheringtons.

When she had put on the new dress she was pleased with her appearance. The only regrettable thing was that she had no footwear other than the plain black boots that she wore every day. A lady going out for tea would have had delicate, elegant shoes to wear. If she went in a carriage, she would pick her way carefully whenever she had to set foot on the ground; if she had to walk, she would wear everyday shoes for walking but carry the neat shoes with her and change into them upon arrival. Emma would just have to wear her plain black boots throughout the tea party.

She knew where Caroline's house was – in the western part of town, not far from Government House where her husband served in the Lieutenant Governor's guard of honour. The town was expanding in this direction, spreading away from the older, eastern area where the Freemans lived. Emma had been to Caroline's house once, to the back door, delivering a message from Mrs. McPhail.

She enjoyed her walk. It was past the middle of May and the weather was summery. The trees were in leaf, and lilacs were in blossom. Dandelions shone bright by the roadside and a few were already fluffy with seeds. The area through which she walked was not fully built up; among the buildings were weed-thronged vacant lots, small coppices, and tiny bits of pasture accommodating someone's horse or cow. In one there was a cow with a very young and woolly-looking calf; elsewhere a part of a vacant lot had been enclosed with a fence woven of withies to make a pen for a couple of dozen hens.

All this, together with the consciousness that she was wearing a new and becoming dress, lifted Emma's spirits. It was a lovely day and she was actually going to have tea with the Heatheringtons.

As she approached the house, however, she found herself in a dilemma. Should she go to the front door or the back door? Last time she had been a servant delivering a message and had automatically gone to the back door. But this time she was coming to drink tea with a lady and gentleman staying as guests in the house – in other words, she was 'gentlefolks'. It was not usual for the same person to be a servant sometimes and 'gentlefolks' at other times; there might be some social rule that dictated what she should do, but Emma didn't know it. She thought she had better go to the front door; it might be disrespectful to the Heatheringtontons for their visitor to go to the back.

So Emma went to the front door and knocked. When it was opened by a parlour maid in a dressy cap and apron, she said, 'I'm here at the invitation of Major and Mrs. Heatherington.'

The maid looked her up and down. 'Do you have a card? A calling card?'

She was referring to the kind of card that Mr. Michaels-Harbottle had given her when checking into the hotel. Ladies always had such things, but Emma did not.

'No. My name is Emma Anderson. The Heatheringtons know me.'

The maid stepped back as a sign that Emma could come in. 'Wait here, please.'

The hall was slightly smaller than the lobby of McPhail's Hotel. Emma knew from what Mrs. Heatherington had told her that Caroline was dissatisfied with the house and considered it much too humble for her. But the hall was a pleasant one, well lit by a fanlight and the windows beside the door, and with a handsome staircase rising out of it.

The sound of talk, with Caroline's voice easily recognizable, came from one of the front rooms. Just as Emma became aware of it, the noise emerged in a sudden rush when the door was opened.

Emma recognized the man who came out; it was Captain Dixon, Caroline's husband. She had seen him several times before but he had never had any reason to notice her. He was clearly surprised to see a stranger standing in his front hall.

'Oh!' he exclaimed. 'Are you...? Have you been...?'

'Your maid let me in. I'm here by invitation to have tea with Major and Mrs. Heatherington.'

He seemed to take her for a gentlewoman; he gave her a civil little bow. 'Quite so. I'm sure one of them will be along soon.'

She smiled. 'Thank you.' Past him, through the open door, she could see Caroline, bulky with pregnancy, lying on a sofa. An elegant man leaned towards her over the back of the sofa, and a young woman in a fashionable hat sat on a chair drawn up close to it.

Caroline saw Emma and stared. They knew each other because Caroline, before her marriage, had stayed in the hotel with her parents. Therefore she knew that Emma worked as a chambermaid, and she seemed annoyed to see her exchanging civilities with Captain Dixon.

Emma returned Caroline's look steadily. No doubt Caroline would tell her husband later that Emma was only a servant and had not deserved his bow, but for the moment all she could do was stare and then give a small nod of greeting. Emma nodded in return.

All this happened in a second, while Captain Dixon was looking around, in a vague but courteous way, apparently hoping to spot one of the Heatheringtons for Emma.

'I hope Mrs. Dixon is well?' Emma asked.

'Oh, yes, yes, it appears that this time .... Ah!' He was rescued by Mrs. Heatherington coming along the passage from the back of the house. Almost simultaneously, Major Heatherington appeared at the top of the stairs and began descending.

'Hello there, Emma,' Mrs. Heatherington said. 'Come along with me to the back parlour.' And she led the way through to the room behind the one in which

Caroline was entertaining her friends.

This room was much less formal than the front parlour. Mrs. Heatherington's sewing lay on a table near the window, and a cat slept on a braided rug in front of the cold fireplace.

The three of them talked about what had happened in their lives recently, sometimes repeating what they had already written in letters. The Heatheringtons gave news and greetings from the Bates and Wilbur families, who lived near the farm on which Emma had grown up and which the Heatheringtons now owned.

'How are the Berrys?' Emma asked. Mr. and Mrs. Berry and their two children had gone to the farm with the Heatheringtons as servants and companions.

'Very well,' Major Heatherington said. 'We have plans for clearing more land and building a larger house.'

Emma watched his face as he spoke and was pleased to see him looking cheerful. When Emma had first met them, he and his wife had had unrealistic ideas about life on a pioneer farm. Emma had helped to give them a more realistic picture; when they actually moved to the farm they were better informed and less optimistic. Since then, during their two previous visits to York and from Mrs. Heatherington's letters, Emma had perceived that they were tackling the problems of frontier life sensibly. Emma very much wished, though, that reality had not crushed their earlier optimism.

Emma told about the Freemans, and the store, and Abner's death, and her trip to Kingston. 'I'm afraid,' she said, 'that it was very foolish of me to suspect John of being involved in smuggling – to suspect him on such flimsy grounds, at least. But somehow, once I began to suspect him of being in trouble, that was all I could see.'

'It's natural to *think* along those lines,' Mrs. Heatherington said, her eyes on Emma. 'The very fact that you're concerned about him, fond of him, makes you fear the worst.'

'That's just it,' Emma said with a little surge of relief at being so well understood.

'Another time, though, perhaps you'll be able to step back and ... and see a larger picture before taking action.'

'Yes, I've told myself that too.'

'But speaking of smuggling,' Major Heatherington said, 'you may be right in suspecting that there's something going on at Blackwood's. We're stabling our horse and wagon there – Caroline doesn't want a farm wagon standing in her yard for her friends to laugh at.' His voice was steady but his eyebrows gave a little twitch of annoyance. 'Well, Friday evening we came back into town late after visiting friends in Richmond Hill. When we drove into Blackwood's yard we couldn't see anyone to look after our horse. But I could hear voices. I traced them to the back and saw two men unloading crates from a cart into a shed.'

Emma nodded. 'That's what I saw, the night I went for the doctor.' Then she gave a start of realization. 'Did you say Friday? John was home late on Friday night, after eleven o'clock. At what time did you see this, sir?'

The Heatheringtons exchanged considering looks, and it was Mrs. Heatherington who answered. 'It was about a quarter after eleven when we arrived here, for I noticed the clock in the hall.'

'So it would be about eleven o'clock when ... I don't

like this,' Emma said in what was almost a gasp of fear. 'Mrs. McPhail says that people can be fined for smuggling, put in jail....'

'But, Charles,' said Mrs. Heatherington to her husband, 'you didn't see John there that night, did you?'

'Oh, no, just two men unloading a cart. No sign of John.'

Mrs. Heatherington turned back to Emma. 'I understand your anxiety, my dear, but don't work yourself into a state over this. It may be just coincidence that John was home late that night. Hasn't that happened before, and hasn't he had good reason for it?'

'Oh, yes, errands for Mr. Blackwood, and once helping a poor man home.'

'There, you see!'

'But never as late as that.'

However, she recognized that Mrs. Heatherington was trying to lead her away from the trap they had discussed earlier. She herself was making the same mistake that had sent her headlong to Kingston.

Her emotions told her that she had reason to be anxious. But last time her emotions had been wrong. Maybe they were wrong this time too.

At any rate it was silly as well as rude to spoil this visit by concentrating on her own worries. She gave herself a mental shake and smiled.

'Well, I'll worry about that later.'

'Not worry too much, I hope,' Mrs. Heatherington said, trying to express her admonition in a half-humorous way.

It was not until she was walking home that Emma remembered her earlier feeling that it might be dangerous to speak to Major Heatherington about John's possible involvement with smuggling. This afternoon she had broken her own rule. But the fact was that when she had actually seen Major Heatherington again it had been impossible to imagine him reporting John to the authorities. He was their friend, and he and his wife were among the very few people whom she felt she could trust completely.

***

The next day she received a bonus. About half past three Charlie told Emma that she could go home. 'I'll be making out the inventory,' he said, 'and I guess I kin weigh out the tea and tobacco for people. If I don't know the price of somethin' I'll ask Mother.'

So Emma walked along King Street enjoying her unexpected freedom. As always, she stopped outside Mr. Lesslie's bookshop to look at the books displayed in the window. Today there was a big folio volume laid open to show a full-page engraving and, facing it, a page of handsome type with broad margins.

The engraving showed a woman in loose robes standing on a pedestal with sky and clouds behind her. She was blindfolded; in one hand she carried a sword and in the other a pair of scales. Across the top of the picture was lettering in a foreign language.

'What are you staring at, Emma?'

It was Miss Morgan, carrying a pile of parcels.

'That picture. What does that writing across the top say?'

'It's Latin, and it means "justice".'

'Justice?'

'She is the traditional image of justice. The scales are for weighing the evidence. The sword is for execution if the person is guilty.'

'Why is she blindfolded?'

'Justice is supposed to be impartial – the same for everyone. It's not supposed to be affected by whether the accused person is rich or poor. She's blindfolded so that she can't tell how the person is dressed or whether he's a famous person or, maybe, a friend of the judge.'

'But justice isn't always like that,' Emma said, remembering stories she'd heard about how the legal system favoured the rich and punished the poor extra hard.

'No, it's an ideal. The human race has lots of ideals. We need them....'

Miss Morgan sneezed, interrupting her own words and causing the pile of parcels to totter. The top one would have fallen if Emma had not caught it.

'I can help you carry them,' she said. 'Are you going home now?'

'It seems I'll have to – or hire a porter to carry my purchases. If you help me, we'll have a cup of tea. Have you time?'

'Today I have. I'm early.'

As they walked, Miss Morgan explained that this spending spree was made possible by her having two new students whose parents were actually paying in money rather than in eggs or firewood. 'In fact, next winter I may be asked to board them, because they live some distance out of town, beyond the Don River.'

'What's their name?'

'Ferguson. Matilda and Louise Ferguson. Their mother....'

'I've met their mother,' Emma said. 'A very self-assured lady.'

'Overbearing, I call her,' Miss Morgan said with cheerful bluntness. 'A bully, in fact. But I won't have much to do with her. For now the girls are being brought in every day by a servant, and the mother writes me notes whenever there's anything I should know. For instance, the girls are not to sit in draughts and are to have places at the ends of the benches so that they do not feel hemmed in.'

'Do you cater to such requests?' Emma asked, remembering how she and Abner Freeman had dealt with Mrs. Ferguson.

Miss Morgan gave a tight little smile. 'For a customer who pays in money, and pays regularly, I'd walk on my hands and yodel.'

Emma laughed but realized that Miss Morgan was almost serious. From working in the store she knew how rare it was to be paid in cash. And although it was possible for someone like Miss Morgan to go to one of the stores and offer eggs in exchange for a pair of stockings, it was awkward and a little degrading.

In any case, the school only just kept afloat, though it was gradually becoming known in York and the surroundings.

As she reflected on this, she had an idea. Charlie had already admitted to needing help with the bookkeeping, and he had made a mistake in addition. Perhaps one reason for his reluctance to become a shopkeeper was that he was not very good at arithmetic. Over tea in the kitchen, she mentioned her idea to Miss Morgan.

'Do you ever take adult pupils in the evening?' she asked. 'Perhaps one evening a week?'

Miss Morgan pursed her lips.

Emma hurried on. 'I know you must be busy enough, teaching all day, but a little extra income might help, in goods or money.'

'Are you thinking of someone specific?'

'Yes, but the idea came to me only this minute, and it's my idea, not his. I thought I'd ask first if you'd even consider it.'

'I would. Who is it?'

'Charlie Freeman. He's taking over the store now that his father is dead.'

'And he needs some more reading and arithmetic?'

'I'm not sure, but I think so. And perhaps some very elementary bookkeeping. Would you be willing to teach him?'

'Yes, I would.' She gave Emma a shrewd but friendly look. 'You really care about those people, don't you? What a mother hen you are! And you're only ... what? ... fifteen?'

Emma blushed. 'Oh, dear, I hope I'm not the bossy kind of mother hen. It's just that people seem to....'

'To need mothering. Quite right. I've been told that I try to teach everyone who comes near me.'

'So you do. You taught me when we first met in the hotel, lending me books and talking about them.'

'Well, that's the way we are. By the way, speaking of the hotel, I saw Mr. Blackwood one evening last week, accompanied by a lady, going into the hotel. Who was the lady? Do you know?'

'That would be his wife, I'm sure.'

'I didn't know he was married.'

'It happened about two weeks ago.' She told the story of her trip to Kingston but did not mention that it was smuggling of which she had foolishly suspected John. 'At first Mrs. McPhail really seemed to disapprove of the marriage but things are better now. I know she once went to call on Mrs. Blackwood.'

'Sensible of her. York is too small for such hostility.'

* * *

That evening Mrs. McPhail went to the Freemans to make a more thorough study of the ledger. As usual when her aunt was out in the evening, Emma sat behind the counter in the lobby of the hotel, ready to attend to people coming in from the street as well as to hotel guests needing service.

When Mrs. McPhail returned, Emma could not restrain her curiosity.

'Did you find anything ... suspicious?' she asked, keeping her voice low.

Mrs. McPhail went into her own room. 'Come in and close the door.' After Emma had done so, she went on. 'We – Rose and Charlie and I – worked together. They sometimes remembered things Abner had said that helped to make sense of what was in the book. We found a few interesting items. Most of the time when people paid in kind – that is, in something other than money – Abner wrote down what it was: three dozen eggs, or two chickens, or whatever. But sometimes he just wrote "merchandise". One man living out beyond the Don River often paid in "merchandise" though Charlie, who regularly delivered beer there, says that his house is a hovel and he seems to do no farming at all. Yet he always had beer delivered and his wife frequently shopped at the Freemans' store.'

'What's their name?'

'White.'

'Oh, yes, I've served Mrs. White.'

'The Fergusons also paid in "merchandise". Charlie said you'd remember Mrs. Ferguson.'

'Yes, I had a ... an encounter with her. Abner Freeman was afraid of Mrs. Ferguson.'

'I'm not surprised, if she and her husband knew that he sold contraband.'

'Miss Morgan says that the Ferguson children are coming to her school and that the parents are paying cash.'

Mrs. McPhail looked at Emma for a moment. 'That's very interesting. You see what it means, don't you?'

Emma nodded. 'What happens now?' she asked. She remembered her reflections last week about reporting smugglers. 'Do you think Charlie should go to the authorities? It's like ... it's handing over his own father to the law. That's an awful thing to think about. And poor Mrs. Freeman, who may have to face disgrace on top of everything else. But if Charlie doesn't report it....'

'He'll be guilty of hiding it. And he'll be at the mercy of the people who know that his father handled smuggled goods.'

'At first I thought he should report,' Emma said. 'Now.... It's terribly complicated, isn't it?' She thought of the picture in the bookshop, of justice holding the scales, weighing the evidence, blindfolded so that the verdict would be fair. It wasn't only judges and juries who had to make judgements. Ordinary people did too, people like Charlie.

'If he does go to the authorities he'll have to stop dealing in contraband. His prices will go up, and he might lose customers.'

'Wouldn't a lot of people admire him for trying to do business honestly?'

'Most people will go to stores that offer low prices. Smuggled goods are usually a little cheaper than those on which tariffs have been paid, though some shopkeepers simply keep the difference for themselves as extra profit.'

'Did you discuss it with him?'

'I discussed it but gave no advice at all. I showed him and Rose some of those dubious items in the books. I told them that I would not take my investment out of the store, at least not for the time being, and that I hoped the store would do well.'

'Did Mrs. Freeman know anything about the smuggling?'

'She says not, and I'm inclined to believe her.' Mrs. McPhail gave a tight-lipped little smile. 'She remembers Abner asking her some years ago for a word that would mean "stuff in general", and she suggested "merchandise". So that's probably when it began. But she had no idea where he got most of his stock.'

'And of course he didn't mention it to you either?'

'To me?'

'When you discussed lending him money.'

'Certainly not.'

'And yet you're involved. If the store fails, Charlie may have trouble repaying you.'

'But if the store succeeds because Charlie continues handling contraband and offering lower prices, he may be caught at any time. Then people would no doubt learn that I had an investment in the store. That could damage the hotel. Success on those terms would be like having an axe hanging over our heads, ready to drop at any moment.'

Chapter Fifteen

The following morning, Emma talked to Rose about Miss Morgan, and very tentatively suggested lessons for Charlie.

Rose's eyes lit up. 'He could improve his arithmetic and learn some bookkeeping? In the evenings?'

'One class a week, probably, and then she'd give him homework – things to work on and practice before the next class.'

But Rose's optimism faded immediately. 'I don't know whether he'd do it. He hated school when he was a boy. He went for about two years. Abner wanted it, and we found the money somehow.' She paused for a moment, staring into space. 'He *hated* it.'

'But now that he has the store to run, wouldn't he see how useful it was?'

Rose gave a discouraged shrug. 'Maybe. I don't know.'

'I think we should mention it to him,' Emma urged, hoping that she sounded tactful and not overbearing. 'I'll do it, if you like. You never know – he may agree.'

'No, I guess it's up to me,' Rose said. 'I'll have to catch him in the right mood.'

Emma longed to mention the matter to Charlie herself. Why hadn't she approached it that way? But she had felt a delicacy about discussing arithmetic lessons with him, and she had expected Rose's whole-hearted support.

Charlie was out for part of that day picking up firewood from a customer who had offered it as payment for his account at the store. He used a neighbour's cart; the loan of the cart was the neighbour's way of paying *his* bill.

He came home towards the end of the afternoon. From the kitchen window Emma saw him drive into the yard and went out to meet him. He seemed to be in good spirits.

'Funny,' he said as he vaulted off the cart, 'how much I remember of what Dad used to say – about how to talk to customers or whatever.'

'Maybe you'll enjoy shopkeeping after all,' she said encouragingly.

'Oh, I dunno about that. Mebbe it's just bein' out on the road today....' Having hitched the horse to a post, he began unloading the firewood.

While he was doing it, Emma reported briefly on the day's business. Mrs. Thorpe had brought only two dozen eggs instead of three because a hawk had been at her hens. Several customers had bought whiskey and the supply was running low.

'And your mother is rather unhappy. I asked her if she had more pain than usual but she said no. I expect she's missing your father.'

'Mebbe. She's had those spells ever since she took to her bed. Feels useless, like no one wants her. Thanks for mentioning it. I'll try 'n' cheer her up.'

* * *

When Emma was getting ready to go to the store the next morning, Mrs. McPhail drew her aside.

'Do you know whether Charlie has decided yet about reporting the smuggling?'

'I haven't heard.'

'Could you give him a message from me? Remind

him that the longer he waits, the harder it will be for him to escape blame. After all, he is at this moment selling smuggled goods so he's committing a crime himself. Every day he delays makes it less likely that the authorities will excuse him.'

'So he should report it soon or keep quiet forever.'

'That's how I see it.'

'But his father died less than two weeks ago.'

'Long enough for his son and successor to have gone over the books and be able to report irregularities.'

Emma thought about it as she walked to work. She was not surprised at Charlie's hesitation. The fact that he had not been on good terms with Abner made it worse, not better. One or two things Charlie had said showed that he would have liked to make peace with his father and regretted that Abner had died before he could do so. That regret and remorse would make it harder, not easier, to report the smuggling and to destroy Abner's reputation now that he could no longer defend or redeem it.

Emma gave the message to Charlie when she arrived. He was in the shop, idly staring out of the window.

He nodded. 'I expect your aunt's right.' But his face revealed nothing about his opinions and plans.

Recognizing how dreadful the dilemma was, she did not press him. Instead she asked about the inventory. He had begun it on Monday, and today was Wednesday.

He gestured at the counter. On it lay a sheet of paper with eight or ten items written on it.

'That's a good start,' she said. She tried not to sound disappointed, but she was. He should have been able to do much more than that.

'I ran out of ink, and there's no more in stock. I'll go

buy some, now that you're here.' He took a few coins from the cash drawer and slouched out of the house.

Emma sighed. The ink was a handy excuse; on the strength of it, Charlie might stay away for the rest of the day. She had not yet spoken to Mrs. McPhail about restricting her hours at the store – the eruption of the smuggling issue had prevented it. But if Charlie went on like this....

Later in the morning, Rose talked to Emma. 'I'm afraid he's not going to be very cooperative about taking lessons,' she said sadly. 'He hasn't made up his mind, but from the stubborn look on his face I'm not hopeful.'

He was home for dinner, and he actually had bought some ink. After the meal, however, he said he had to mend the catch on the door of the hen house. When Emma went out to ask him something, he was sitting on a small barrel next to the chicken run whittling.

Her feet made no sound on the soft dust of the yard, and he didn't hear her coming. His hair had fallen over his eyes, and his whole body conveyed concentrated attention on what he was doing. The knife was nearly hidden in his big hand with the hairy back, but the hand moved nimbly, flickering around the little piece of wood in the other hand. When he held it up to look at it and decide what to do next, she saw that it was the head and neck of a rooster. There, vividly depicted, were the bird's challenging eyes, the comb slightly bent, the arrogant angle of the head. With decisive flicks of the knife, Charlie scored the wood so as to show how the feathers lay on the bird's neck.

Then he noticed her. In the first instant, as he met her eyes, she saw the look of absorbed attention lingering there. He held up the carving for her to see, but even as he did so his expression faded to a kind of rueful apology for whittling instead of working.

She smiled over the little carving. 'He looks as though he'd peck your eyes out.'

'And he's only an ordinary barnyard rooster like that one over there,' he said, pointing the knife at the rooster pacing in a dignified way among the hens, 'not even a fighting cock.'

'I can see that. A fighting cock looks much wilder, more savage.' She had seen a cockfight one day in the market square. 'But even a domestic rooster can be proud and masterful. He's a more useful creature than a fighting cock.'

'I guess so. But you didn't come out here for that. I expect you've got work for me to do.'

Later that afternoon the smuggling issue came up again. The two of them were in the shop together working on the inventory. Charlie had just sold a quarter pound of tea to a customer.

'The tea supply will be running low soon,' Emma said when the customer was gone. 'If you aren't going to handle smuggled tea, you'll have to find a different source of supply. I don't know if....'

He flushed and looked angry; she realized that she hadn't been very tactful. 'I'm sorry. I only meant....'

'Oh, I know,' he said, not looking at her. 'I've got to decide.' He looked up. His mouth was twisted in a crooked smile, but his eyes were troubled. 'It's not easy. If I don't handle smuggled stuff, I'll lose customers. The store might not survive, and it's pretty important to Mother 'n' me, probably the only way I can make a living at home so's I don't have to pay someone to look after Mother.'

'Suppose you had someone.... Could you get someone to live in? A widow, perhaps, glad of a room – your dad's room – who'd look after your mother and help in the shop?'

He considered it. 'Where would I find someone like that?'

'You could ask Mrs. McPhail. She knows a great many people.'

'Then I could go out to work again. But it won't be easy finding someone....'

No, it wouldn't, Emma admitted silently. She'd have to be educated enough to keep the books, and she'd need to make decisions while Charlie was out. It was necessary for Rose to like her because they would be together almost constantly. She would have to be a single woman or a widow with at most one small child because there was only the attic bedroom available for her. It was essential that she live in, because the room and board would be a large part of her wages. The Freemans could never afford to hire someone and pay her a full wage in money. Nor could they afford to hire a man, even should there be someone interested in the position – and that was unlikely because there were so many more profitable things for men to do.

Charlie had been right to wonder where he would find someone. Such women did exist but there was an enormous demand for them as wives, companions, or servants.

'Mother says I should get married!' Charlie burst out with a big laugh. Then he looked shocked and abashed, no doubt regretting the words as soon as they were spoken. He blushed and shook his hair over his eyes.

Married! Emma had thought of Charlie as a boy but he might easily be eighteen.

'Well, Charlie' she said, trying to put him at his

ease, 'you'll just have to find a young woman, then.'

* * *

That night, lying in bed staring at the paler blackness of the quarter-pie window, she thought about Charlie's embarrassment at having mentioned marriage. Was he embarrassed at the very thought of marriage or at the fact that he had spoken of it to her? Probably it meant that Charlie and Rose had discussed Emma as a possible bride. Why shouldn't they? There she was – the right age, a willing worker, on the spot and already familiar with the store and the family. They'd be blind and foolish not to consider her.

What did she think about the idea?

Instinctively she shied away from it.

Why did she react that way? He was nice-looking, and just that day she had felt a real affection for him as he was concentrating on his carving of the rooster.

But....

However much she might want to help Rose and Charlie through their present difficulties, taking them on for the rest of her life was a different matter.

All the same, things might improve. She did like Charlie, most of the time. (Well, *some* of the time.) It was only these problems about the shop and the smuggling that had made him seem indecisive and stubborn. If the problems were solved, he might be a changed person.

Thinking like this, Emma suddenly missed her mother again. For two years she had been managing without her parents, sizing up the world by herself, making decisions without being able to discuss them with a trustworthy person. But every now and then something came up which she felt unable to handle. A few weeks ago she had not known how to deal with whatever trouble John was in, and she had made a wrong decision.

Now she was out of her depth again. She had hardly thought about marriage for the last year or so, not since Isaac Bates had made an offer to her a few months after her parents' death. He was just beginning to clear a farm for himself in the bush and had suggested that they marry in a year, when he had a shanty built. She had weighed that future against one in York with her aunt and, for better or worse, had chosen the latter.

She had made that decision – an important and difficult one – alone. Since then she had become more accustomed to decisions and also more aware of the consequences of making a mistake. Before deciding about anything so momentous as marriage, she needed someone to talk to.

Mrs. Heatherington! She could talk to Mrs. Heatherington about this. The Major had gone back to the farm – this was a busy season for farmers – but his wife was staying until Caroline had her baby. Now was the time to talk to Mrs. Heatherington before she too went home.

The next morning, therefore, on her way to the Freemans' store, she called at Caroline's house. She hoped to see Mrs. Heatherington herself and arrange a time for a talk but, in case she didn't see her, she had written a note.

This time she went to the back door. She found everything in disorder.

'Oh, the mistress is having a baby!' said a dithery young serving maid. 'Right this very minute!'

'Can I see Mrs. Heatherington?'

'No, no, you can't see nobody. Everyone's busy!'

'Be sure you give her this note, then.' The girl, younger than Emma, was wearing coarse clothing and a huge, filthy apron. Clearly her normal work was scrapping pans and scrubbing floors, not answering the door. Emma, anxious that her letter should not be lost or forgotten in the chaotic household, would have welcomed the disdainful parlour maid who had opened the front door to her on Sunday. But there was no other servant in sight, and all she could do was again urge the little scullery maid to remember that the note was important.

***

When Emma got back to the hotel late that afternoon, she found a message from Mrs. Heatherington inviting her to come again on Sunday afternoon. She did so and was shown up to Mrs. Heatherington's bedroom where there were a couple of chairs by the window.

After asking about Caroline and the new baby, and congratulating Mrs. Heatherington, Emma explained her problem as clearly as possible.

'I think Mrs. Freeman and Charlie might be discussing whether Charlie should ... should marry me.' She blushed. 'It would be convenient for them.'

Mrs. Heatherington gave Emma a speculative look. 'Would you like to marry him?'

'Do you mean do I love him?'

'Well, if you loved him that would probably make your decision easier, though not necessarily wiser. But people marry without love. They marry because they get a good offer, or because they like a person, or because they need a home and a position. Love sometimes helps, but it can get in the way as well.'

Emma thought for a moment.

'The trouble is,' she said at last, 'that I can't picture the man – or boy – that I'd want to marry. My parents ....' She glanced at Mrs. Heatherington's face, then down again at her own lap. 'My parents were gentry, even though they were poor and were working hard clearing a farm. But I'm a servant now. I don't meet many boys, and certainly none of the kind that ... that my parents would have liked me to marry. And even if I did meet them, they wouldn't want to marry me because they'd see me as a servant. So what can I do? Marry someone like Charlie, just to be married? Or stay as I am and...? As long as I'm single, I *could* still find someone suitable. Once I married someone like Charlie, I'd be ... be *fixed* at that level. For ever.' She looked up again. 'I know this sounds dreadfully snobbish, but I think I'm being sensible. I'm not thinking only of position but also of ... of tastes, attitudes, interests. If I did it wrong I'd suffer for the rest of my life.'

'I think you're being very wise, my dear,' Mrs. Heatherington said. She thought for a moment, then went on. 'You're probably right to feel that a small shopkeeper like Charlie would not be a very good match for you. But at least he owns the shop and does not work for someone else. If Charlie were enterprising, he could become a prosperous merchant, and your parents would probably have felt such a marriage to be fitting – always assuming that he was a suitable *person* as well. Is Charlie enterprising and ambitious?'

Emma smiled at that. 'You don't know Charlie! He's happiest driving a dray and handling beer barrels.'

Mrs. Heatherington looked very thoughtful, and the silence lengthened. Emma didn't interrupt. It was just such reflection and contemplation that she had hoped for.

'If you were very ambitious, my dear, and hard-headed and a bit callous, you'd marry Charlie so that you could gain control of the store yourself – not legal control, perhaps, but control in practice. Then you could become a prosperous merchant yourself – *you*, not Charlie. You'd just use him.'

Emma had never thought of such a possibility. Before she could find anything to say, Mrs. Heatherington continued. 'Such things have been done before. But I'm not sure that you have the hardness for it. And you would need to be tough. If you let scruples and conscience stand in the way, you would not only fail to advance yourself and your husband but you might sink to his low level of ambition and achievement. Or the marriage might fail. Or you might become very unhappy.'

'That's a frightening thought.'

They were silent for a while. Then Mrs. Heatherington sighed. 'I don't feel very capable of advising you about this, Emma. For one thing, Charlie hasn't actually made you an offer, and he may never do so.'

'I wanted to be ready in case ...'

'Of course, very wise of you.'

'... and to take advantage of your being here in town to talk to.'

'I wish I could be more helpful. But you've been making your own decisions for ... how long is it?'

'Two years. And it wasn't really ... I mean, I wasn't expecting you to make the decision for me.'

'No, my dear, I know that. I can do this much. I can advise you not to be in a hurry. Even if he asks you, take time to think about it. And also I'd like to meet Charlie while I'm here – in an informal way, you understand. I'll come to the shop one day this week. Then, if we continue this discussion by letter, I'll have a mental picture of him.'

The matter was left there. Emma had known that she would have to make the actual decision herself, but it was a relief to have talked about it.

Chapter Sixteen

Mrs. Heatherington visited the shop on Wednesday. The excuse she gave for coming was to bring Emma word that she intended to go home early the following week, now that Caroline and the baby seemed to be doing well.

Charlie was in the shop; he had just brought full barrels of whiskey and molasses in from the store-room at the back of the house and was putting them in place against the wall. Emma made introductions and admired Mrs. Heatherington's ability to express her condolences for the loss of Charlie's father while at the same time observing him with her keen, kindly gaze.

She stayed for only a few minutes. Emma walked out to the road with her, looking for pretexts to keep her talking. The news of Mrs. Heatherington's return to the farm depressed her and she had a strong urge to hold on to her.

'What did you think of him?' she asked.

'A good-looking young man, and quite agreeable.' Mrs. Heatherington smiled. 'I can see that he likes handling barrels, as you said the other day.'

'But what do you really think?'

'I'd need to see a great deal more of him. All I have to go on is what you've told me. As I said, you'll have to make up your own mind. But at least now I know what he looks like, and I've seen the shop. I'll be eager for your letters in the coming weeks and months.'

Emma realized that for the moment she would have to be satisfied with that.

***

On the Monday of the following week, the weather turned very warm. In the morning, when Emma walked to the store, the air was fairly cool, but it felt as though it would be hot later in the day. There was a touch of heat in the breeze and in the haze that dimmed the blue of the sky while still letting the sun burn through. The warmth aggravated the smells of garbage piled in vacant lots and of the pools of stagnant water in ditches along the road. It seemed to breed even more millions of mosquitoes than usual. Emma remembered what John had told her in Kingston about the connection of garbage with cholera; the York newspapers had contained several editorials lately about the filthy state of the town and of the bay from which many people drew their drinking water. Emma agreed that the town was dirty but had no idea how it might be cleaned up.

But the weather produced pleasant effects as well. It would be good for the gardens, such as the one she was passing at that moment, a sizeable vegetable garden with beans trained up poles and peas climbing up branches stuck butt down in the soil. There were rows of other vegetables, many of the plants too small still to be identified. She had passed this garden regularly all spring and had admired its neat rows and its promise of abundance to come.

The rapidly warming weather lured Charlie outdoors. In the afternoon he invented an excuse, and Emma stayed to watch the store and keep Rose company. She helped Rose to look over her wardrobe, which was stored in the little chest in her bedroom. Because she was bed-ridden, Rose owned only nightgowns and a few underthings, and bed-jackets and shawls.

As Emma reached the bottom of the chest, she came across a bed-jacket that looked as good as new. She held it up. It was pink with yellow ribbon threaded through the eyelet lace – an unattractive colour combination – but it looked wearable.

'Don't you ever use this?' Emma asked. 'It looks nearly new.'

'Oh, that! Someone made it for me, but I think it's so ugly. Pink and yellow!'

'It just needs new ribbon – blue, maybe, or maroon.'

'Well....'

It was decided that Emma would go to one of the stores on her way home to pick out the ribbon. Charlie would go along to pay for it; he had in any case to go as far as Dr. Widmer's house to deliver a gallon jug of whiskey. Rose could be left alone for half an hour; because of the warm weather, the fire would be so low as to be safe.

The day had indeed turned hot, and there were many people on the street. Emma enjoyed being with Charlie; she remembered their trip to Mrs. Ferguson's house, which would have been so pleasant if she had not had to apologize at the end of it.

Emma chose the ribbon and Charlie paid and put it in his pocket. When they were outside again, they stood for a moment watching the scene in front of them, the talking groups of people, the children playing, the ladies with parasols, a man riding by on an exceptionally handsome horse.

'Well, I'll see you tomorrow,' Emma said. She would turn north from here while Charlie went eastwards back to the store.

But Charlie wasn't listening. He was staring past her head, his eyes fixed on something farther along the street.

'There's that man who came to the store,' he said quietly. 'The one with the saddle-bags of tea. He's got the bags with him. Come on, just walk along talkin' so we can get closer before he spots us.'

The first words had startled Emma and she had nearly whirled around to follow Charlie's gaze. But his quiet, tense voice and his instantly planned strategy caught her attention and drew her into his plan. Giving a nod, she turned to walk alongside him, saying something about the weather and the mosquitoes. Although there were several small groups of men standing on the street and talking, she recognized their man at once by his height and by the saddle-bags hung over his right shoulder. He was talking to someone who, when he turned his head, proved to be Mr. Michaels-Harbottle.

Emma abandoned the subject of the mosquitoes and mentioned to Charlie that she and John had already become suspicious of Mr. Michaels-Harbottle.

'You haven't reported him?' Charlie asked, keeping his eyes on his quarry.

'No evidence.'

'Well, I'm not interested in him. I'm gonna grab my man and take him to the customs house – it's just down there.' He gestured towards the lake; Emma remembered that it was against the wall of the customs house that she had sat while waiting for the schooner to finish loading.

'Won't it be closed? It's past six o'clock.'

'Don't think so. They always have to be ready to meet ships from the American side.'

By now they were within about fifteen yards of the

man with the saddle-bags. Emma understood very well that Charlie wanted to get as near as possible before being noticed. She remembered the man's short visit to the store and his abrupt departure when he found himself face to face not with Abner Freeman, whom he presumably knew and trusted, but with two strangers.

They walked a little closer, and then he saw them. At first his gaze was impersonal; either he did not recognize them or he was going to treat this as a casual encounter with people whom he had barely met.

But Charlie's determined face and stride must have warned him. He said a word to Mr. Michaels-Harbottle, who instantly vanished between two buildings. Then he himself turned and began rapidly walking away. Charlie broke into a loping run and caught up with him. He grabbed his left elbow; Emma, when she reached them, could see the taut cords in Charlie's hand and wrist.

'What's all this?' the man demanded, trying to pull his arm free but apparently not yet completely grasping Charlie's intention.

'I'd like you to come with me....'

Abruptly the man guessed what was happening to him. He twisted out of Charlie's grasp, but the effort dislodged the saddle-bags from his other shoulder. They fell in a heap at his feet and tripped him up. Charlie was on the man in an instant, pinning him down.

'Get me some help, Emma!'

Several men were already crowding around but they simply watched curiously. Charlie was doing his best but the other man looked as though he might break loose.

'Someone help Charlie!' Emma cried. 'That man's a

smuggler! Someone help Charlie hold him!'

'*I'm* not going to help turn in a smuggler,' one bystander said with a laugh. 'Smuggled brandy's all I can afford to drink.'

But two of the others did help. In a minute Charlie and the smuggler were on their feet and Emma picked up the saddle-bags. They were unexpectedly heavy. She couldn't lift them to her shoulder but hugged them in both arms; they enveloped her in a smell of sweaty horse and something that might have been tobacco.

They made a little procession down to the customs house, where they found George Savage, the collector himself, just preparing to leave for the day. He stayed to hear Charlie's story and to inspect the saddle-bags, which contained contraband tea and tobacco. He enlisted Charlie's help to take the smuggler to the court house; Emma went along because it was on the way to the hotel. At the court house they were taken to the office of the magistrate on duty, where Charlie again told his story. The man with the saddle-bags, whose name was Edward Miller, was taken to the jail next door.

When he was locked up, and Mr. Savage had taken leave of them, Emma and Charlie were left alone standing in the open space in front of the jail and court house.

'It looks as though you made up your mind to report the smuggling,' she said. The story Charlie had told to the collector of customs and the magistrate, though it would have to be filled out with more details later, suggested clearly enough that Abner Freeman had dealt in smuggled goods.

'I guess so,' he said, looking surprised.

'You mean you hadn't made up your mind?'

'No, it was just when I saw that man, knowing he was a crook, standing around as bold as anything with his damn bags over his shoulder.... It was like my feet decided for me.' Now that the action was over, but consequences had still to be faced, Charlie looked puzzled and bewildered rather than satisfied.

'As Mrs. McPhail said, the longer you waited the worse it might have been for you. And a man like this could have turned you in at any time.'

'Yeah, that's so.'

'Now you'll have to tell the whole story.'

'And go honest. Well, I guess that's best anyway. But I don't know what we'll do if the store fails.' He looked very gloomy for a moment. 'You'd better let Mrs. McPhail know about this.'

'All right. See you tomorrow.'

'Sure.'

***

Not until she came in sight of the hotel did Emma remember that it was Mr. Michaels-Harbottle to whom the man with the saddle-bags had been talking. Now she tried to imagine how the arrest might affect him. Would he know that Miller was in jail? She was pretty sure that Mr. Michaels-Harbottle had seen her with Charlie heading for him and his friend. He had certainly disappeared fast enough. He might well consider himself in danger too.

Dinner was over at the hotel. 'I saved you and John something to eat,' Mrs. Jones said.

'Isn't John home yet?'

'No. Maybe he's out enjoying the weather.'

But Emma's main concern now was to talk to Mrs.

McPhail. She set down her bundle and went through the kitchen to the lobby. There she knocked at her aunt's door and was bidden to enter.

'I'm sorry I wasn't here to help serve dinner, Mrs. McPhail, but something important happened.' She described Charlie's capture of the man with the saddle-bags.

'So Charlie decided to report what his father had been doing.'

'He said he hadn't planned it, but when he saw the man he just went after him.'

'Well, I'm glad he caught him.'

'We didn't catch Mr. Michaels-Harbottle.'

As she spoke, Emma realized that she hadn't mentioned that Miller had been talking to Mr. Michaels-Harbottle. And she certainly had never told her aunt that she and John had already become suspicious of him earlier.

'What do you mean?'

'Mr. Michaels-Harbottle was talking with the smuggler when we first saw them. He dashed into an alley when he spotted us.'

'What makes you think that Mr. Michaels-Harbottle is involved?' Mrs. McPhail demanded, suddenly indignant. 'It may have been a perfectly innocent, casual conversation. He's a respectable gentleman.'

'He bolted like a guilty man, though. John and I have been wondering about him for some time. In Kingston we saw him talking to....' Then she realized that Mrs. McPhail also didn't know about the goings-on in the shed behind Blackwood's livery stable. At least, Emma hadn't told her.

'... talking to whom?'

'To someone whom John suspects of smuggling.'

'This is ridiculous! Mr. Michaels-Harbottle is an ordinary, upstanding businessman. I've talked to him often during meals here – a most polite and agreeable person. I won't have you and John going around slandering people like that. It's malicious and untrue, and it can only make the hotel look bad. I won't have it, Emma, do you hear?'

'I've seen things....'

'There's nothing to see. You're *imagining* things, inventing excitement for yourself. All this nonsense about smugglers standing in public places talking! It's absurd!'

'It makes perfect sense to me. There are always little groups of people standing talking on the street. No one notices them.' Then, before Mrs. McPhail could reply, she asked. 'Was Mr. Michaels-Harbottle at dinner this evening?'

'No, he sometimes isn't.' But as she spoke, Mrs. McPhail's eyebrows twitched in a tiny frown of puzzlement, as though she were remembering something.

'But...?' Emma prompted, as though her aunt had actually started to speak.

'Now that I recall, I saw him out on the street just before dinner.' She gestured towards the street in front of the hotel.

'But he didn't come in?'

'I don't think so.'

It was obvious that something had undermined Mrs. McPhail's earlier assurance.

'Go upstairs, Emma, and see if he's in his room.'

'What should I do if he is?'

'Ask him if I may have a word with him. I'll invent an excuse. Go on, now.'

Emma went up to the small front room, which Mr.

Michaels-Harbottle had occupied since the day when she had signed him in earlier that spring. She knocked, waited, and knocked again. When there was still no answer, she went in.

The room was empty. Not only was Mr. Michaels-Harbottle not there but neither were his belongings. She glanced around at the neat emptiness – he was one of the tidiest guests she had ever known – and, feeling justified by the suspicious circumstances, looked through the chest of drawers. Each drawer, as she pulled it out and pushed it in again, gave a hollow rattle.

Only in the bottom drawer had something been left behind. Hard to see on the old newspaper used to line the drawers, but noticeable to Emma who was looking for something of the sort, were a few black specks. They might have been taken for dried-up mouse droppings but when she picked them up, she saw that they were tea – little black curled leaves just like the ones she had taken off the counter at the store after the man with the saddle-bags had left. Again, as she had done then, she laid them on the palm of her hand.

From where she was squatting in front of the bottom drawer she noticed something else left behind. Lying far under the bed was a crumpled handkerchief. She reached for it and recognized it as one of Mr. Michaels-Harbottle's. It was pale grey and had an unusual type of stitching along the hem.

She went back to Mrs. McPhail's room.

'He's gone,' she said. 'Took everything except this handkerchief and ... have you got a sheet of paper? Ordinary writing paper.'

Mrs. McPhail took the paper out of her desk drawer and Emma carefully slid the tea-leaves onto it from the palm of her hand. As she did so, the door behind her suddenly burst open. It was Ruth.

'Emma, can you come? John's hurt!'

'Hurt!' Emma cried, whirling around. 'Where is he?'

'In the kitchen. He's....'

Emma didn't wait for the details.

John was sitting on one of the benches alongside the kitchen table. He had a bleeding cut beside one eye, and a bruised lip. His left arm was lying limply on the table.

Emma had barely reached him and begun examining the damage when Mrs. McPhail came up to them. 'What's this, John?' she demanded.

'There was ...' He winced as he moved his lip. 'There was a fight behind Blackwood's.' He looked at Emma. 'Bick and ...' He shifted his glance to Mrs. McPhail, '... and that man who's staying here. Mr. Harbottle or whatever his name is.'

Emma glanced up at Mrs. McPhail and saw again that small furrow between her eyebrows.

John went on. 'They were fighting. Mr. Harbottle had a heavy stick, a sort of club. I came on them by accident. He ... Mr. Harbottle ... thought I was spying. He hit me. Bick was lying on the ground by then. Mr. Harbottle ran away.'

'When was this?' Mrs. McPhail asked.

'Just a few minutes ago. I came straight here.'

Emma spoke. 'I can put a bandage on this cut, but I think a doctor should look at his arm, see if it's broken. Can we send Joe Tubb to fetch Dr. Ross?'

'Certainly.'

For once Joe was there when he was wanted. He was staring goggle-eyed at John. Mrs. McPhail used Mrs. Jones's ink and paper to write a note and sent Joe to get Dr. Ross. Meanwhile, Emma had filled a basin with warm water and was delicately dabbing the bloody cut on John's face.

'I'd like to finish our talk, Emma,' Mrs. McPhail said when Joe had gone. 'Look after John first and then come to my room when you can.'

The women in the kitchen did what they could for John. They moved him to Mrs. Jones's chair by the fireplace and laid a folded towel along the arm-rest for his hurt arm. Mrs. Jones made him a cup of very sugary tea. Emma discovered that he also had an ugly scrape on one knee and cleaned that. After hovering about in a state of combined anxiety and excitement, Mrs. Tubb and Ruth went back to the scullery to finish washing the dishes.

Dr. Ross, when he came, reported that John's arm was not broken but that the wrist was badly sprained and that there had been a heavy blow near his elbow.

'Looks as though you lifted your arm to protect your head, son,' he remarked.

'That was one thing,' John said; presumably he meant that there had been other blows as well.

Dr. Ross tied up the hurt wrist tightly and also bound the cut on John's temple, which Emma had left unbandaged so that he could see it. The bruised lip and the scraped knee did not need bandaging.

When he was finished, Emma walked out into the yard with him.

'What should I do for him, Doctor – besides what we've just done?'

'I wouldn't worry too much, Emma. He's a sturdy lad. I don't think he'll develop a fever, but of course let me know if he does.'

'How long should he stay away from work?'

'See how he feels. He may have a fair amount of pain

tomorrow and feel wretched. Is he the sort to take advantage of this to get a few days off?'

'No, the very opposite. He'll probably insist on going.'

'Well, the pain may persuade him to stay home for a day. But I don't think he'll do himself any harm if he goes to work. Of course that arm won't be good for anything. I guess the two of you will just have to see.'

When she went indoors she helped John to bed. She decided – and he made only a feeble protest – that he should sleep in her bed that night, not on his pallet on the attic floor. So she moved her nightclothes and washing things out to the open attic where he usually slept. When she had him settled, she went back to Mrs. McPhail's room where, with a sigh, she sat down in her usual chair. The upsets of the evening had exhausted her, and in any case it was already past ten o'clock.

'Now, Emma,' said Mrs. McPhail, 'let's go over all this. You found these in Mr. Michaels-Harbottle's drawer. I agree that they look like tea. You're suggesting that they are evidence of his smuggling.'

She nodded. 'Ruth and I cleaned the room very thoroughly this spring and put down fresh newspaper in all the drawers. He – Mr. Michaels-Harbottle – is the only one to occupy it since then. And why would a man keep tea in a hotel room?'

Mrs. McPhail's lips pinched in a narrow line. Carefully she folded the paper around the tea-leaves and fastened the package as though it were a letter, with a drop of sealing wax which she imprinted with the small stamp that she used for her letters. Across the front she wrote, 'Leaves found in bottom drawer of room occupied by Mr. Michaels-Harbottle. June 4, 1832, 9:30 p.m. Thought to be tea.' She signed it and silently handed Emma the pen to add her signature.

'I'll keep the handkerchief in case he comes back for it.' She folded it and laid it and the package of tea-leaves on a small table that stood near her desk. The newspaper packet of tea from the shop already lay there. 'Now. Do you think John is right in saying that it was Mr. Michaels-Harbottle who hurt him?'

'I'm sure of it.'

'You attended to Mr. Michaels-Harbottle's room this morning, tidied it and made the bed. Were his belongings there then?'

'Oh, yes. Otherwise I'd have told you. He must have decided to leave when he saw us capture Edward Miller. You said you saw him outside on the street just before dinner.'

'Do you think he could have come in and packed and left without my seeing or hearing him?' Mrs. McPhail was thinking out loud rather than asking Emma's opinion.

'I think so, don't you? The only tricky part would be walking out with the valise, and he could do that while you were presiding at dinner. After that he must have gone to Blackwood's and got into a fight with Bick and hurt John.'

'That puzzled me when John said it. What would Mr. Michaels-Harbottle be doing at Blackwood's? Unless he went there to hire a horse, and that would probably draw too much attention to his sudden departure. He'd want to leave town with as little notice as possible, I would have thought.'

'No, he'd go to Blackwood's because of the contraband in the shed. Oh! you don't know about that.' Emma was too tired now to be tactful. Besides, the whole story was obviously going to come out.

'About what?'

'The smuggling was happening at Blackwood's – or rather, the smuggled goods, some of them, were being stored in a shed behind the livery stable.' As she spoke, she thought of the business connections between Mr. Blackwood and Mrs. McPhail. For a nightmarish moment she wondered whether both of them were involved in smuggling, whether indeed Mr. Michaels-Harbottle had been staying at this hotel *because* he was in league with Mrs. McPhail. But then Emma remembered Mrs. McPhail's disapproval of smuggling and her awareness of the punishment for those who were caught. Her own reputation and that of the hotel were, Emma concluded, too important for Mrs. McPhail to endanger them in that way.

Mrs. McPhail looked indignant. 'Mr. Blackwood wouldn't....'

'We don't know whether he did or not,' Emma said wearily. 'Someone else may have been using the shed secretly.'

There was a silence.

'Well,' Mrs. McPhail said at last, 'there's nothing more to do tonight, and you ought to be in bed. We'll think about it further tomorrow.'

Emma agreed. As she left the room, she caught a glimpse of her aunt's face settling into lines of deep anxiety.

Chapter Seventeen

John did prove to be obstinate about going to work the next morning. His face was pale under the piratical bandage that covered the wound on his temple, and he admitted that his arm was sore. But he insisted that he must at least tell Mr. Blackwood about the fight he had seen. When Emma offered to go herself and repeat to Mr. Blackwood what John had told her, or to ask Mr. Blackwood to come to the hotel and hear John's account, he just looked mutinous and kept on clumsily dressing himself.

Emma, seeing that her well-meant efforts were making it even harder for him, let him go. She herself was almost unbearably tired; she had not slept well and was worried about John and about Charlie and the shop.

She had finished her usual morning chores in the hotel and was about to set off for Freeman's when a carriage pulled up. From it emerged Mr. and Mrs. Blackwood, and John. Mrs. Blackwood had her arm around him. They came in through the front door; Mrs. McPhail, who was behind the counter, opened the door of her private room and, with a twitch of her head, summoned the Blackwoods and John in. Emma, who had been in the lobby asking Mrs. McPhail something, followed.

Mrs. Blackwood helped John to one of the rocking chairs beside the fireplace and looked at him for a moment before turning to Mrs. McPhail and Emma.

'This boy needs a rest. He fainted this morning.'

Emma went up to him. Worried as she was, she was determined not to fuss, but she pulled up a footstool and sat down close to the rocking chair.

'Well, he was hurt yesterday....' Mrs. McPhail began.

Mr. Blackwood interrupted. 'I know. He told me about last night's fight. And about Ralph, and Ralph's brother Bick, and the use that has been made of my shed. *Without* my knowledge, I may say!' He glared at them all, defying them to contradict him. 'He took me there, and we saw the blood on the ground. I traced this fellow Bick – asked Ralph where he lived – and found that he had come back to his boarding house in the middle of the night. He's very badly hurt. The landlady says that the doctor couldn't believe that he'd actually been able to drag himself home.'

'Is he still alive?' Mrs. McPhail asked.

'Delirious. Apparently the doctor isn't prepared to say whether he'll pull through.'

Emma understood the reason for her aunt's concern. From John's account it seemed clear that it was Mr. Michaels-Harbottle who had given Bick such a beating. If Bick died, their former guest would be not merely a smuggler but a murderer as well.

'When I came home after seeing Bick,' Mr. Blackwood said, 'I had another look at that shed. Florence and I,' he added, including his wife with a glance. 'There were certainly signs that it had been used. Marks in the dirt on the floor. Tracks of wheels and horses outside. And the hinges of the door had been oiled.'

'Tea-leaves?' Emma said, forgetting to be cautious.

Both the Blackwoods stared at her.

She blushed, realizing that she had come dangerously close to revealing what Mrs. McPhail would, no doubt, prefer to keep secret for as long as possible. She hurriedly scraped together an explanation that wouldn't involve Mrs. McPhail and the hotel. 'Charlie Freeman turned in a suspected smuggler yesterday. He had left tea-leaves on the counter at the shop. Just a few that fell out of his saddle-bags. When we caught him his saddle-bags were full of tea and tobacco.'

'We didn't look for tea-leaves,' Mrs. Blackwood said, 'but I'll do it as soon as I get back.'

'But,' said Mrs. McPhail, 'there was no actual contraband in the shed?'

'Nothing at all,' said Mr. Blackwood. 'However, one of my carts and a horse are gone. Stolen!' He paced about in self-righteous indignation.

'Probably borrowed,' Mrs. McPhail answered. 'They may be found abandoned in a day or two. Obviously one of the smugglers emptied the shed.'

'But why should they abandon my horse and cart? Why not take it to wherever they're going?'

'Because I think they'd use the horse and cart only to get to the lake – to whatever landing place they use. Their real escape would be by boat, just the way they bring the contraband in. They'll leave the horse and cart somewhere when they've transferred the smuggled goods to their boat.'

Emma noticed how careful Mrs. McPhail was to leave Mr. Michaels-Harbottle's name out of it. The Blackwoods had not mentioned it either; maybe John hadn't named the man who had hurt him. It would no doubt come out in the end, but Mrs. McPhail was going to protect the hotel's reputation for as long as she could.

'Well,' Mr. Blackwood admitted reluctantly, 'I suppose that makes sense. Be nice to get them back, I must say.'

It was Mrs. Blackwood who reminded them of John. 'Can this boy rest for a day or so?'

'Of course,' said Mrs. McPhail.

They decided that John did not have to be in bed but should stay quietly in or near the hotel. Emma said that if he felt faint he should lie down on her bed. She had a word with Mrs. Jones, asking her to keep an eye on him during the day. Then she went to the store.

As she walked, she thought about the smuggling. She tried to put herself into the mind of Mr. Michaels-Harbottle. There he was, yesterday evening, in the shed behind the livery stable. That afternoon one of his associates had been arrested. Now he had hurt Bick, who was probably still lying there and might die of his injuries. He'd given John a beating but allowed him to escape. He had to get away. He wanted to take with him whatever smuggled goods were still in the shed. Following Mrs. McPhail's suggestion, Emma imagined him 'borrowing' Mr. Blackwood's cart, harnessing a horse to it, loading it with the contraband in the shed, putting his valise into the cart as well – and probably the wounded man – and driving off. He delivered Bick to the boarding house. Then he drove out of town.

Where would he go? No doubt, as Mrs. McPhail had suggested, to wherever the smugglers' safe landing place was, somewhere along the lakeshore. Some private little cove or the mouth of a creek, a densely overgrown bit of marsh.... There'd have to be a shed or barn where the goods could be stored safe from weather, theft, and the prying eyes of the preventive men.

Somewhere like the Fergusons' farm. It was far enough out of town so that their comings and goings would be private, yet near enough to bring merchandise into town easily. The property went down to the shore. As for signs that the Fergusons might be involved – well, they were well-off and could afford to pay cash to Miss Morgan for the little girls' schooling. They ran up large debts at Freeman's store – just the sort of debt which might be paid off periodically with smuggled merchandise which would then be sold in the store. And Emma and Charlie, on their way back from the Fergusons' farm that day, had met Ralph, Blackwood's hired man, driving an empty cart in that direction late in the afternoon.

She knew that this was not conclusive proof, that there were no doubt many others besides the Fergusons who might have provided the required landing place and barn. But it certainly made the Fergusons a possibility.

All right, then. Mr. Michaels-Harbottle delivered the injured Bick to his boarding house and drove to the Fergusons. If he were lucky there would be a boat there, at that hidden wharf, into which the contraband could be loaded. If there were no boat, the contraband would be stored in a building or in the woods, the same place where incoming stuff would be kept until it was moved to Mr. Blackwood's shed.

Then, last night, the unloaded cart would be driven to a place where it could be abandoned without incriminating the smugglers, including the Fergusons. Back into town? But that meant that it would be found in the morning, almost at first light. More likely it would be taken further east, away from town, where it might go undiscovered for longer.

***

When Emma reached the store, she told Charlie about John's beating. That led to her mentioning her conjectures about the horse and cart. After all, he was involved in the whole affair.

Charlie looked thoughtful. 'I might try to find that horse and cart. Do you think Mr. Blackwood would give a reward?'

'I've no idea.'

'Worth a try. I'll go out lookin' today.'

'Can I come?'

He frowned. 'Well, there's the shop to look after, and mother....'

She nearly said, 'It was *my* idea, and it's *your* shop and *your* mother.' But, watching his face, she saw him working it out for himself.

Instead she suggested, 'We could go together, after we close the shop this afternoon. Maybe you could get one of the neighbours to look in on your mother.'

He agreed, though still not very graciously. By the end of the afternoon, however, he seemed to be reconciled to her coming. He had arranged for one of the neighbours to sit with Rose, and then he and Emma set off, heading for the Don bridge. The late afternoon was very warm and still. They walked steadily, crossing the bridge and keeping on eastwards past the Mill Road and, some distance further, the Ferguson farm. After her thoughts of that morning, Emma examined it covertly. The house was set quite far back from the road and there were several substantial barns and sheds. There was an ample cleared area around – pasture, and fields green with the new crops coming up – but forest blocked the view to the lake. There was, of course, nothing to support her suspicions, but neither was there anything to cast doubt on them.

Just beyond the Ferguson farm was another one, much more modest, where a few hens were fluffing their feathers in the dust of the driveway.

'Tuckers',' Charlie said. 'I used to deliver there. Old man and a young one – no womenfolk.'

Shortly after that, they encountered a rider coming towards them. Charlie asked him if he had seen a horse and cart abandoned anywhere, but he hadn't.

'They needn't be in plain view, o'course,' Charlie said gloomily to Emma as they walked on. 'They could be hidden anywheres, in the woods, behind a shed.... Or the smugglers could have killed the horse.'

'Or taken it along. You were the one who thought it was worth looking for them.'

'You wanted to come.'

After that they were silent. Their steps were nearly noiseless on the dusty road. The bush now closed them in on both sides, except where, here and there, it had been cut back to make a farm. On most of these farms the farmer and his whole family were working in the fields, among the stumps, planting or weeding.

They had been walking for perhaps an hour, and Emma was beginning to think that they might as well give up, when they reached a hollow with a small, marshy stream running through it. The hollow was filled with dense cedar bush. There was no bridge, only a rough ford with, beside it, some stepping stones. When the stream was high it would be difficult to cross. Even now two of the stones were under water. Charlie, with his long legs, jumped so as to touch only the dry stones, but Emma got one foot wet.

Among the dark cedars, beyond the stream, it was more silent than ever. A bird sang one short phrase. Then, after a profound silence, they heard the tiny clink of harness up ahead. It might have been made by a single horseman riding along, but in that case there would surely have been a continued clinking.

Alongside the stream, among the shadowy cedars, the road was not dusty but muddy. Without a word, Emma pointed to a pair of wheel-tracks that led away from the ford, along the road for a few yards, and then into the bush towards their left. They followed them, though Emma had an odd sense that it was not from this direction that the clinking had come. Insects besieged them in a cloud, and an invisible rustle almost under their feet suggested a snake or some other creature making off in a hurry.

A short distance into the marshy cedar bush they found a cart. The horse was nowhere in sight. The cart's shafts rested on a fallen tree so that the two-wheeled vehicle was more or less level. In it was a mound of loose hay.

'Hay?' Charlie whispered. 'Why put hay in it? Mebbe this ain't the cart we're looking for.'

'But why would anyone put a cart here, except to hide it?' Emma heard the edge of irritation in her own voice; she could barely concentrate on the cart because she had to keep waving the flies and mosquitoes away from her face.

Then she noticed that near the cart there were not only mosquitoes and blackflies but also the big bluebottles that are always drawn to garbage. Their blue-green bodies shone in a streak of sunlight that found its way among the cedars and touched the ground just beyond the cart.

She moved closer to the cart, very cautiously, until she saw what the bluebottles had come for, and why there was hay in the cart. At the back, where the hay was thinner and where the tailgate of the cart was missing, she saw a booted foot, its toe pointing upwards.

'There's someone in the cart,' she whispered to Charlie. 'Lying down.'

Charlie joined her and they stared at the boot. 'We'd better check if he's dead or only hurt.'

He walked around to the side of the cart and reached over to push aside the hay at about the place where the man's head would be.

'Oh!' Emma said. The man was Mr. Michaels-Harbottle, and his throat had been cut. There was no question at all that he was dead. Charlie pulled the hay back into place.

'We'll have to take him into town,' he said. 'We need a horse.'

'We heard a horse's harness, remember? That clinking sound? It didn't come from here.'

'They'd have hidden the horse a little way off. Horses don't like the smell of blood.'

They went back to the road and, without much trouble, found the horse's tracks leading into the bush on the other side. The horse, hearing them, gave a soft nicker.

The animal was still harnessed and bridled and had been tied to a tree at the foot of which was a dark little stream that curled in a sinister way among the cedars to join the creek in the ravine. Charlie untied the horse, led it to the cart, and hitched it up. The animal did indeed become restless near the cart, but Charlie gentled it along with a constant murmuring and stroking.

Emma hated climbing up onto the seat, among the cloud of flies, close to the remains of Mr. Michaels-Harbottle. But Charlie wanted her there and, when she was on the seat, handed her the reins to hold loosely.

He himself stayed at the horse's head, leading it by the bridle out onto the road, through the ford, and up the slope onto the level road. Not until then did he climb onto the cart and take the reins.

'I hope the horse'll be okay now,' he said. 'Once we're moving and out in the open, the smell ought to lie behind us and not bother the horse.'

'I suppose you're driving to the court house?'

'Yeah. To the magistrate. Like yesterday.'

'I can't believe that it was only yesterday that we were there.'

After that they travelled in silence. It seemed to Emma that, in spite of the warm June sun declining ahead of them, they brought with them a cloud of the same ominous gloom that had hung over the cedar swamp.

Chapter Eighteen

When they reached the court house, they found a different magistrate on duty. Charlie had to tell his whole story of the smuggling again before beginning to recount the events that led to the discovery of Mr. Michaels-Harbottle's body. Almost at once he mentioned Emma's part in these events. 'Emma here thought the cart might be out east of town....'

'Your name is Emma?' the magistrate said, turning to her. 'What is your surname?'

'Anderson, sir. I'm the niece of Mrs. Harriet McPhail and I work for her.'

The magistrate nodded; as Emma had expected, her aunt's name was recognized.

'What made you think that the cart might have been left east of town?'

To explain that, she had to tell what she knew about Mr. Michaels-Harbottle, about the bits of evidence that she and John had put together, about John being hurt, and about what had been found – and not found – in Mr. Blackwood's shed.

'We've heard something of this,' the magistrate said. 'The man Bick Davies has died and his landlady came to us. We will certainly speak to your aunt and Mr. Blackwood. But you haven't told us what made you think that the cart might be abandoned east of here.'

She went on with her story. At the first mention of the Fergusons, the magistrate and his clerk exchanged glances.

'Be careful what you say, Emma,' the magistrate said. 'I'm sure you know that it's wrong to spread untrue and slanderous rumours about people.'

'I haven't spread any rumours, sir. Some of this is guessing, but some is fact.' She went through the list of items about the Fergusons which she had compiled in her head that morning. 'Some of it is true, sir,' she said in conclusion. 'And we *did* find the horse and cart east of town, where I thought they would be.'

The magistrate let them go, saying that no doubt he or some other authorities such as the customs officers would be in touch with them later. Then Charlie went back to his mother and Emma to the hotel, where once again she had to report to Mrs. McPhail on the day's events.

* * *

The next morning at the hotel, while the servants were having their breakfast, Mrs. McPhail came to the kitchen.

'Emma, can you come to my room, please?'

In Mrs. McPhail's room Emma found George Savage, the collector of customs, and one of his men whom he introduced as Bill McKee.

'We wanted to see you, Emma, to check a few things. Early this morning, at first light, we searched the Fergusons' farm and the Tuckers' next door for contraband.'

'Did you find any?'

'Nothing at all at the Fergusons'. They were offended but didn't prevent our searching.'

'Clean as a whistle,' added McKee gloomily.

'But next door?' Emma said, sensing what had not yet been said.

'They'd left. The place was deserted. Apparently

there'd been the old man, and his son who was about twenty-five. They'd gone. But there were signs of hasty departure – some things left in the house. Horseshoe tracks by the water trough – we're going to check the hooves of Mr. Blackwood's horse that was "borrowed". Also there was a small loading dock with a shed on it, a good tight shed much better built than the house. Tea-leaves in the shed, and marks on the floor of crates being dragged and barrels rolled. And something shoved under the door-sill which you might be able to identify.'

He opened a leather satchel and drew out a cloth bundle folded in a peculiar way. Emma took it. It was a fine-quality pale-grey handkerchief with an unusual pattern of stitching along the hem.

'Don't....'

He spoke the warning even as she shook the bundle loose and gasped. It was obvious why the handkerchief had been folded in such an awkward way. The folding was designed to hide a heavy brown encrustation.

'Blood?' she asked.

'I'm sorry – I didn't want you to see that. Do you recognize the handkerchief?'

'It's Mr. Michaels-Harbottle's. All his handkerchiefs were this colour and had this sort of stitching. It was found in that shed? Like this? Bloody?'

He nodded.

'So Mr. Michaels-Harbottle was killed there.'

'We think so. It looks as though the handkerchief was used to wipe the knife – that's why the blood is in that funny pattern.' He took it from her and spread it out. The blood formed a very irregular star pattern. 'Which makes it look as though the Tuckers killed him. But as for our finding them.... They probably left by boat. By now they could have landed anywhere along the American shore and have disappeared for good. They'll have friends over there to help them, smuggling contacts....'

'Poor Mr. Michaels-Harbottle.'

'He was a smuggler, Emma.'

'Maybe, but I sort of liked him. He was polite and looked rather pleasant. Mrs. McPhail liked him too, didn't you?' she asked, turning towards her aunt.

'A considerate guest, and good company at dinner,' Mrs. McPhail said.

McKee shrugged, but Mr. Savage nodded gravely.

'It happens. Just because a man's a criminal doesn't mean he's bad all through.'

The two men got up to go, taking the bloody handkerchief as well as the one which Emma had found under Mr. Michaels-Harbottle's bed. They also took the two little packages of tea-leaves, which Mrs. McPhail gave them with a short explanation. As she got to her feet and prepared to usher them out, she asked Emma to stay for a moment longer.

When she returned, she sank into her chair with a sigh.

'Just now before you joined us,' she said, 'Mr. Savage told me that yesterday they searched Mr. Blackwood's premises. Besides what Mr. Blackwood told us about, there were some tea-leaves in the shed, as well as signs of brandy having been spilled at one time. Mr. Blackwood still swears that he knew nothing about it, and in fact the customs people found nothing to incriminate him personally. The shed is apparently easy to reach from the side farthest away from Blackwood's house, and it's not closely overlooked by the neighbours. Mr. Savage thinks that if the neighbours heard anything they would either put it down to legitimate after-hours activity at the livery stable or, if they thought of smuggling, they might be the sort of people who protect smugglers and make it so hard for the customs officers to catch them.'

Mrs. McPhail looked disapproving; but Emma, after all her thoughts on the subject, found it impossible either to praise or condemn anyone who protected smugglers.

'After this, I don't suppose smugglers would think of using Mr. Blackwood's shed again,' she said.

'Probably not. And Mr. Blackwood has vowed to keep a closer eye on it in future, and to be more careful about the men he hires. Mrs. Blackwood has said that she will help him.' Mrs. McPhail smiled. 'It's just possible that he may have acquired more "wife" that he had bargained for.' She seemed to be genuinely but pleasantly amused at the idea.

Mrs. McPhail's words suggested that that was the end of the conversation. Emma made as though to get up but paused before doing so. 'I must be on my way to the store,' she said, 'but I'd like to talk to you some time about how long I should continue working there.'

'You yourself would be the best judge, Emma. What do you think?'

Something in Mrs. McPhail's look and voice caught Emma's attention. Not only was Mrs. McPhail asking her advice, but she spoke to Emma as she did to other adults, her friends and equals.

Emma took a moment to choose her words. 'Charlie is able to manage the store now, more or less. He has a chance to learn more arithmetic and some bookkeeping from Miss Morgan. He and Mrs. Freeman are ... are taking up their lives again. Charlie said he might put up the sign-board by the road again – you know, the picture of the scales, to identify the store and maybe bring in more customers.'

'That sounds as though he means to carry on.'

'I think we should wait and see if he really does put up the sign.'

'Do you think he should continue with the business?'

'Well, that's up to him and Mrs. Freeman, isn't it? I suggested once that they might try to find a boarder who would use Mr. Freeman's bedroom and help look after Mrs. Freeman and the shop. They can still do that. But if I keep going there....'

Emma met her aunt's eyes.

Mrs. McPhail nodded. 'They will never work things out for themselves.'

'No.'

'Today is Wednesday. Tell Charlie and Rose that you'll continue coming for the rest of this week but that I *may* need you here in the hotel full-time from Monday on. That will give them a few days to get used to the idea. But if you think you should still go there next week, let me know.'

'Thank you, Mrs. McPhail.'

Emma got up and went to the door.

'And, Emma, I'd like to say that you've handled this assignment very well.'

'Oh!'

'It has required tact and sensitivity and inventiveness. I'm pleased with you.'

For one stunned moment Emma stood where she was, with her hand on the doorknob, her eyes riveted on her aunt's face.

'You *are?*'

'Certainly. Now you'd better be off to the Freemans'.'

The last words were uttered in Mrs. McPhail's usual brisk way. But the praise had been spoken.

As Emma walked to the store, weighing these things in her mind, she found that what she treasured most was not, after all, the praise of her handling of the assignment but the earlier part of the conversation. Stunning as the words of actual praise were, it had been an even greater compliment – and perhaps one which Mrs. McPhail had made unawares – to be treated as an equal, to be asked for advice, and to be told that Mrs. McPhail would trust Emma's judgement.